Adam Millard is the author of twenty novels, ten novellas, and more than a hundred short stories, which can be found in various collections and anthologies. Probably best known for his post-apocalyptic fiction, Adam also writes fantasy/horror for children, as well as bizarro fiction for several publishers. His "Dead" series has been the filling in a Stephen King/Bram Stoker sandwich on Amazon's bestsellers chart, and the translation rights have recently sold to German publisher, Voodoo Press.

For Louise

Hope you enjoy !

AM

MILK

ADAM MILLARD

A CIP catalogue record for this book
is available from the British Library

ISBN: 978-0-9954537-4-6

Crowded Quarantine Publications
34 Cheviot Road
Wolverhampton
West Midlands
WV2 2HD

For everyone at Birmingham Children's Hospital and The Encephalitis Society. I apologise in advance for what you are about to read.

"Never cry over spilt milk, because it may have been poisoned."
— W.C. Fields

MILK

1

The scorching sun ruthlessly beat down upon Oilhaven, a dot of a town in the middle of a desert no longer possessed of a name. Its inhabitants slunk through the streets, dripping with sweat and grime, fully aware that washing was simply a waste of time. Out here, the water had a tendency to be dirtier than the air. You were much better off leaving it well alone.

Such unbearable heat was nothing new to Oilhaven, or anywhere else on this godforsaken ball, for that matter. Ever since The Event, the sun's assault had been relentless, penetrating the stratosphere and troposphere with prodigious ease. Even the most enthusiastic sunbather now covered up, for there was a fine line between a nice tan and terminal skin cancer.

Out here, if the heat didn't kill you, the UV would, and if the fiery ball in the sky's rays didn't finish you off, a million other things were waiting in line, for life had changed drastically since The Event.

Imagine, if you will, an ant's nest. Now set fire to that nest and set upon it God's most rapacious creatures.

That...*that* was Oilhaven.

And in the middle of that no-named desert, in the centre of that town (twinned, unsurprisingly, with Hell; and also with Sana'a, Yemen) stood a convenience store. The only one within five-hundred miles, LOU'S LOOT was as dilapidated as the rest of the town. The only difference between his building and those surrounding it was the flickering neon light hanging above his door, powered by the battery from a dismantled Ford Cortina. Without said light, one might simply walk right past LOU'S LOOT, none the wiser, which was why he often switched it off and put his feet up...

Lou was a portly man, something of an irregularity in a world struggling to catch and kill its next meal. If you were to ask him how he did it, he might say something along the lines of, "It's my metabolism," or, "Daddy was a fatty, too," but the truth of the matter was, Lou didn't go short of food. Concealed in the basement of his ramshackle convenience store was enough tinned goods to feed the town of Oilhaven for the next ten years, but what they didn't know wouldn't hurt them, and what they *did* know would most certainly hurt him, and so he kept it to himself, lest he be brutally beaten about the head and thrown to the bandits.

Lou was also a grey, balding man, which made him look a lot older than his fifty years. One might say he had an air of Churchill about him, a soupcon of Eisenhower, but such comments were, at best, attempts at flattery. Lou Decker looked more like the late, great Australian entertainer, Clive James, than any president or prime minister. His head was perfectly round; so round, in fact, that whenever people needed to draw a circle, they asked if they could borrow it.

One thing he had over the rest of Oilhaven – apart from the vast quantity of canned spam and asparagus beneath his establishment – was his knowledge of the *old* world, and the artefacts and workings of said artefacts that had survived The Event. Whenever someone salvaged goods in the desert, it was *he* they brought them to. When one of the 'haveners stumbled upon a mechanical-looking thingamajig, with whatchamacallits and bobs and bits, it was Lou with the stories of how such a thing had been created, of what it could do (if only they had the right batteries). It was Lou they trusted to put the guts of the object back in – for a *price*, of course – and it was Lou that traded the item for food when its owner fell hungry a few weeks later.

He was clever like that.

His store was lined with mechanical wotsits, lengths of plastic pipe and steel tubing, with cloth and bolts and nuts of every size (in case anyone was feeling creative), with almost everything you could imagine in a post-apocalyptic wilderness. If you were to walk into LOU'S LOOT and not find what you were looking for, a quick word in his shell-like and there was a very good chance he could get it for you within twenty-eight days, including free delivery. In a world gone to hell in a hand-basket, that was quite a trick.

Undeniably Lou's bestselling items, though, were his sex toys. Men and women no longer fornicated, at least not in the old sense of the word. Perhaps it had something to do with the heat, or the grime perpetually painted upon one's person, which was terribly off-putting to the opposite sex. Maybe people had simply

9

forgotten how it went. You put that thing in this thing and repeat until beset with tingliness. How hard was *that?* The 'haveners, it seemed, would rather not bother, and it was there that Lou made the majority of his money.

He had toys of all shapes and sizes. Some were even returnable if they didn't fit, but only if the purchaser had retained the receipt – in most cases, a small slip of parchment with the item's description scratched into it.

Oh, yes, LOU'S LOOT was doing quite well, considering the unfortunate circumstances. News had filtered through shortly after The Event that most retailers had burnt to the ground, or exploded as a result of such an apocalyptic blast. Those that hadn't perished in The Event had been looted to within an inch of their lives in the following weeks. But LOU'S had survived, due mainly to the fact that out there, in the middle of nowhere, it was awfully difficult to assemble an army of plunderers without people becoming suspicious.

It was even harder to order the necessary ski-masks to complete the job, since Lou was the only man capable of attaining such scarce objects, and he wasn't born yesterday...

"Morning," said a voice.

Now Lou was clever enough to know that the voice belonged to the gangly man that had just walked into his store, since there was no-one else around. He had the look of a spider about him. An incredibly ugly spider, with holes where there should have been teeth and an empty socket where there should have been an eye. The one eye he *did* have darted around the place, as if following a rather excited fly.

"Good morning," Lou said, which was the done thing when welcoming a potential customer pre-noon. He placed his mug down on the counter – chai, for anyone interested – and pushed his not-so-small-frame up from the rat-eaten armchair he called home. "Welcome to LOU'S LOOT, where we have everything you need, providing you don't need weapons, ammo, posh nosh, thrush cream, soap, or toothpaste." It was his usual spiel, and each of the 'haveners must have heard it thousands of time by now, but *this* guy…

This guy didn't *look* like a 'havener. Lou certainly didn't recognise him, not that that meant anything. Out here, people changed from day to day. Beards were grown and shaved overnight (and that was just the women). One minute you could be feeling exceptionally good about yourself, the next you were gaunter than Karen Carpenter during Lent. Wrinkles had the propensity to appear from nowhere, and when you least expected them to. There were three children in Oilhaven (not everyone had forgotten how to make sex, but these three had been the result of unsuccessful withdraw methods) and each of them bore wrinkles upon their faces. It was the *sun*, you see. The sun…and the amount of *frowning* that people did.

The man – if indeed that's what he was, for his spiderlike affectations could not be underestimated –

wandered up and down the aisles, occasionally picking things up before replacing them just as quickly.

Lou could see where this was heading, and he didn't like it, not one bit, uh-huh, not today, thank you very much...

"Is there something you're looking for in particular?" Lou said, slapping a clay-and-latex vagina down on the counter. "This is Susie. Susie, say hello to Mr...?"

The man glanced down at the object and grimaced. "She doesn't look clean," he said, dipping his head to take a better look at her innards.

Lou was annoyed at the man's reluctance to impart his name, but tried not to show it. "She's cleaner than any walking around out there," Lou said. "I can give her a quick spit-polish, if you're worried about catching something, but I can assure you—"

"I'm not interested in your carnal contraptions," the man said, pulling from his waistband what appeared to be a very large knife. Yes, so large was this knife that Lou could see his entire face in it, and what an annoyed, round face it was, too... "Tobacco," he grunted. "*All* of it. And alcohol, and don't try to fob me off with that piss-water you fools drink around here. I want the *good* stuff. The golden stuff. The stuff that makes you go '*eeeehhhhhhhrrrrrr*' as it slips down your throat."

The knife, Lou noticed, was trembling in the man's hand. His long, slender fingers dripped with sweat; the hairs upon his knuckles swayed back and forth, as if the store had suddenly become electrically charged, which was impossible, since electricity was a thing of the past, deader than disco and dodos combined.

"You don't have to do this, son," Lou said, calm as you like. This wasn't his first run-in with a bandit, and it sure as hell wouldn't be his last. Or maybe it *would*. That knife was awfully sharp. He tried not to think about it.

"Just put everything on the counter," the arachnoid bandit said, slicing the air in front of Lou's face with his blade. "And no fucking funny business. I've had a really bad morning; it will mean nothing to me to kill you."

And Lou saw that he was telling the truth. This was a boy having an absolute *shocker* of a day, and it was only going to get worse.

"There is no tobacco here," Lou said. There was no sense in telling the bandit about the crate of woodbine at the foot of his basement stairs. No, no sense at all. "And when was the last time anyone heard of the golden liquid of which you speak? I assume you're referring to Whiskey?"

The bandit nodded frantically. "Yes! *Whiskey*! That's the one. Put it all on the counter, along with the tobacco, and I promise you won't get stabbed in the face."

Lou sighed, for it seemed like an appropriate time to do so. "Let me put it another way," he said, pushing the shaking knifepoint to the side ever-so-slightly, lest his nose be punctured. "There be no whiskey here. There be no baccy here. These things are gone forever. If you like, I know a very good addiction counsellor, though he might not be able to do anything about your apparent mental instabilities."

The spiderlike crook visibly shrank, which was good news as far as Lou was concerned, for he was a lanky bastard. "You must have *something* for me to steal," he said. "What about guns? Do you have guns, and ammo?"

"Did you not hear my little patter as you came in?" Lou said. "The Vatican has more guns than me. Feel free to try there, but for now, I suggest you run very fast in any direction." And with that, Lou straightened up to reveal a pair of pistols. Very nice pistols they were, too, with filigreed barrels and wooden grips. Once upon a time, they might have cost a bob or two, but now…well *now* they were absolutely priceless.

The bandit glared down at the pistols, incredulous. "I thought you said you didn't have any guns," he said, tucking the knife back from whence it came. The colour had drained from him, which only served to make the dirt on his face stand out even more.

"Don't believe a word *I* say," Lou said. "Other than *this*: I will shoot you in the kneecaps and feed you to my dying mother if you don't piss off, right now."

And piss off the bandit did, running from the store so rattled that it would take Lou several hours to get the stench out of the air.

"Fucking bandits," Lou said, lighting a cigarette and holstering his pistols. Pistols that hadn't been fired in over a decade. To the faux pussy sitting atop the counter, he said, "Looks like it's just you and me again."

He picked her up.

He closed up the store and took her through to the back room, where sweet love was to be made.

2

In an office one street over from LOU'S, a suited man sucked languidly on a cigar. The room was drenched in a grey-blue fug; you could hardly see the tropical aquarium that made up one wall of the office. Inside the aquarium, the fish moseyed back and forth, espying the smoking man with no small amount of suspicion, for he was the type of fella one was best keeping an eye on, fish or not…

Kellerman was his name, and mayor-ing was his game. While the rest of the world had fallen apart, leaving the majority of The Event's survivors crying into their now-dusty cornflakes, Kellerman had sensed an opportunity. He'd always fancied himself an authoritative figure, and so he had wasted no time in seizing control of Oilhaven. It didn't take long – three days, give or take a few hours – as most people were too busy coming to terms with the apocalypse to notice him slip into office. By the time they did notice, it was far too late. Kellerman was mayor.

He had the suit and the cigars to prove it.

A *good* mayor? An honest mayor with the people's best interests at the forefront of his agenda? Not on your nelly. Kellerman was a rogue, the kind of guy that, if he was in a James Bond movie, would have a British accent and stroke a fluffy, white pussy. The suit he now wore had been torn from the back of an investment banker less than an hour after The Event. He would have had the shirt, as well, had it not been plastered in blood and viscera. The cigars he now smoked had been procured from the back of a fleeing Mexican's Prius the day immediately following The Event, and the Mexican buried in the desert, where by now he would be nothing but bones, a torn and bloodied sombrero and, perhaps, a moustache.

Oh, Kellerman was a scoundrel of the highest order, but that, he thought, was what Oilhaven needed. You couldn't just put any blockhead in charge of a surviving municipality; you needed someone with a little oomph, a little – how did it go? – *va va voom*...Someone not afraid of making the important decisions, such as 'should I shoot him in the kneecaps or the spine?'.

The people of Oilhaven knew where they stood with Kellerman; usually as far away as possible. While many of them disagreed with his policies on taxation ('you give me three quarters of what you make, and I won't pick-axe you in the nethers') and his ability to make people disappear (and not in a cute David Blaine-Dynamo-David Copperfield way), they knew better than to rebel, lest they find themselves with a hole in the head or waking up in the desert next to a cigarless Mexican.

A knock upon the door startled Kellerman, who had been partaking in a staring-match with one of his more courageous angelfish. "Come in," he said, blinking tears away before resuming the battle.

Two burly men entered, which was fine as he knew them both very well and had been anticipating their arrival. If Kellerman was the head honcho – and he most certainly was – then Smalling and Harkness were his footsoldiers. As ugly as they were big, Smalling and Harkness (never *Harkness* and *Smalling*! Oh, no, that would never do) bore more scars per square inch than most burn victims. The bits that weren't scarred were tattooed, and some of the tattooed bits had since become scarred. Both men were bald, and neither of them had ever considered wearing a toupee, such was the stigma that came with it.

"Give me a second," Kellerman said, lifting a hand to his subordinates. The angelfish was really going for it now, and there was no way Kellerman was backing down. If he lost…well, the fish would be supper, but then all the other fish would start getting cocky, and the last thing he needed was an aquarium on the brink of revolution.

Smalling shrugged at Harkness, who arched his eyebrows in response. They would wait, and as it turned out, they didn't have to wait long as the angelfish finally gave up the ghost and swam under a rock.

"Ha!" Kellerman said, clapping his hands enthusiastically. "Did you see that? Fucking fish has been giving me evils all morning!"

"You sure showed him, boss," Smalling said, tapping at the aquarium's glass frontage with a stumpy, grimy finger. There was a childlike innocence about his expression, as if he'd never seen a fish before, or indeed one so embarrassed that it had hidden itself away from the rest of the tank in fear of derision.

Kellerman whizzed across the room on his castor-wheeled chair, landing almost perfectly behind his desk. He had to drag himself the last few inches, but you couldn't nail it every time. "I take it you've brought me some money," he said, rubbing his hands together so fervently that something sparked.

Harkness pulled an envelope from his dirty, leather satchel. It was quite remarkable that envelopes – being *paper*, and all – had survived The Event, but so had stamps and those little yellow notes you could stick on things, proving that you should never underestimate office supplies. "We've got half of this month's," he said, dropping the envelope onto Kellerman's desk. "It's fucking scorching out there. We thought we'd pop back for a glass of filthy water before continuing our rounds."

Kellerman peeled open the envelope and emptied its contents onto the desk. Coins clattered, and so did a few of the notes, which were so thick with grime you could have used them to wedge doors open. "Who's left to pay?" he said as he began to count the grotty cash.

"A couple of the miners," Smalling said. "Oh, and Abigail. And Lou."

Kellerman sucked in air through his teeth, which were in need of exigent attention. That was the thing about the apocalypse; never any dentists around when you need them. "The miners shouldn't be too problematic," he said, shoving the half-chewed cigar into the thin slit of his mouth. "I hear they've uncovered some good stuff this month." By *good* stuff, he meant quality dirt and a handful of indiscernible objects. Abigail, on the other hand, would be tricky. She was the only whore in Oilhaven, and since everyone had either gone off sex, or chose to take care of themselves, she had about as much income as a used tampon salesman.

"The whore has *some* money," Harkness said, glancing sheepishly at his buddy. Smalling rolled his eyes.

"Do you mean to tell me, young Harkness, that you put your winky in the whore's kitchen sinky? Not only that, but you paid for the privilege?" Kellerman looked about ready to upchuck.

Harkness shrugged. "Needs must, sir."

"Yes," Kellerman said, shaking his head with disgust. "Well, I hope you have since given your member a damn good wash in the radioactive well-water, and don't come crying to me when it decides to leave your body completely."

Smalling laughed. Harkness, for perfectly good reasons, did not.

"And that just leaves Lou Decker," Kellerman said, stuffing the crispy notes back into the envelope. Lou *always* did well, which meant that *Kellerman* always did well. He didn't trust the store's proprietor as far as he could throw him, and he knew very well that the fat prick was hiding goods in his basement, but that was none of his concern.

At least, not yet.

"Do you want us to baseball bat him, sir?" Harkness said, somewhat eagerly.

Kellerman frowned. "Has he displayed any reluctance to pay this month's tax?" he asked.

Harkness shook his head. "Not that I know of, sir."

"Then why would I want you to *bat* him?"

"I'm not rightly sure," Harkness said, scratching his bald pate. "To make an *example* of him?"

Kellerman stood and walked around the desk; Harkness shrunk a little, but despite that he still towered over his boss. "And when Lou's lying crippled on his store floor?" said he, "who would run the place? Who would bring in the money? Who, my dear friend, would provide this tumbledown shithole of ours with the necessary goods to survive, thusly lining our pockets by proxy?"

Harkness shrugged, for there were an awful lot of long words in there he didn't understand.

Sensing his underling didn't quite comprehend the question, Kellerman slapped him gently across the face and smiled. "If you are intent on batting anyone, might I suggest you start with the whore? Not the face, though. She's ugly enough."

Harkness perked up.

"Is there anything else, sir," Smalling asked, for he was the brains of the group, and his bladder was giving him some right gyp. If he didn't piss soon, he was pretty sure he would never piss again.

"As a matter of fact," Kellerman said, retaking his seat at the desk, "there is." He smiled and sucked hungrily on his cigar. Once the room was back up to what he considered to be an acceptable fogginess, he said, "How old is that Fox girl, now?"

"Zee?" Smalling said, as if there were any other daughters belonging to the Foxes. Kellerman nodded. "I'd say...she must be...if I had to venture a guess...well—"

"Was it not her birthday last week?" Kellerman impatiently said. "And did you not attend?"

Smalling nodded. "We both did, yes. Rita Fox made a wonderful cake, albeit a little dusty..."

"And how many candles would you hazard were planted in this cake?"

"Seventeen," Harkness said. "I remember counting them, because I thought it was an awful shame we didn't have anything to light them with."

"So she's seventeen?" Kellerman said.

Smalling and Harkness nodded in unison.

"In that case," Kellerman said. "I would like for you to bring her here. I have some jobs that need taking care of, and she is in need of employment."

"These *jobs*, sir?" Smalling said. "They wouldn't be of the 'blow' and 'hand' variety, would they? Only Roger and Rita Fox might not be best pleased with that situation."

"These *jobs*," Kellerman said, the irritation palpable upon his face, "are of the 'cleaning out the aquarium, emptying my ashtray, pouring me a large glass of gin and tonic' variety, not that it's any of your concern. If Miss Fox does, in fact, fall in love with me as a result, then that is entirely up to her. I'm not in the business of forcing women's hands, or mouths, for that matter."

Smalling nodded, for he quite liked Zee Fox and would have hated for anything bad to happen to her. Turned out that the worst she could expect was a cigar-burn, a couple of fish bites, and perhaps a pinch from the hinges of Kellerman's drinks cabinet as it shut.

"We'll bring her by this afternoon," Harkness said. "If that's okay with you, sir?"

Kellerman was already working himself up for a rematch with the angelfish, but he could easily make time for the arrival of Zee Fox. "Yes, that'll be fine," he said. "And if Lou *does* give you any grief over this month's payment, do feel free to clobber him once, but nothing to grievous. You don't bite the hand that feeds you, but the occasional slap is often necessary."

And there was, not even by Shakespeare or Keats or David Bowie, never a truer word spoken.

3

Lou emerged, flustered but ultimately satisfied, from the back room to his store to the sound of frenzied knocks upon the door. It always amazed him how impatient the people of Oilhaven were, given that many of them didn't have jobs or things of import to be getting on with. The Event had caused more unemployment than Margaret Thatcher.

The incessant pounding upon the door continued, and as Lou pulled his fly up and re-shelved Susie, he said, "Yes, alright, I'm coming. Honestly, it's like you've never seen a convenience store before." Of course, if the person knocking was a drifter, then the chances were that they hadn't.

Lou reached the door and unlocked it. The person/s on the other side must have sensed imminent openings, for the knocking died down ever-so-slightly.

The door opened to reveal a young girl with whom Lou was well acquainted. Her long, red hair was so dazzling that Lou had to avert his eyes momentarily, by which time Zee Fox had already blurted out something about her younger brother, Clint.

"Slow down," Lou said. "Start from the beginning, and try to enunciate." The girl was clearly agitated, for she had forgotten to include a lot of vowels in her original tirade.

"It's *Clint*," she said.

"Go on."

"He's been throwing up all morning, and it's a terrible colour. Almost *black*. Mom sent me to see if you had anything that could help him." She moved past Lou and began to examine the shelves, where she found a length of hosepipe, a cheese-grater, and a box of watch batteries.

Lou allowed the door to shut. "Can you be more specific?" he asked the girl. "I mean, was the vomit chunky or runny? Did it smell of cheese? Is your brother allergic to anything? Can you put that hosepipe down? We're not in the business of colonoscopies."

Zee placed the hosepipe back from whence it came and turned to face the shopkeeper. She grimaced. "I'd say it was the consistency of tar," she said. "Yes, tar with bits of Lego in it."

Lou frowned. "Were there bits of Lego in it?" he said. If there were, he had a feeling his diagnosis would be a speedy one.

"Not real bits of Lego," Zee said, smiling slightly, as if Lou was the densest person in the room. "But there were *chunks*, and he hasn't eaten anything with chunks in for a good few months."

"Hm." Lou wandered the length of the store and took up position behind his counter. "I'm going to assume he's been drinking the well-water and that something has perhaps died down there again."

"That's one hell of an assumption," Zee said.

"Yes, it *is*, isn't it?" Lou said, reaching below his counter. "Get him to take a spoonful of this twice a day," he said, slamming a large bottle of golden fluid onto the counter. "You may have to restrain him, because I'm not going to lie to you, it tastes like the devil's shit."

"What is it?" Zee said, picking up the bottle and examining its barely discernible label.

"Have you ever heard of something called *paracetamol*?" He articulated the last word as if he was talking to a monkey, and not a young adult.

For a moment, Zee bore the expression of someone whose sole method of travel was the short bus. "Pa-ra-cee-ta-mol," she said, slowly and deliberately. Lou had to hand it to her; for her first time, she'd really nailed it.

"That's right," he said. "Once upon a time, a long time ago—"

"Is this going to take long?" Zee said, clearly concerned about her bilious brother.

"It'll take a lot less if you don't interrupt," Lou said, forcing a smile. *Kids*, he thought. *Who'd have them?* And the answer, thankfully, was hardly anybody nowadays... "Now, where was I?"

"At the beginning I think," Zee said.

"Oh, yes. Well, a long time ago, before The Event, before you and your brothers were even born, there were places of medicine, places filled with decades-old magazines and calming fish-tanks. Places where people went to seek advice for their ailments."

"Magic?" Zee asked, hopefully.

"No, not *magic*," Lou said. "Science. You see, when these diseased people arrived at these magnificent monuments, most of which looked just like houses or office buildings, they were sent through to rooms where men and women of knowledge sat waiting, usually crunching on an apple or scribbling on bits of paper that could be swapped for pills and lotions."

"Sounds amazing," Zee said, checking her wrist for the time, even though she didn't own a watch. "Do go on."

And so Lou went on. "These doctors – that's what they were called – would listen to the infected, the diseased, the people with the bones jutting from their bodies, and do you know what they would say?"

Zee shook her head.

"They would say take two paracetamol every four hours with a glass of water and get the hell out of my office." Lou shrugged. "They were very busy people, you see, and back then, a lot of people were simply trying to get out of work. Paracetamol did the trick on most things, and that's what is in *this* bottle. I'm pretty sure that your little brother will get better if he takes it."

The girl removed the bottle from the counter and tucked it beneath her arm. "What do I owe you?" she said, reaching into her pocket and coming out with a handful of silver buttons.

Now, under normal circumstances, Lou would have counted the buttons in her palm and told her, "How strange! That's the exact amount I was going to ask for!" But not today. Today he was feeling generous. Today he was feeling…charitable. The wank he'd just had might have had something to do with it. "Just make sure Clint takes the medicine twice a day," he said. "And put those buttons away before anyone sees you. I've already had a bandit in here this morning."

"Oh, thank you, Lou!" Zee said, pocketing the silver buttons. Her mother would be ever so pleased with her. "You're a saint to this town. A gen-u-ine saint."

Lou had been called many things – tosser, cheat, buffoon, tubby, halitosis-head, cock-knocker, among others – but he'd never been called a *saint* before. It felt, he had to admit, quite nice. Not as nice as the thing he'd done in the back room five minutes ago, but nice, nonetheless.

As Zee skipped toward the door with a childlike innocence, Lou thought it was only right to say, "Don't go telling anyone about this. I might be a saint, but we don't want every Tom, Dick, and Larry coming in here expecting free paracetamol."

Zee turned and smiled. "Your secret's safe with me, Lou," she said, and with that, off she went, carrying with her a bottle of ultra-diluted painkiller that wouldn't cure a gnat's haemorrhoids.

Still, that was all he'd had to offer, and at a fair price, he thought. "Nice girl," he mumbled. She was the only *real* girl in Oilhaven. There were, he hoped, others like her out there in the world, but that was something he might never know.

For fifteen minutes, Lou set about cleaning his store, removing the thin film of grime that coated everything, and would continue to coat everything, for no apparent reason. Post-apocalyptic Oilhaven was no place for people suffering from OCD, for they would never have time to catch their breath.

"And how is business treating you, mister Decker?" said a deep, and not altogether welcome voice.

Lou stood, forgetting, for a moment, the half-polished shovel he'd been working on. When he saw the two men standing there, like a pair of bald bulldogs, he visibly shuddered. It wasn't that they frightened him; he always got like that when he was about to be relieved of his takings.

"Business is piss-poor," Lou said. "I'm starting to think someone's opened up a Walmart out in the sticks." He was, of course, lying. Business was great. Not exactly booming, but he was making enough to get by on, and the stuff coming in was in good condition, too; a veritable mish-mash of oddities and consumables.

Harkness – at least, Lou *thought* it was Harkness, for they were very much interchangeable, as far as he was concerned – did a thing with his mouth that wasn't quite a sneer and wasn't quite a smile, but something inbetween. It was the look that cats get when stricken with wind. "Now now, Lou," he said. "You know what day it is, and you know that Kellerman won't be too pleased if we go back there lighter than usual."

Kellerman, Lou thought, and now it was his turn to use the windy-cat face. Who did he think he was? Setting himself up as mayor, taking people's hard-earned wages for himself, beating those that didn't pay up (or at least getting his follically-challenged goons to do the beating) like some sort of middle-eastern despot.

"Well, as you know," Lou said, leading the men toward the counter. Slowly; what was the point in rushing? "There have been a lot of deaths around here recently. Some of my most valuable customers have, how can I put it? Ceased to exist."

Smalling reached into his jacket pocket and came out with a set of brass knuckles, which he proceeded to force over his stumpy, tattooed digits. When he was done, his hand looked like someone had dressed a bunch of sausages in elastic bands. "You don't want this to get messy, Lou," he said. "Trust me."

And Lou, who didn't trust Smalling as far as he could throw him (not very far at all), had to agree with the bald giant. He didn't want things to get messy. Messy meant blood; messy meant broken bones. Worst of all, messy meant that Smalling and Harkness would ransack the store. There was a chance, during said ransacking, that they would stumble upon his hidden stash, and that…well that simply wouldn't do.

Lou sighed and reached down below his counter. As well as bottled medicine and the pair of pistols that might or might not work, below the counter was where Lou kept Kellerman's seventy-five percent. As his hand hovered over the bag, he had the sudden urge to go for the pistols. *Why the fuck not? If they work, they work. If they*

29

don't, I'll be dragged out to the desert and… yes, *that* was why the fuck not.

"Attaboy," Harkness said as Lou dropped the bag onto the counter. "What is it this month?"

"A bit of everything," Lou said. "Some cash, a couple of rings, a jewel-encrusted music-box." Not to mention a jar of toenail clippings, some dead guy's cock-ring, and a fine selection of silver cheese-knives. Trading after the apocalypse was nothing if not interesting.

"Kellerman will be pleased," Smalling (or was it Harkness?) said. "And you, my friend, get to run your store on his land for another month. Why the long face? You look like you want to have a pop at me. Look at that face, Harkness. Is that the face of someone who looks like he wants to have a pop?"

"That's a very angry face," Harkness concurred. "It would look ridiculous peppered with bruises."

Lou allowed his features to soften and took a deep breath. If the men standing before him hadn't been built like Roman towers, he might have had a go, but they were, and so he swallowed his pride (and a little bit of sick) and kept his mouth shut.

"That's better," Smalling said. "Now. While we're being civilised, and whatnot, I was wondering if you'd seen that young Fox girl about the place?"

Yes, you just missed her. She's a lovely girl, so it's no wonder you're seeking her out for what, I assume, are insidious purposes, was what Lou should have said. What he *did* say, however, was nothing like that. It was more like, "No, I haven't seen her," and judging by the expressions on the glabrous gorillas' faces, that wasn't what they wanted to hear.

"Well, let us be frank," Harkness said, though Lou was quite happy being Lou. "If you see her, you are to contact Kellerman. I know she's something of an outdoorsy girl, so if she comes this way, we need to know about it."

Lou nodded. "I'll close the store and walk across town to Kellerman's office myself," he lied. To hell with Kellerman and his devious plans, which now seemed to include the poor Fox girl. Whatever he wanted with her, it couldn't be good. Kellerman was not in the business of showing respect, and the last thing Lou wanted was for Zee Fox to fall into the maniac's grasp.

"Okay," Smalling said, hoisting the bag up from the counter and slinging it across his shoulder. It clinked and clanked as the goods contained within knocked against one another. "We'll leave you to it. I can see you've got a lot of dusting to be getting on with."

Story of my life, Lou thought.

"Oh, and you might want to towel yourself down," Harkness said, pointing to a damp patch on Lou's shirt. "Looks like your titties are leaking. Not had a baby recently, have you?"

Lou laughed, and never a faker laugh had there been. He ran a hand across his chest, ignoring the strange warmth he found there. And *stickiness*… "Thanks for dropping by, fellas," he said, leading the way toward the door. "Be sure to drop by again. Say, in thirty days or so."

Smalling and Harkness stomped across the room behind Lou; they were of a size where stomping was only natural. "We will," Harkness said. "And don't forget, if you see the Fox girl, send her straight to Kellerman's office. It's a matter of national security."

"Is it?" Smalling asked. He looked terribly confused. "I thought the boss just wanted a *slave* girl?"

"Shhhhhhhhh," Harkness said, shaking his head and widening his eyes, the internationally recognised signal for *Shut the fuck up!*

So he wants to make a slave of her, Lou thought. *Slimy prick. Well not on my watch…*

"I'll pretend I didn't hear that," Lou said. "Now, if you could just fuck off so I can get the place dusted, that would be fantastic."

So off they fucked, leaving Lou to his own devices, which included worrying about Zee Fox, dusting the paraphernalia, and wiping down his strangely-tender boobies with a damp cloth.

Just another day in paradise…

4

A mile or so away from Oilhaven – there was no way to be sure of the actual distance, but it *felt* like a mile – stood four dirt- and pock-marked motorcycles (and one horse). Beside each vehicle stood a bandit. Sweaty and scarred, these bandits were, for want of a better word, ugly. They were the kind of bandits – not that there was any *other* kind – that one would go out of one's way to avoid. And if one *was* unfortunate enough to make their acquaintance, one would shudder and wince and most probably vomit, for these bandits were, as previously mentioned, rather unsightly.

These bandits, as most did, went by a name, a collective epithet that separated them from other bandits, and that name was:

LOS PENDEJOS

Now, for non-Spanish-speaking people, that name might conjure up images of sun-drenched beaches, margaritas, suntanned beauties pulling themselves through the water like centuries-old mermaids, and suitcases full of money and passports.

You couldn't be further from the truth, for Los Pendejos could be roughly translated as The Assholes, an apt, if not endearing, name for a bunch of bug-ugly marauders.

The leader of Los Pendejos, and therefore the owner of the cleanest and least damaged motorcycle, was El Oscuro. Now, again, those non-Spanish speakers amongst you might, upon hearing his name, think of dark things, for it does sound a lot like *Obscure*, and obscure things are seldom flamboyant. His name, roughly translated (*why is it always roughly translated? Does nobody own a Spanish-English dictionary anymore?*), means The Dark One. An odd choice, really, since El Oscuro was the only albino bandit in the state.

"Are you telling me, Samuel" El Oscuro said, clicking his fingers in a way that could only be described as diva-*esque*, "that you didn't grab a thing. That you were chased from the store by the proprietor, who appeared to be wielding a pair of antique pistols? That said store owner tried to sell you a fake vagina, and that you weren't even a little bit tempted?"

Samuel nodded; that was *exactly* what he was telling his superior.

"This is why *you* get the horse and we get the motorcycles," El Oscuro said, lighting a cigarette filled with tobacco that had been used so many times, it couldn't really be considered tobacco anymore. "Did you manage to take a good look around the town, though?"

"As I was running away," Samuel said, "I bumped into a kid throwing up black stuff in the street."

"That's hardly going to win the place any awards," Red, the female bandit, said. Red was, as one might imagine, as blonde as they came. El Oscuro's first lady, Red was a violent little minx. She'd once poked a hedgehog with a stick until it squeaked. Oh, yes, Red was not to be messed with, lest you find yourself on the wrong end of a particularly large stick.

"How many?" El Oscuro said. "How many civilians did you see as you were running away from the man with the antique pistols that might or might not have been loaded?"

Samuel did the maths in his head, which wasn't his strong point. Eventually he shrugged. "I wasn't really paying much attention," he conceded. "Other than the vomiting kid and the storekeeper, I didn't see anyone else."

"You see?" said one of the other bandits. This one was called Blink, due to the fact that he never did. "This is what happens when you send a boy to do a man's job. If you'd sent me—"

"If I'd've sent *you*," El Oscuro said, "you would have frightened everyone in town with your strange googly eyes."

"That's right," said Thumbs, who unsurprisingly didn't have any, and was therefore one of the worst pickpockets that had ever lived. "Look at all this sand out here, floating around in the air. Doesn't that make you want to blink? Not even *once?*"

Blink shook his head. "People spend five years of their lives just blinking," he said. "Which means I'll live longer than everyone else."

El Oscuro was on the verge of stabbing them all where they stood. "Can we just stop talking nonsense for a few minutes?" he said. "I've got a terrible headache, and you lot are driving me up the proverbial wall."

The bandits fell silent, apart from Samuel whose trousers audibly squeaked.

El Oscuro reached into one of his motorcycle's panniers and pulled out a map. He set about unfolding it, which was like trying to finish a Rubik's cube blindfolded. After three minutes of cursing and struggling, he screwed it up and shoved it back into the pannier from whence it came. "Okay, we've got two choices," he said. "We can skip this shitty little town and continue west. With a bit of luck we'll come across a nice city; plenty of pockets to pick and businesses to pillage. Or, we can all take a little looksee at Oilhaven. We're running low on supplies, and Blink's going to need more eye-drops soon. Now, according to the map—"

"The one you just crumpled up and stuffed in your bike?" Thumbs said.

"Yes, that's the one," El Oscuro said. "According to *that* map, there might be nothing to the west for a few days."

"A void?" Blink said. "Like a black hole?"

El Oscuro sighed. It seemed appropriate. "No, *not* a void," he said. "I mean, there are no other towns or villages. We're out in the middle of nowhere and it could be a while before we're in the middle of *somewhere*."

"That makes more sense," Blink said. "But for all we know, people have built new towns. That map's an old one."

"*Finally*, he speaks some sense," El Oscuro said. "There have been no new maps since The Event, which means we have no real way of knowing if any reservations have popped up in this area. What we need to decide is whether to risk it. Do we continue west, and hope to come across somewhere to pillage and plunder, or do we sneak into Oilhaven like the pitiful little creatures we are and have a bloody good time?"

There were mumblings and mutterings as the members of Los Pendejos chewed it over. Red took this moment of deliberation to relieve herself behind a dead cactus. When she returned, it seemed that the decision had been made.

Fucking typical, she thought. *Pop out for a piss and all of a sudden you lose your right to vote.*

"It's settled then," El Oscuro said, throwing a leg across his mechanical steed. "As soon as it gets dark, we'll sneak into Oilhaven and find somewhere to hunker down. Then, first thing in the morning, we'll have a good look around. Since the only things we know about are a bilious child and a storekeeper with pistols older than all of us put together, we should have a lot of things to discover."

"Won't they hear us coming?" Samuel said. "I mean, *I'm* alright. I've got the horse, but won't they be suspicious if four Harley's come a-rolling into town in the middle of the night? They're pretty noisy, and noise tends to wake people up."

"Which is why we're going to bury them here," El Oscuro said, climbing from his bike and silently cursing himself for not thinking about that before now. "Yes, I'd already thought about that," he lied. "Start digging. At least a foot down. We don't want to be known as the bandits whose bikes were stolen by other bandits."

And so Red and Blink, Samuel and Thumbs, all began to dig. Since they had no tools, they dug with their hands, and the sand was awfully dry and took a fair bit of digging.

"No, not the *horse!*" El Oscuro exclaimed, for he had taken his eyes off the diggers for just a moment. "Get him out of there before he chokes to death on sand."

And the horse did some whinnying as he was pulled from the freshly-dug hole. He also did some headshaking and some sighing, for Mordecai had once belonged to a very sensible farmer from Ohio, and knew very well that he was in the company of idiots.

When the holes were dug and the motorcycles buried – in a fashion – El Oscuro took a step back and inspected his crew's handiwork. "Not bad, not bad," he said, though it wasn't *good*, either. "Looks like someone got fed up of *Take That*, but it'll have to do."

And the sun began to drop toward the horizon, as was its wont, and the heat…well, that remained, for The Event had royally fucked up the climate. Even at night-time the temperature levelled off at around ninety. Many pyjama factories had shut in the months following The Event, as had boxer-shorts warehouses, nightie distributors, hot-water bottle manufacturers, and cuddly toy plants. Across the world, however, cold-water bottle sales had tripled, and liquid-nitrogen duvet sets were now an actual thing, thanks to an investment from the three surviving members of Dragons' Den.

"So what do we do now?" Thumbs said, plunking himself down in the sand.

"Give it another half hour," El Oscuro said. "And then Oilhaven will be ours."

5

The Fox house was built on good foundations, meaning it didn't fall down quite as often as everyone else's. It was also built right at the edge of town, which gave the family a great 180-degree view of the desert, not that anything ever happened out there, though Tom Fox, the unfortunate middle-child, had once watched a plastic bag float from east to west, which had killed ten minutes.

As the only parents of young children in Oilhaven (Zee, Tom, and Clint) Roger and Rita Fox knew a thing or two about sleepless nights, and bore the wounds to prove it. Thirty-nine and forty respectively, Roger and Rita Fox looked twice their age. Both were grey and brittle, a result of going without for so long. They were, in fact, the perfect advertisement for why the apocalypse was no place for raising kids.

Roger, when he wasn't trying to sleep, worked at the Oilhaven mine. It was his job to sift out the bad dirt and bag it up, a thankless job if ever there was one. There weren't many uses for the bad dirt, but like fluffing midgets for porn movies (*Snow Tight and the Seven Whores, The Gobbit, Lord of the Brown Rings*), someone had to do it...

Rita Fox was a stay-at-home mother, which meant that she had the unenviable task of chasing two prepubescent boys around the yard, occasionally hitting them with broom-handles, whilst trying to keep a seventeen-year-old girl from going off the rails. Roger moaned about his job on a daily basis, but he wouldn't have swapped places with his wife for all the dirt in the mine.

As a family, they sat around the youngest member with concerned expressions etched upon their countenances. In other words, Rita hoped Clint stopped being sick soon; she'd spent the majority of the day sweeping it out the front door, and it was getting to be quite bothersome.

"He's starting to look a bit better," Roger said, noting the colour upon his exhausted son's cheeks. "That medicine Lou gave you seems to be doing the trick."

Zee smiled and stroked her youngest brother's head. "He said it was something called pa-ra-*cee*-ta-mol," she said.

At the mere mention of the magical remedy, Rita and Roger's faces lit up. "Well, *that's* a blast from the past," Roger said. "Do you know, I haven't heard that word for almost…must be *twenty* years."

"We used to take paracetamol all the time," said Rita. "Usually to stave off the effects of a particularly nasty hangover."

"What's a *hangover*, Mommy?" Tom asked, pulling his favourite dirty blanket around him. It wasn't cold, but Tom sure did love his blan-kee, more than he loved *not* dripping with sweat.

Roger and Rita exchanged knowing glances, as was their custom when recalling things from the past. It usually meant something long and tedious was about to follow, something of absolute inconsequence.

"Well," Rita said, "back in the day, *before* The Event, alcohol was in abundance. You couldn't move for the stuff. In fact, there was so much of it that people were addicted to it. They would spend all their benefits on cider and whiskey and vodka and lager and, if they were feeling really flush, mojito."

"But didn't they need to eat?" asked Tom.

"They *did*," Roger said, stroking his face in that way father's do – with a dirty, half-chewed fingernail. "But these people eschewed food in order to buy more alcohol."

"They were what we called alco-holics," Rita said.

"Or *pissheads*," Roger added. "But for the social drinkers, such as your mother and I, we reserved our drinking for the weekends."

"That's right," Rita said, smiling up at the empty space in front of her as if in fond remembrance. "Your father and I would go out on a Saturday night, and we would dance. And drink. Often at the same time, which meant a lot of spillages on the dance-floor."

"But that didn't matter," Roger said, reaching across and taking his wife's hand. "As your mother said, there was plenty of the stuff."

"And so we would drink and dance until the early hours of the morning before hailing a taxi," Rita said.

"Mommy, what's a tax-ee?" Tom asked, for he was quite the inquisitive little runt.

"A taxi," she said, "was a car that smelled of sick and dog-shit. What you would do is, you would signal a taxi down, and then you would climb in and tell the driver where you wanted to go. Then, when you got there, you would pay him."

"Sounds ridiculous," Zee said, shaking her head. "Why would anyone want to get into a car that stank of shit and sick?"

"Nobody *wants* to get into a car that stinks of shit and sick," Roger Fox said. "But at three in the morning, when your kebab's going cold, the smell isn't all that important." He stroked Rita's hand with sickening affection; Zee gave Clint another spoonful of medicine, just so she didn't have to watch their hands fucking.

"So what's a *hangover*?" Tom asked, for he was still waiting for an answer.

"A hangover is how you feel the morning after all that drinking and dancing," Rita said. "It's like a headache and a stomach-ache rolled into one."

"It's what paracetamol was originally invented for," Roger said, though whether that was true, he didn't know.

"Did the alco-holics take it?" Tom asked. "When they had a hangover?"

Roger stretched and yawned. "Well, the thing with the pissheads," he said, "was that they drank so much of the stuff that they became immune to it. Some of them, the really bad ones, well they didn't stop drinking long enough for a hangover to set in. A hangover's what happens when you stop drinking, so a lot of them kept it up around the clock."

"Clever bastards," Zee said as she walked across the room and emptied Clint's sick-pan out of the window.

"I don't think *they* thought so," Rita said, wringing dirty water out of a mouldy facecloth before draping it across her son's face. Her son was too young and too sick to protest.

"I can't believe Lou Decker gave you the medicine for *free*," Roger said. "I had him pegged as the kind of guy that would charge you three silver buttons just to use his commode." And, Roger thought, with good reason, since he'd once paid three silver buttons just to use Lou's commode…

"Well, he was really nice," Zee said, placing the empty sick-pan down beside her brother. "I think he's getting soft in his old age, and having to look after his poor, dying mother, too."

Rita tutted. "Freda Decker has been dying for the last twenty years," she said. "It all started because of an ingrowing toenail, and since then she's been on her back. I think she's one of those Munchausen women."

"What?" Roger said, scratching his head. "You mean she's *barren*?"

Rita didn't have time to correct her husband – or reproach him for such a terrible joke – as there came a heavy knock upon the door. It was the knock of

43

someone who clearly wanted to come in, as most knocks were.

"Don't all get up at once," Roger said as he climbed to his feet. His knees audibly cracked. He walked across the room, which was lit only by three candles, but they were nice candles; the kind of candles that gave off a spicy smell.

"Wait a minute," Rita said, suddenly concerned. "You're not going to answer that, are you?"

Roger looked at the door, and then at his wife, and decided that, yes, he was going to answer it, as was the done thing with knocked doors. "It's probably nothing," he said, more to convince himself than anyone else.

Another knock, this one more impatient than the last.

"Well, that nothing's making a helluva racket," Rita said. "I don't trust it, and at *this* time of night." She looked at her wrist and, lo and behold, she didn't have a watch, but the moon was high in the sky, and that was good enough for her.

Now Roger was uneasy. Rita was right; they weren't expecting anyone, and there was a certain *I'll huff and I'll puff and I'll blow your house down* vibe about the knocking. Maybe they were overthinking it, but maybe they weren't. Maybe there were bandits at the door. Big ugly bandits that rode motorcycles and had silly names. Maybe...

"We know you're in there," said a voice, and it was a voice they all recognised. It belonged to Smalling, one of Kellerman's turds, though quite what it was doing hammering on their door in the middle of the night was anyone's guess. "We can see the candles flickering beyond your curtains. What's that smell? Cinnamon?"

"Go out through the back window," Rita told Zee. "Take Tom with you, and stick to the shadows."

"But Mo—"

"Do as your mother says," Roger interrupted, keeping his voice as low as humanly possible. "They're probably only here for this month's taxes."

Then why am I being tossed out the back? Zee thought. Still, there was no point in arguing. She climbed to her feet and took Tom's hand in her own. "How will I know if it's safe to come back?" she said.

Roger considered it, then said, "I'll put one of these smelly candles on the back windowsill."

Zee rolled her eyes, for it was a code that Alan Turning would surely laugh at. "Okay then," she said, and to Tom, "Come on. We're going to have a little walk in the dark. Let's just hope we don't get attacked and buggered by bandits."

"Don't be such a drama queen," Rita hissed, though the thought had already crossed her mind. "Take your machete with you, and if anyone tries to bugger you or your little brother, you have my permission to lop off their buggering tools."

At that, Zee brightened. She picked up her machete from the corner of the room and dragged Tom out through the rear window, which wasn't difficult as there was no glass in it.

There came more banging upon the door, to which Roger Fox said, "Alright, alright! I'm coming! Honestly!"

The banging stopped and was replaced by conspiratorial whispering. Roger didn't waste any time in opening the door after that, as there was nothing more dangerous than conspiratorial whispering.

"Ah, Harkness, Smalling," he said cheerily as the candlelight from within reflected on their bald pates.

"Actually, *I'm* Harkness," Harkness said. "He's Smalling."

"That's very interesting," Roger said, though it really wasn't. "I take it Kellerman has spent last month's tax and would like some more?" It wasn't funny, but neither was turning up at one's door in the middle of the night, unannounced.

The one called Smalling climbed into a pair of brass knuckles and grinned. "Please, Mr Fox, give me a reason to use these. It's been a very boring day so far, and I've got all this pent-up aggression." He pinched the bridge of his nose between thumb and forefinger. Roger considered sending him to LOU'S LOOT, where he knew for certain the knucklehead could find himself a reasonably-priced painkiller.

"That won't be necessary," Roger said. Across his shoulder, he called, "Rita! Could you bring the envelope from the bureau? The one with the picture of the sad face on it?"

A few seconds later, Rita Fox stood at the door, wielding a small brown envelope with considerable skill.

"Is *this* the one?" she said, gesturing to the envelope. "I only ask because there's a picture of a sad face in one corner, and in the other, a rather nifty sketch of a pair of tits."

"That's not a pair of *tits*," Roger said, accepting the envelope from his wife with a smile. "That's a picture of Smalling and Harkness here. Our friendly local bruisers. Granted, it's rudimentary, but I think I captured the essence of them both."

"Give me *that*," Smalling said, snatching the envelope from Roger with so much force, the corner tore away. "It looks nothing like us. It looks like a pair of tits."

Roger Fox nonchalantly shrugged. "Will there be anything else?"

"Actually," Harkness said, peering past the Foxes into the candlelit room. "We came by earlier today, but there was no-one home."

That made sense. Roger had worked a twelve hour shift at the mine, and Rita had been too busy tending to their sick son to answer the door. "And what was it that you came by for earlier?" Rita said, suddenly apprehensive. Roger reached down and took her hand, which was clammier than a jogger's butt-crack.

"Oh, nothing to worry about," Harkness said, with a grin that suggested it was something to worry about a lot. "Kellerman has a proposal for your daughter, that's all."

"He can fuck off!" Rita snapped. Roger squeezed her hand, and her next words were a little cooler. "I mean, why would he want anything with Zee? She's about as useful as an ashtray on a motorbike."

"Is she here?" Smalling said.

"She's *never* here," Roger said. "Spends more time outdoors than the stars, that one."

"Do you know when she'll be back?" Harkness said, clearly growing impatient. He was already thinking about what they might tell Kellerman upon returning to his office with the collected money...and no girl.

Rita Fox huffed and crossed her arms. "Have either of you ever met a seventeen-year-old girl before, other than Zee?"

They shook their bald heads in unison.

"Well, seventeen year-old girls," Rita continued, "are like volcanoes. Entirely unpredictable and liable to erupt at any moment."

"But at least you always know where a volcano is," Smalling said, rather cleverly for him.

"Indeed you do," Roger said, "but that doesn't make them any less dangerous."

Harkness frowned and lit a roll-up. "I have no idea how we got onto the subject of volcanoes, but I'd rather we didn't continue," he said. "If you could send Zee to Kellerman as soon as she returns..."

"Of course," Roger said. "Send her straight to Mayor Kellerman, gotcha!" Behind his back, both hands were possessed of crossed fingers.

"Mommy!" a tiny voice whined from the room behind. Then there was retching and groaning, and then a splat, which meant that Clint had managed to miss the sick-pan and had, once again, upchucked on the floor.

"You'll have to excuse us," Rita said, tugging her husband back by the arm and easing the door shut. "We've got a very sick boy at the moment, and…" That was as far as she got before the door closed in the henchmen's faces. "Shit, Roger, what does Kellerman want with Zee?"

Roger seemed to be staring past her. "I have no idea," he said. "But one thing's for sure."

Rita clutched at the pendant hanging around her neck. "What? What is it, Roger?"

"We need to get a bigger sick-pan."

6

Lou locked up the store when the moon was directly overhead. It wasn't the most accurate way of telling the time, but you worked with what you had. He took the leads off the charger which powered his neon sign (currently reading LOU'S LOO due to a broken T) and gave the place a once over, just to make sure everything was just so. After deciding there were no ninja bandits hiding out in the shadows, he made his way upstairs, to where his mother lay dying.

"Good day?" she asked as he tried to slip by her room unnoticed, a feat he hadn't managed in over twenty years. Dying or not, there was sod all wrong with her hearing.

"Didn't get *killed*," he told her, easing the door open just a little, just enough to see her partially mummified face by the candle in his hand.

"That's nice," said she. "Did we sell much?"

We? That never ceased to amaze Lou. "Couple of things," he said, yawning. "How are you feeling today?" He hated to ask but, as her only son and confidant, he felt obliged.

"Like shit warmed up," she said, which made a change from 'Like a sack of turds in a tumble-drier'. One of these days she would surprise him. One of these days she would answer the question with, 'I feel much better today, thank you, son,' and he would drop down dead where he stood, for portly men are known for their inability to handle sudden shocks. "Can you bring the fan closer?"

Lou sighed and entered the room proper. The fan sitting in the corner of the room hadn't worked for fifteen years, but she liked to lie there and imagine the blades going round. "Is that better?" he said, setting it at the bottom of her bed.

"You're a good boy," she told him. Her gummy grin would have unsettled most people, but not Lou. "I don't think I have long left, son—"

"Mother," he said, anything to stop her from going off on another 'I don't have long left' speech. "You were saying that twenty years ago, and look. You're still here. And twenty years from now" – *God, I hope not* – "you'll *still* be saying it."

Her inelastic bones creaked as she clambered up onto her elbows. She weighed no more than six stone, which was five and a half stone more than she would have weighed had she succumbed, as promised, and made her way into the urn Lou had been polishing for the last two decades. "No, you go on to bed," she said. "Don't worry about your silly old mother."

And there was the guilt trip she liked to slather him in just before bed, which made it almost impossible for him to sleep. And if the guilt wasn't enough, her muffled sobs usually did the trick. On the bright side – Lou was an optimist, except when it came to wild mushrooms – if she was *crying*, then she wasn't *dying*.

"Can I get you anything before I go?" he asked. "I've got a half-gallon of purified water in my room. Are you thirsty?"

She *was* thirsty, and she knew all about her son's basement stash. She often went down there on the days he went out. In fact, she was the most active bedridden person she knew. "Do you have any of that brandy left?" she said, knowing full well that he did, and that he was intent on bartering with it in the near future. For some reason, bandits loved a nip of brandy. "The stuff that pulls your lips back over your gums?"

Lou sighed. She was talking about his apricot brandy moonshine, the most potent drink he'd ever managed to brew. "I've only got a little bit left," he said.

"That's okay," she said, grinning gums once again. "I only *want* a little bit."

And so Lou headed down to the basement, and when he returned, Freda Decker was sat up in bed with a glass in one hand and a cigarette going in the other. "You never know," she said, pushing the empty glass toward her son. "This might be my last drink."

Somehow, Lou thought, *I highly doubt it.*

With his mother placated, for now, Lou headed through to his room and collapsed onto the bed, which in turn collapsed onto the floor. He was too tired to do anything about it now, though, and was soon slipping into a deep, deep sleep, where he hoped to dream of a world without bandits, a world without corrupt mayors and bald-headed goons, a world without an ailing mother who wasn't ailing quite as badly as she liked to make out. A world in which The Event had never happened.

And then he heard it. His mother's melodramatic sobs from the other end of the hallway. He pulled the pillow over his head and closed his eyes.

7

Kellerman chewed upon his cigar as he counted the month's takings out on his desk. It wasn't a bad haul considering, and yet the one thing he'd been looking forward to all day remained absent.

Zee Fox. Not too shabby to look at, and not too far gone to be disciplined. She was what Oilhaven needed; what *he* needed. A matriarch. Someone to point the finger at when things went wrong. Someone to bring him tea and cigars while he settled down after a long day of unethical dealings.

Every gangster had one – a Frances Kray, a Mae Capone, a Hilary Clinton – and was he not a gangster? Was he not running Oilhaven as he saw fit; with an iron fist and a pair of tit-headed maniacs? Was he not the boss? And didn't the boss deserve a woman, one that hadn't been dragged kicking and screaming through the apocalypse?

Why yes, Kellerman thought. He certainly did...

He wasn't looking for love, or someone to fornicate with on those cold nights (*which* cold nights?). As far as he was concerned, love was just a word now. It was no longer 'all around' as one long-dead band had put it. Nor was it 'all you need' or something that you should tell Laura. It was a four-letter-word, and Kellerman knew plenty of those.

No, Zee wasn't going to fill a space in his heart; she was going to fill the space in his cupboards, hopefully with cleaning products. She was going to do all the running around, for he wasn't as young as he used to be, and anyone that was should make an appointment with a doctor, if they could find one that hadn't been evaporated by the apocalypse.

There was only so much time one could spend discussing current affairs with tropical fish – eighteen minutes and thirty-six seconds, to be exact. But Zee Fox could be educated, taught everything he knew, and they could play chess and draughts and, if she was really in the mood, *Clue*, and they would rule Oilhaven (80-20 in Kellerman's favour, of course) like a couple of British monarchs, only without all that hoity-toity crown and throne nonsense.

"We could change its *name*," he said, forgetting for a moment that he was utterly alone. And they *could*. They could change the name of the town to one of those annoying portmanteaus that the old people used to favour so much on their cottages and caravans.

KellerZee?

Zellerman?

Kellermanzee?

"Yes, we could do that," he said, once again out loud. Or they could stick with Oilhaven and not be known as 'that irritating pair of cunts who think they run the bleeding place'.

Either way, things were looking up for Kellerman, and for Oilhaven (Zellerkee?).

If only, he thought, *we knew where she'd pissed off to...*

*

"It won't be for much longer," Zee said, stroking Tom's sweat-drenched head. Her brother was tired, and ready for bed, but she knew they had to wait. To go back now was insane. Her parents had sent them out to the desert for a reason, though what that reason was, she didn't quite know.

"Do you think they're okay?" Tom said. "It's been a long time since we left."

"It *has* been a long time," Zee said. "A really long time, but we promised that we wouldn't return until we saw the candle in the window, and we're going to keep that promise." She drew her brother in close, and then pushed him away just as fast, for he was sweatier than a gypsy with a mortgage.

"What if something terrible has happened?" Tom asked, glaring up at her with sad, puppy-dog eyes. She knew exactly what he was saying. *What if Mom, Dad, and Clint have been butchered and are currently dripping down the living-room walls?* She preferred his understated question more than her own translation.

"Dad wouldn't let anything bad happen to the family," she said. "And I don't think Smalling or Harkness would do anything to hurt them, or *anyone* for that matter." They were, she thought, like a couple of castrated pitbulls. Sure, they *looked* nasty, but you were more likely to be attacked by a clique of meandering kittens.

"He *likes* you, you know?" Tom said, far more knowingly than any eight-year-old boy had the right to.

"Who?"

"The *bald* one?" Tom said.

"They're *both* bald," she said.

"The one who always stands on the right."

"Oh!" Zee said, suddenly realising which one he meant. "Smalling! No, he doesn't, and don't say things like that out here in the dark. It's creepy as hell."

Tom smiled. "He does. I've seen the way he looks at you. Like he wants to *sex* you."

"Thomas Edgar Fox, you take that back right now!" Zee couldn't believe what she was hearing. "And anyway. What do *you* know about sexing? You're barely old enough to know about *walking*."

"I've heard Mom and Dad *sexing*," he said. "I know what it is. It's when a man climbs onto a woman and..."

"Can we not do this?" Zee said, looking anywhere but at her brother, who seemed to know more about sexing than she did. "Mom and Dad don't sex, and they never have. Sexing's something people used to do before the world fell apart." It had crossed her mind, on more than one occasion, that the world had fallen apart *because* of sexing. The Event, from what she'd heard about it, was like a big explosion, and sexing, from what she'd *also* heard, was pretty much the same. Maybe too many people had been sexing at the same time, thusly blowing the world to kingdom come. It was a theory, anyway.

They sat in silence for a few minutes, which suited Zee just fine, and stared out into the darkness, toward the house that they called home.

It was very dark over there...

Almost as if...

*

"Shit!" Rita Fox said, lurching forward in the marital bed.

"What?" Roger said, following suit.

There was something they'd forgotten, but Rita couldn't quite put her finger on it. "Did you empty Clint's sick-pan?" she said into the darkness.

"Twice," Roger replied. "There was a lot less on the second one. I think he's going to be alright."

Rita relaxed back into her pillows. "Good, good," she said, closing her eyes. No, there was something else…something of utmost import that they'd forgotten. "Have you set an alarm?" she whispered.

"Not since two-thousand and twenty-five," Roger replied, slapping his lips noisily together. "But if it makes you feel better, I can wake up a little bit earlier than you and do some beeping."

Rita shook her head. "No, that's fine, but I'm sure there was something we needed to OH MY FUCKING GOD WE FORGOT ABOU ZEE!"

For a minute, Roger Fox lay motionless, as if he recognised the name, and yet couldn't remember where from.

Then it hit him like a ten-ton-hammer, and he did lots of *oopsing* and cursing as he stumbled about in the dark in search of candles, matches, and something to protect him from their angry daughter when she got back.

8

The horse trotted quietly and slowly into Oilhaven. Upon its back, five bandits argued and whispered at one another over which one of them had guffed.

"Everyone just pipe down," El Oscuro said, pulling on Mordecai's reins. "It doesn't *matter* which one of us farted. There are more pressing matters afoot."

"That means it was El Oscuro," Red muttered from the back of the horse. She dismounted in a spectacular fashion – somersault, cartwheel, up into a pirouette – and straightened up her dress, which bore more stains than an ex-president's trousers. "So this is Oilhaven," she said, taking it all in. "Doesn't look like much."

Samuel climbed down from the horse, though not as gracefully as Red had (foot caught in stirrup, moan of despair, ass hit the floor). "They have the store," he said, dusting himself down. "Which is more than most shitty Podunk towns have in this day and age."

"What do *you* think, Thumbs?" El Oscuro said, taking Mordecai up to a canter.

The answer was, of course, not a lot. "I think we could do some real damage here. I mean, I wouldn't suggest setting up shop, or anything, but it'll do for a couple of days. Like you said, we're running low on supplies. I think we'll find what we need here."

From within the shadows to their right, something smashed. In response, the bandits pulled out small blades and sharp sticks, except for El Oscuro, who unsheathed a samurai sword. Being the leader certainly had its perks…

"Over there," Red said, pointing at the darkness between two ramshackle huts with her cleaver.

Surely enough, something shifted within the nebulous space; a dark pink mass, sliding along the floor like a giant filthy worm. Since there were no such things at giant worms, filthy or otherwise, the bandits wasted no time in making their approach.

"We know you're there," El Oscuro said, slicing the air in front of him with the sword. Mordecai nervously whinnied as the wind from the swinging blade whispered into his ears. "Don't make any sudden movements, and I promise no harm will come to you."

Blink, Thumbs, Samuel, and Red walked a few feet ahead of the horse, who was, in turn, quite grateful. The closer they got, the more panicked the writhing pink shape became. It was a man…a *naked* man…not what any of them had expected to see upon their arrival, but it *was* a hot night, and it wasn't as if there were any police to arrest the starkers native.

"Is that what I think it is?" Thumbs said, squinting.

"If you're thinking it's a shrivelled penis," Red said, "then yes."

"We're not going to hurt you," El Oscuro said to the trembling shape. "And you clearly have nothing for us to steal, at least nothing that would feed us for very long." He climbed down from the horse and moved to the front of his gang.

The man – if one could call such a deprived creature a man – pressed himself as tightly to the wall between the two buildings as he could. "I don't have anything," he said. "Please don't hurt me."

El Oscuro frowned. "I just told you that…never mind. Listen, naked man. Do you know somewhere around here that would put up a weary band of travellers? We're a tidy bunch, and not averse to leaving a ridiculous tip." He sheathed the sword; the man cowering in the shadows was clearly not a threat.

"You…you could try…try Abigail," the man said. Despite the heat, he was shivering, as if afflicted with something incurable, something that none of the bandits wanted to catch a whiff of.

"You'll have to be more specific," Samuel said, flicking the poor man in his tiny junk. "We're not from around here. Is Abigail an inn-owner?"

"Close," the defrocked chap said. "She's the resident whore."

Glances were exchanged between the bandits, many of them filled with disgust. The naked man sensed he was losing them and decided that what Abigail needed was a generous sugar-coating – not to mention a de-fleaing, a good bath, and a liberal application of thrush cream.

"No, she's *okay*," Nudey Nuderson said. "She has space at her place for the likes of you, providing she hasn't got any clients tonight."

"Does she get a lot of clients?" Blink said, as wide-eyed as ever.

"Does a bear shit on the *pope*?" said the naked man. When all he got for his efforts was confused stares, he added, "No. She hasn't been busy recently. It's not that there's anything wrong with her. I mean, I wouldn't, personally, but she's a lovely old lady, if you can see past the glass eye and the hair lip."

"I'm sure we can pretend not to notice," El Oscuro said. "Where can we find this delightful dolly?"

"She lives just down yonder," said the naked man. His finger pointed in the direction of 'down yonder'. "But I doubt she'll be in at this time of night. She'll be out touting her goods to anyone brave enough to touch 'em. You'll most likely find her at The Barrel."

"You have a bar here?" Red said, incredulous. "An actual bar?"

The naked man tried not to laugh. "If you could call it that. The Barrel sells watered-down drinks—"

"*How* watered-down?" Thumbs said, suddenly excited.

"There's probably more alcohol in the rain," said the naked man. "But people like to think they're getting tanked. It's amazing how tipsy you can get by sipping at a glass of 0.2% water."

"Sounds *wonderful*," Blink said. "Let's go and get fucked off our faces and have a chat with an old hooker."

"Or *Saturday night*, as it used to be known," Thumbs added.

"If you just tell her Mickey sent you, she'll…" He trailed off, then added, "You know what? Don't mention me. Just tell her you're looking for a place to stay for the night. I'm assuming you have the means to pay for said lodgings?"

"We'll not slaughter her in her sleep, if that's what you mean," Red said, though she knew very well that wasn't what he had in mind.

"Yes, most people accept 'not dying' as a currency where we're from," El Oscuro said. "But this is Oilhaven. Who are we to come in here and start breaking the rules? Of *course* we will recompense Ms Abigail for the use of her floor."

"You haven't seen her *floor* yet," the naked man said.

"And so, on that non-joke, we will bid you adieu." El Oscuro mounted Mordecai. "Now…where might we find this lightweight bar?"

The naked man stepped, momentarily, from the shadows, his tiny thing blowing gently in the wind. "If you go to the end of this street, you'll see a dead crow. Take a right, and you'll notice a barrel leaning against a wall.

"Ah, so that's why it's called The Barrel?" Blink said, nodding.

"No, it's because the owner's built like a *dalek*."

"Oh."

And they all laughed.

"Okay, put your game-faces on, people," El Oscuro said. "We're going to The Barrel to catch us a whore."

You'll be lucky, thought the naked man as he slunk back into the darkness, *if that's all you catch…*

9

Fields. Beautiful green fields on all sides. It was, it had to be, a dream. A wonderful dream from which he would regret waking, but for now he would enjoy it. He would revel in its glory, for dreams like this didn't come around too often. More often than not, his dreams were filled with wretchedness; with images of his dying (was she?) mother. With visions of those terrible moments immediately following The Event. This dream, this beautiful dream, was a breath of fresh air.

Speaking of air, the air here was breathable. More than that, it tasted of syrup. A sweet, delicious syrup that one could eat forever and never grow tired of. He inhaled, and inhaled, and ignored the saccharine lumps at the back of his throat. Anything was better than the dust and sand he'd gulped on for the last twenty years.

I never want to wake up, *he thought.* Please, let this be it. Let me remain here forever, with these fields, and those...

Cows.

Lots of cows. Mooing at him, but not in a threatening fashion. He wasn't afraid of them, and why would he be? They were part of a dream – part of his marvellous dream. There was nothing to be scared of.

There are a lot of them, though, *he thought, taking a few tentative steps forward. The grass felt good beneath his feet; a luxurious carpet of damp timothy.*

The sun was up, but it wasn't unbearable. He wasn't sweating, which made a nice change. Out there, in the waking world, you couldn't move without excreting thick, slimy sweat, but here...here, he could walk around in the daylight, with the sun at its zenith, and not have to worry about where the next towel was going to come from, or if he was going to wake up the following day peppered with zits.

Out here, everything was perfect.

Except…

Something wasn't quite right. The cows were regarding him with something akin to circumspection, as if they knew something that he didn't. Lou didn't like it. No, this is a nice dream! Please don't fuck it up for me!

But it was already fucked up; he just didn't know it yet.

At the edge of the field to his right, a farmhouse stood. Its red roof and swinging barn door would have been considered clichés if there was anyone else there to witness them, but Lou didn't mind. Sometimes, a cliché was the only way to go.

He moved closer to the farmhouse, wary of the cows in the surrounding fields, which appeared to be conversing with one another in the only way they knew how. Moooooooo! "Look at this twat. Who does he think he is? Coming into our field, walking around as if he owns the place."

No, it's a nice dream! Leave me alone.

As he reached the edge of the field, he met the fence separating him from the farmhouse. The scent of something wonderful drifted across from the open back door, something cooking on the hob, or, he thought, in one of those industrial-sized ovens. Whatever it was, it overpowered the sweet, sweet air for just a moment. It was delightful, and exactly what one might expect to sniff at the back door of some pre-apocalyptic farmhouse.

Mooooooooo! "He doesn't get it," one of the cows said, though Lou knew that cows didn't speak. *It was the surreal part of his dream; all dreams had them. You could be having the most logical dream ever and then, bam! In pops Elvis Presley for a little singsong and a fried banana sandwich. That was how dreams worked, and it explained the talking cow element of his perfectly.*

He turned his attention back to the farmhouse, and not a moment too soon, for a man was leaving, now, via the back door.

"Excuse me," Lou said, *hoping the man could hear him as he trundled across the path.* "I couldn't help noticing the wonderful smell emanating from your back door. Would it be terribly forward of me to offer up my services? I'm extremely good at eating food, and it would be an awful shame if you didn't get an outside opinion on your wife's cooking."

The man mustn't have heard, for he headed into the barn at the side of the house without so much as a sideways glance.

Mooooooooo! "Listen to him. Thinks Barry's going to let him have some soup. Who does he think he is?"

Shut up, Lou said. If you don't ask, you don't get. *He didn't know why he was explaining himself to a fieldful of cows, but it seemed appropriate since they were mocking him so implacably. What was it with these cows, anyway? Were they jealous of him? They were lucky he hadn't dreamt a barbecue into the field and started hacking them up. It had been a long time since he'd had a decent burger – one not made from squirrel or, god forbid, tofu – and here was a field filled with cows, the main component of a decent burger.*

Was it too late to imagine a grill and a bag of charcoal?

Ah, here came the farmer again, carrying a pair of iron buckets. "Excuse me, Barry, is it? I'm Lou, and this is my dream, so you can stop acting for the time being and fetch me a bowl of that special soup you've got going on in the house."

Barry opened the gate, stepped through onto the grass, and pulled it shut behind him, making sure it was locked.

Why am I locked in here with these…these animals? Only now did he find it odd that he was standing in a field; only now did it strike him as a little unusual that he wasn't sat at the dinner table with a napkin around his neck and the farmer's wife staring at him with pure lust as he filled his cheeks with pea and ham broth.

The farmer walked across the field, toward *Lou, and yet persisted with his silly game of ignorance.* "Erm, Barry? Bazza? Baz? Whatever, look, I know you can hear me, so you might as well knock it off and answer."

Nothing.

Mooooooooooo! "He doesn't know," *said one of the talking cows.* "He's an idiot," *said another.* "He's about to get the shock of his fecking life," *said a third, for it was an Irish cow.*

What are they talking about? *Lou thought, staring around at the cows as they muttered conspiratorially at one another.* "Oi! You lot! If you've got something to say, say it to my faaaaaaaa…."

And that was where the dream took a turn for the worse as something yanked on Lou's cock. At least, he thought it was his cock. That was the only thing down there worth yanking on, as far as he was concerned.

"Keep still," *the farmer, Barry, said. He'd dropped to his knees; the buckets had been placed underneath Lou.*

"Look, mate," Lou said. "I don't know what your game is, but I'm not into all that. If you could just take your hands off my..."

Udder?

Lou pushed his head as far forward as he could, and it was then that he saw his legs – all four of them – and at the end of each leg was a black hoof. And the thing that Barry was tugging on was not his cock, after all, and though he was grateful for that, he was a little disturbed by the hanging sack of mammary glands that made up his undercarriage.

Mooooooo! "By jove, I think he gets it!" said one of the cows.

"What the fuck is going on!?" Lou yelled, trying to move away from the hand frantically jerking beneath him. But he was stuck fast, for this was that part of the dream when paralysis sets in. "No, this can't be happening! This isn't real! It's just a dream!"

A really, really bad dream.

Lou (moo?) closed his eyes and counted to ten, ignoring the farmer's hand as it continued to milk him for all he was worth.

One, two, three...

Just a dream. A nightmare. An awful nightmare in which Lou was a cow...

Four, five, six...

Nothing to worry about, apart from Barry's ring finger, which was pinching his teat...

Seven, eight, nine...

Everything was damp, now...damp and cloying, as if he'd been the centre of attention at a bukkake party.

Ten...

*

Flinging himself forward in bed, the first thing Lou realised was that he was sweating dreadfully, despite the bed not having any covers. The malodorous stench of perspiration filled the room, but it wasn't just the smell of sweat he noticed in the air. There was something else, commingling with the sweat. Something he hadn't smelt in a long, long time.

Milk.

But that wasn't possible, was it? Men don't produce milk, do they? That would be like a woman squirting semen, wouldn't it? All good questions, none of which he knew the answer to.

He ran a tremulous hand down his front, through the sodden, coarse hairs that had graced his chest since his tenth birthday. Sure enough, there was a stickiness there, one that you wouldn't associate with sweat.

"No," he laughed, shaking his head. "Not possible."

But, apparently, it *was* possible. It was *very* possible because it had happened.

His chest-hair was matted, thick with…dairy? He ran a finger over one of his nipples (the left one, not that it mattered) and watched as a jet of still-warm milk fountained out, pattering upon his mattress with a noise like raindrops on an umbrella. He snatched his hand away, as if it was acid pouring from him and not something you could quite happily drink by the gallon.

"This can't be happening," he said. "This…this can't be real."

The dream wasn't real. Standing in a field with a herd of acerbic cattle, that hadn't been real. Being tugged at by Barry the farmer, that wasn't real…

But this…

This…

He didn't have time to agonise as his head met the saturated pillow once again, and he was pulled down into an unconsciousness that was, he considered, more than welcome.

10

Before The Event had changed the world forever, people liked nothing more than to visit huge buildings with massive screens. They would eat something called 'popped corn' and what they didn't eat would be tossed at the bald man's head ten rows in front. Now, on these big screens, the owners of the establishments would project movies, or films, to the layman. There were all sorts of films (even ones about sparkling vampires, if you can believe that) but one of the most celebrated genres was the western. Cowboys doing battle at the O.K. Corral – which was essentially a thirty second shootout, so quite how they managed to get a two-hour movie out of it was anyone's guess – and John Wayne, a much-loved actor, walking around as if he'd shat his pantaloons, telling people to 'get off your horse and suck my dick' or something to that effect. These films usually had a main hub, a place for the cowboys to sit down with a drink and a deck of cards, ready to play a few hands. Now, whenever a stranger entered these places, these *saloons* – not to be confused with *salons*, which were places you could get your nails filed and your asshole waxed – the rest of the room fell silent and all eyes fell upon the outsider. The pianist in the corner would stop playing, and the bartender would cease with his counter-wiping and throw the towel over his shoulder in anticipation of the inevitable trouble that would follow.

And *that* is exactly what happened when the five members of Los Pendejos stepped into The Barrel, except for the piano player bit. But Gerry the guitarist did the best he could with what he had and placed his ancient acoustic down next to the stage.

"I don't think we're welcome here," Blink whispered. "I think *they* think we're bandits."

"We *are*," Red surreptitiously said from the corner of her mouth.

"Everyone just leave the talking to me," El Oscuro said. "My father was a trained negotiator for the LAPD." To the people of The Barrel, he said, "People of The Barrel! We come in peace!" A second later, an apple bounced off his head and rolled away, its thrower loath to make themselves known.

"I thought you said you were a good negotiator?" said Samuel, edging toward the door behind.

"No," El Oscuro said. "I said my *father* was a good negotiator. I take after my mother, who was a shoplifter from Kentucky."

In the corner of the room, a darts player threw wide of the mark before angrily turning on the new arrivals. "You made me miss," he said.

"Erm, *sorry*?" El Oscuro said.

"I've never missed that board before," said the darts player, still incredulous.

"Well, you can add it to your CV," said Thumbs, who wasn't in the mood for any nonsense. "Come on. Let's get to the bar. I'm gasping." And with that, he made his way across the room, through the tables and chairs that had been seemingly dropped anywhere they would fit. The rest of the bandits followed, aware that you could have cut the atmosphere with a blunt spatula.

The bartender, an angry-looking man with eyes that seemed to look in two directions at the same time, regarded the Johnnie-come-latelies with no small amount of suspicion. All around, people returned to what they had been doing before the bandits arrived, and the bandits were grateful for the resuming noise.

"We're looking for a…" El Oscuro said, trailing off as he tried to figure out which one of them the bartender was scowling at. When he realised it was none of them in particular, he continued. "We're looking for a whore. Goes by the name of Abigail. From what we've heard, she's not much to look…" He trailed off again for fear of offending the visually-impaired barkeep. "She has a glass eye…" Fuck, it was harder than it sounded.

The bartender plucked the filthy towel from his shoulder and set about wiping down the dust- and grime-coated counter. "You want information, you're going to have to buy a round of drinks first." He spat on the towel and began polishing a used glass.

El Oscuro nodded thoughtfully. "In that case, what'll it be?" he said, turning to his band.

"I'll just have a glass of water with a nip of vodka," Red said, perusing the chalkboard hanging over the bar. There wasn't much to choose from; and water seemed to be the main constituent of everything.

"Can I get a millilitre of whiskey, topped up with your finest rainwater?" Thumbs said.

"Make that two," added Blink. "And I don't suppose you've got any bar snacks, have you?"

The barkeep growled. The Barrel hadn't seen so much as a pork scratching or a bag of peanuts in over twenty years.

"I'll have a Drambuie light," El Oscuro said, which, according to the specials board, was a quarter of a mil of Drambuie, topped up with water and finished off with a cocktail umbrella. It would be just like the old days, except that in the old days you didn't have to buy a thousand drinks to get a bit tipsy.

"Coming right up," said the barkeep as he placed the spit-polished glass back on the shelf behind the bar. Then, without even a pause, he took it back down again and half-filled it with water from a rusty boiler at the end of the counter.

"Wouldn't want to be the one to get *that* glass," El Oscuro said, laughing and nudging Thumbs in the ribs.

When the bartender syringed a nip of golden fluid into it and dropped a cocktail umbrella in the glass, El Oscuro stopped laughing. "Oh, for fuck's sake," he said. "I'm going to have to get a tetanus when we get out of here."

When all the drinks were poured – there was nothing pretty about it; it was like watching a thalidomide clown juggle swords – the bartender lined them up on the counter and scribbled something down on a piece of paper.

"That'll be two gold bars or the equivalent," he said, dropping the pen with some finality.

El Oscuro almost spat out the Drambuie part of his drink. "Excuse me?" he said, wiping his chin.

"Two gold bars or the *equivalent*," said the barkeep. "I know I've got dodgy eyes, but stuttering's never been a problem for me." He stared them up and down, and two at a time, which was a remarkable feat.

"I wish you'd told us that *before* you made the drinks," El Oscuro said, snatching Red's drink from her just before she downed it. "We're just a humble band of travellers. Surely you can see we're not nobility? That we don't have two gold bars to rub together?" And if they *did*, The Barrel would have been the last place on earth they would have been spending them.

"If you don't have the means," the bartender said, "then you're in a lot of trouble."

"Really?" Blink said, glancing around the room. "Because we haven't seen a cop, a deputy, or sheriff since we got here, and you don't look like the type of guy to—

" He was cut off mid-sentence, which was understandable due to the large fist wrapped around his throat.

The bandits took a step back, apart from Blink, whose feet were several inches off the ground. On the end of the giant fist wrapped around their comrade's throat was a giant arm, and attached to that was…well, you get the idea. This hulking mass of rock and sinew was visibly steaming, and not in the way one might expect in an establishment of alcohol.

"Do you want me to break his neck, Roy?" the giant asked the barkeep, who was smiling now, happy that he had acquired the upper hand.

"I don't think that will be necessary, Tiny," replied the barkeep. To El Oscuro, he said, "So, where were we? Oh, that's right. You were about to pay for your round." He held out a hand, palm up, knowing that it wouldn't remain empty for long.

El Oscuro sighed and rolled his eyes. "Can somebody pay the man?" he said. "I've left my wallet at home."

"We didn't even want the drinks to begin with," Red said, reaching into her bra and coming out with a handful of freshwater pearls. She slammed them down on the counter, eschewing the barkeep's open palm altogether, just to be a nuisance.

Tiny growled and released Blink, who crumpled to the floor like a sack of mouldy cauliflowers. "Is that enough, Roy?" asked the giant.

The bartender scraped the pearls into his hand and, after inspecting one with a magnifying eyepiece, stuffed the lot into his ass pocket. "Just about," he said. "Enjoy your drinks, folks, and then might I be so bold as to suggest you piss off elsewhere?" He turned his back, as if to go about his business, but El Oscuro was having none of it.

"Hang on," he said. "You didn't tell us where we can find this whore…this Abigail."

Roy the bartender turned around. "She's sitting in that corner over there," he said. "You walked right past her when you came in."

They all turned and cast disapproving glances toward the mess sitting in the darkest cranny of the room. It was, if they were being honest, the best place for her. Abigail the whore must have been on the wrong side of seventy. Her boobs were sitting on the table; inbetween them was a pint glass, half empty (or half full, depending on which way you looked at it). The woman looked hopeless, desolate, and liable to kill herself if one more person rejected her.

"Come on," El Oscuro said, picking his glass up and taking a long gulp. "Let's go and secure us somewhere to sleep."

And so, across the room they went, nursing their expensive drinks as if they were apt to explode if treated too carelessly.

*

It had been a long week for Abigail Sneve. A long and demoralising week. It had been the kind of week she should have, as a whore working in a world that no longer saw sex as a viable business model, been used to by now. And yet she could *never* get used to it. All the knockbacks, all the excuses, all the dirty looks from disapproving survivors – The Event could have done her a huge favour all those years ago and wiped her off the face of the planet along with the seven billion others that had perished.

Her only bit of luck that week had come in the form of one of Kellerman's goons; which one, she wasn't quite sure. And it had been...*fun* while it lasted. The goon had paid her, which was always a bonus, and so here she was, drowning her sorrows in the only bar within a hundred miles, maybe more.

"Excuse me?" a voice said from somewhere above. At first, she thought it was God, calling her home, and her hopes were falsely raised, for when she looked she found four rough-looking fellas and a blonde girl staring down at her. It was the one at the front that did the talking. "We were told you might be able to help us."

Abigail couldn't believe her luck. Her sadness dissolved quicker than her first husband's penis on their wedding night. "'Ere, I knew it!" she said, clearly delighted. "Don't tell me. You all want a piece? A slice of old Abigail? Well, let me tell you, there's plenty to go around, ain't that right?" she said, somewhat proudly to the entire room. When nobody answered, she pressed on. "Anyway, what'll it be? Ain't nuffink out of bounds, let me tell you. I've had it in every 'ole, so I have, and I've even 'ad new 'oles put in, just in case. Oh, this is gonna be so fuckin' *great*! Listen…" Now she was only talking to Red. "I've 'ad birds before, you know, but nuffink quite like you." She licked her lips, and Red, who couldn't quite believe what he was hearing, swallowed down a mouthful of bile. "So, where do you wanna do it? We can go back to mine, if you'd like. O'course, I'll wanna come back 'ere afterwards, you know? Spend me winnings, and all that. You lot look a bit sick? You ain't gonna give me nuffink, are you? I'm as clean as they come, I am."

El Oscuro sipped furtively on his drink, and arrived at the conclusion that there was nowhere near enough alcohol in it. "We're not here for an orgy," he said. "But we were pointed in your direction by a naked alleyway man, who said you might be able to help us with a slight accommodation issue we're having, and will continue to have, for the next few days."

The whore visibly deflated. "Oh, you've been talking to Bollock-Naked Mick, 'ave you? And 'e reckons I can 'elp you, does he?"

The bandits nodded in unison, and also in hope.

"If you could put us up for a few days, I'm sure we can come to some sort of arrangement." El Oscuro didn't know what that arrangement might be, but he was almost positive there would be no sexual intercourse involved.

Almost positive.

Abigail licked her lips, something she'd been doing for many years, if the scabs surrounding her mouth were anything to go by. "You're not from around these parts, are you?" she said, and then without waiting for an answer, added, "Nah, didn't think so. 'Ere, you ain't gonna tie me up and steal me stuff, are you? I don't have a lot, but what I do 'ave, I'm quite fond of."

Red, wide-eyed as if affronted by such a remark, said, "I, for one, am appalled. Appalled that, in this day and age, a band of bandits can't walk into a town without the finger being pointed. It's this kind of small-mindedness that prevents us from making a decent, honest living."

Abigail waited for the woman's diatribe to finish before saying, "But you just said you were bandits, and I ain't stupid. Bandits is bandits is bandits."

"Okay," El Oscuro said. "If you let us crash on your floor, I'll make sure that Samuel over here makes use of your, er, *services*."

At that, she brightened. Somewhere behind, Samuel almost choked on his water-vodka.

"Deal," the whore said, holding out a liver-spotted hand, which El Oscuro shook, albeit reluctantly. "Give me 'alf an hour and we'll get you settled in."

El Oscuro grinned, for they now had a base of operations, and it had cost him nothing.

It had, on the other hand, cost poor Samuel dearly.

11

Sleep had never been a problem for Lou Decker. As a child, he'd dozed through earthquakes, terrorist attacks, volcanic eruptions, and the mailman; his mother used to call his name from the bottom of the stairs, "*Lou! Lou! Looooooooooouuuuuuuuuuu, you lazy fucker!*" and even that wasn't enough to rouse him. Eventually, Freda Decker would take a more hands-on approach: a bucket of water, a sack of rats, thirty-thousand volts. Oh, yes, Lou Decker was well-trained in the art of sleep.

But, it transpired, pissing milk from one's nipples was more than enough to keep him awake for the rest of the night. What started out as a trickle, easily dealt with by his sheets and a filthy towel he kept at the foot of his bed for 'other' purposes, became so much worse. A deluge. A flood. There was only so much of it he could drink himself, and so in the end, he'd made his way down to the kitchen, where he now stood, surrounded by pots and pans and cups and jugs and upturned hats, all of which were filled with milk...

His milk.

Milk from *his* nipples; nipples that had no right to be producing milk, or anything else, for that matter. In just a few hours he'd filled every receptacle he could find, and several gallons had been lost to the sink, for there was nowhere else to put it.

As well as sleep, Lou had always been good at speaking. Words were his forte, inasmuch as he used them on a daily basis, and seldom got lost for them.

But *this*…this had rendered him dumbstruck. No matter how hard he tried, nothing would come, and so there he stood, tits dripping like a snotty-nosed dachshund, mouth opening and shutting like a fish out of water, trying to get his head around what was happening to him. He was still standing like that an hour later when a voice from the door behind said:

"What in the name of all that is good and pure is going on in *here*?"

Lou spun, so quickly that milk from his teats geysered across the room and slapped into the face of his mother, who recoiled in horror, as was her wont.

"Mom!" he said, suddenly very embarrassed. Though not because of his naked body; she'd seen all that malarkey before. "What are you doing out of bed?"

She wiped the white liquid from her eyes and gagged. "I…I heard you moving about down here," she said. "I thought you were a *bandit*." Indeed, the hatchet in her hand suggested that, if he had been a bandit, he would have been leaving in several parts.

"Not a bandit, mother," he said. For some reason, the milk was coming thick and fast now. It was almost as if his mother's presence hastened the flow, as if the sight of her, standing there covered in it, provoked his nipples to *'Make more! Make more milk, you lactating sonofabitch!'*

"What in the…" She stepped off the stairs and cast her eye over the overfilled receptacles haphazardly spread around the room. "What *is* all this? All this…*stuff*?"

"It's nothing, mother," Lou said, though it was very clearly *something*. "Go back to your deathbed."

Freda walked through the kitchen, nudging pots and pans with her gnarled feet. She, too, was naked; her skin was almost…serpentine, as if she could shed it at any moment. That was one of the downfalls of spending so much time dying in bed. The sores.

"Mother, this is very embarrassing, and you being here is just making it worse." Lou leaned over the sink just as a long gush of milk evacuated his body. "In fact, none of this is real. Go back to bed. You're dreaming. All of this is a dream. A very fucking *bad* dream."

"It's not a dream," his mother said, crouching next to an upside-down fedora. She dipped a long, gnarly finger in and then pushed it into her mouth. It was Lou's turn to gag. "Is this…is this *milk*?" she said, astonished.

"Mother, can we talk about this in the morning?" Lou said, plonking himself down at the kitchen table. The spray no longer mattered; what mattered was that he was going to be the laughing stock of Oilhaven. "What have I done to deserve this?"

Freda Decker cupped her hands and drank freely from the fedora. She hadn't tasted milk – or *seen* it, for that matter – in over ten years. She'd forgotten just how lovely it was, how sweet and earthy and delightfully creamy; it all came flooding back to her in an instant, and she had to cross her legs to prevent the orgasm that threatened to buckle her knees and send her sprawling into the myriad pots and pans.

"Oh my God!" she gasped. "It is! It's milk! You're making milk! How the fuck are you making milk!?" She drank some more, only coming up for air when it was absolutely necessary.

"Can you not do that?" Lou said. "It's very distracting."

Wiping her thin, hairy lips, Freda Decker smiled sheepishly.

"It started yesterday," Lou said. "I thought it was just sweat. I mean, you know how warm and sticky it gets in the shop. Then, a few hours ago, I woke up covered in the stuff. I could feel it pumping through me, like some creamy enema." He wiped the tears from his eyes; milky tears that were warm and sticky to the touch. "I tasted it," he said. "God, I tasted my own milk, and it was…better than I expected, actually."

"It's fucking gorgeous!" said his mother, lapping at her palms with a black and repulsive tongue. Lou shot her an exasperated look and she stopped.

"Anyway, I was in a right mess, and there seemed to be no end to the milk, so I had to get up, and I came down and…" He gestured to the filled vessels all around. "The rest is history."

Freda Decker let all of that sink in for a moment. And while it was sinking in, she walked across the room and picked up an aluminium flask from the countertop. Lou had already filled it up with his milk, and Freda Decker emptied it in just three long swallows. "Okay," she said, wiping the white from her lips. "Let's look at this scientifically. Nothing has changed. Your diet is the same? You haven't noticed any strange marks, say, a *666* on your scalp?"

Lou shook his head. "*Nothing's* changed," he said. "Other than the fact that I'm leaking semi-skimmed at a remarkable and terrifying rate."

"Okay, okay," Freda said, waving a hand dismissively in the air. "I've heard of this phenomenon before. It's pretty rare, but not beyond the realm of reality."

It was, unfortunately, beyond the realm of Lou's comprehension. "Are you saying that this has happened to other men? How is that even *possible*?" He cupped his hands and collected the milk seeping from his right nipple, before dropping it onto the kitchen floor.

"Son, there are plenty of things we will never understand. The best way, in my experience, is to stop trying." She put the empty flask down and picked up a mug. She drank down its contents before saying, "Ahhhhhhhhh. That's beautiful, that is. You make quite a nice milk, for a man who's never been pregnant before."

"What am I going to do, Mother?" This wasn't something he could just get used to, like an ingrown toenail or a bunch of itchy piles. This was, for want of a better word, ridiculous.

Freda Decker sat down at the kitchen table, studying her son intently. "The world hasn't seen this much milk for decades. The Event put a stop to farming, and the majority of the cows were wiped out in the initial blast.

Women are no longer interested in sex, and therefore unlikely to get pregnant. Milk has become an endangered beverage, and you, my son, you sit there, feeling sorry for yourself with your titties leaking what most people would see as liquid gold."

Lou did some frowning. "What are you saying? That I should be *grateful*? That this couldn't have happened to a nicer guy?" It did taste like pure heaven; he couldn't deny that. It had been ages since he'd touched the stuff, and now, for some strange reason, he quite fancied a bowl of cereal.

Freda Decker's lips curled into a thin slit of a smile. "I'm saying that we should embrace this. That *you* should embrace this. Just think, we live in a world where people are constantly dying of thirst. A world where the well-water is only marginally safer to drink than anthrax-laced piss. This is a miracle, Lou. A sign from God that he wants us to continue as a species, and you...you are the messenger."

"That's odd," Lou said. "Right now I feel like a moo-cow." If God was trying to make a statement – and Lou didn't believe for one moment that he was – then why didn't he simply purify the water? Why didn't he make the rain less acidic, and therefore less likely to melt your throat if you tried to make a nice cup of tea with it?

"You're looking at this all wrong," said his mother. "Just think about what we could do with this, huh? Just think about all those people out there. They would kill for just a quick suckle on your teat—"

"I would prefer it if you never said anything like that again—"

"Yes, but you get what I'm trying to say." Freda Decker's smile faltered for a moment. Lou knew exactly what was going to fall out of her mouth next, for he'd seen that expression before, on many occasions. "I don't have long left upon this earth," she said. Lou mouthed along with her, such was his familiarity with her self-pitying nonsense. "I would like to go to my grave knowing that you are happy, that you have enough to get by on."

Grave? Lou thought. She was going in the incinerator, with the rest of the recyclables.

"That's all very well and good," Lou said, "but there are no circuses left for me to join."

"I'm not talking about you setting up shop with some carnival," Freda said, her smile returning. "I'm talking about creating a brand; a brand that will make us, er, *you*, rich beyond our, er, *your* wildest dreams."

Lou didn't quite grasp what she was getting at. A *brand?* Milk wasn't brand-able, was it? Milk was, and always would be, just milk, no matter whose nipple it dripped from. But she was right. Things *had* changed. People would likely give their right testicle for a gallon of the white stuff. There was, after all, only so much infected water one could digest before it caught up with you; only so many Drambuie Lights one could sup before your giblets dissolved.

He had fresh milk pouring from his tits. It was sweet, and rich, and had a brief aftertaste of honey and kittens. It was a *very* brand-able product in a post-apocalyptic world.

"So, what you're saying," Lou said, and now even he was smiling, "is that we should bottle this stuff up. Sell it by the quart, by the gallon, by the tonne, and get very rich in the process?" His nipple gave out a little squeak, as if sentient and quite happy with the situation.

Freda nodded. "It would make this dying woman very happy," she said, "if we were to build this up into a sustainable business. You can be the boss, of course, and whatever you say goes."

Lou liked the sound of that.

"The 'haveners are going to go *mental* for this, I just know it." His mother ran a hand across the kitchen table, through the milk pooled there, and then licked it with her almost bovine tongue. "We could even flavour it. Remember when people used to drink those shakes? Chocolate? Mmmmm. Banana? Strawberries?"

Lou shook his head. "We haven't had any of that stuff for years," he said.

"Then we'll *improvise*," said his mother. "There are three crates of tinned pilchards in the basement. We can use those."

"Fish and milk?" Lou said, disgusted and intrigued in equal measure. "Would that work? I mean, would…" He paused, long enough to consider his mother's previous sentence once again. "How did you know about the pilchards in the basement?" he said.

Freda Decker sighed. "Never mind all that bollocks. Are we going to do this, or what?"

Lou nodded. "I think we are."

"Fantastic!" Freda jumped to her feet and clapped her hands excitedly together. For a dying woman, she looked awfully chipper. "Now, get a mop and clean this mess up. I refuse to work in such gross conditions."

12

The sun rose over Oilhaven like a volcano in the sky. It was going to be another scorcher – the seven thousandth in a row – and many of the 'haveners were already seeking out the shadows in which to plonk their deckchairs. Those of Germanic descent had woken early and draped towels over the areas they wished to claim, which was why there was now a long row of yellow, red, and black stretching across the shadier side of the town.

Mickey, the naked alleyway man, had spent the better part of an hour fighting off a young couple intent on setting up a picnic in his living room, or what would have been his living-room if the alleyway had had a roof.

"You can't eat your pickles here," he'd informed them. "You're going to have to find shade elsewhere."

The man of the couple – though the woman of the couple was *also* pretty manly – had decided aggression was the only way to deal with Mickey, and had managed to get three heavy-handed slaps in before Mickey pulled out a tenancy agreement.

"Look!" Mickey had said, pointing to the sheet of paper. "This is my *home*. It states here that the area between *A Cut Above* hairdressers and *Six Feet Under* funeral parlour is mine." He wiped blood from his nose. "You're about to set up your picnic in my front room."

The man had apologised profusely before dragging his girlfriend/wife/life-partner and their wicker hamper away, but not before presenting Mickey with a mouldy sandwich of spam and spam (it's what's for dinner, *and* tea, apparently). Mickey had passed the sandwich on to a rat that lived at the end of the alleyway – in Mickey's toilet, as a matter of fact – in the hope that, one day soon, the rat would die and he could have a proper meal.

In Abigail Sneve's hovel, four aching bandits scraped themselves up from the floorboards and stretched. A fifth bandit, Samuel, sat whimpering in the corner of Abigail's boudoir. For him it had been a night of utter terror, of gummy blowjobs and anal beads, of genital warts and vaginal guffs. It was, as far as he was concerned, the worst night of his entire life.

Take one for the team, had been the general consensus, which was all very well and good for those *not* taking one for the team.

"Come back to bed," Abigail croaked from the soggy mattress at the other end of the room. "I only got up to thirty-two in my fifty best ways to please a man."

Samuel pushed himself up onto unsteady legs; legs that threatened to break beneath him. "I'll take your word for the other eighteen," he said, pulling his trousers on and trying his hardest not to cry any more.

Upon making his way into what looked, *sorta*, like a lounge, Samuel was met with cheers and applause from his colleagues, not to mention several pats on the back, and even, in one case, a "How the fuck did you manage that without throwing up?" Well, the truth of the matter was: he didn't. But, as if by a stroke of sheer fortuity, it turned out that vomit-play was number twenty-seven on Abigail Sneve's list of ways to please a man.

"Right, everyone," El Oscuro said once the plaudits for their comrade died down. "We've got a busy day ahead of us today. A very busy day, indeed."

"We going on the rob?" Thumbs said, simulating the very thing with his thumb-less hands.

"That we are," El Oscuro said. "But lay off the pickpocketing, Thumbs. We don't even know if this place has a prison for us to bail you out of yet. For all we know, they're instructed to kill bandits on sight, which means we need to keep a low profile."

"That's easy for you to say," Samuel said, still shivering from his carnal encounter with the seventy year-old *fille de joie*. "The store owner knows me, knows what I look like."

"But that was *yesterday*," Red said. "Today, if you don't mind me saying, you look like *half* the man you were. Barely recognisable. Last night was the best thing that could have happened to you. It's given you a sort of…*ashamed* aspect. A 'please, just shoot me now' kind of vibe. It's better than any mask. You bump into that storekeeper today, he'll greet you with a smile before trying to sell you something for your ailments. I guarantee it."

"She's right," Blink said, scratching at his right eyeball with a used matchstick. "I didn't recognise you when you walked out of that bedroom. Did you have that limp yesterday?"

Samuel shook his head. Number sixteen on Abigail's list had involved a breezeblock. "So you don't think I need to hide out? Lay low?"

"By all means," El Oscuro said. "Stay here. Keep our landlady happy for the duration—"

"I'll risk being recognised," Samuel said.

"That's what I thought," El Oscuro said. "So, here's what we're going to do."

Now, El Oscuro wasn't great at making plans, at setting goals and sticking to them, or at coming up with viable heists, ones that were worth the hassle, and more than that, worth being collared for. It was a wonder he was in charge of *anything*, let alone a ragtag band of merry thieves. But what he lacked in wisdom, skill, and dependability, he made up for in sheer enthusiasm. Oh yes, El Oscuro couldn't get enough of the job, of robbing the rich to feed himself, and today an entire town would be at his mercy.

Today, Los Pendejos would leave their mark on Oilhaven, one way or the other. What kind of mark, and how big, remained to be seen.

13

Something was happening in the street outside LOU'S LOOT. There was a queue; a phenomenon not seen since Lou had a special on squashed squirrels. A line of people stretched all the way back to The Barrel, where Roy Clamp stood smoking a clay pipe. Don't ask what was in the pipe; even he didn't know.

"What's going on?" Roger Fox asked as he walked past the pub's proprietor on his way to the mine.

Roy chewed anxiously on the bit of his pipe before speaking. "You mean, what's with this fucking ridiculous queue that's blocking the entrance to my establishment?"

"That's exactly what I mean," Roger said.

Roy, clearly as irate as he was perplexed, said, "That flaming Lou Decker's up to his old tricks again. I haven't been down there, but I've been listening to the Chinese whispers as they work their way along the line, and apparently, Lou Decker has started selling silk."

"Silk?" said Roger Fox.

"Silk," replied the barkeep. "Don't know how he's got hold of a load of silk, or why, all of a sudden, everyone in Oilhaven is interested in buying the stuff. If you ask me, silk's the bastard cousin of polyester. Give me a yard of leather over that shit any day of the week."

Roger shrugged, for he was indifferent to fabrics. "He'll make a *fortune* out of it," he said. "Honestly, I don't know how he's managed to keep that place going for so long, but I'm of the opinion that somewhere, the devil has a piece of paper with Lou Decker's signature on it."

Roy laughed; it sounded like a tin of ball-bearings being rattled. "He does always seem to land on his feet," he said. "They don't call him *Lou the Cat* for nothing."

"No they don't," Roger said, because nobody called Lou 'The Cat', not even that death-bedridden mother of his. "Well, I must be getting on. That dirt isn't going to mine itself."

"Have a good one, Rog," Roy said. "And give my regards to that lovely wife of yours."

"Will do," Roger said as he walked away, though he wouldn't. Nobody ever passed on regards to their wives. Ever.

Roger continued along the line, occasionally saying hello to those he knew (but not stopping to chat; he didn't know them *that* well), and as he walked, he became increasingly aware of a few words that might have suggested Roy Clamp had, somewhere down the line, got his wires crossed.

Words like cow, and cheese, and *halloumi*, whatever the hell that was. These were not words one would associate with silk. It was certainly a conundrum, and by the time Roger reached LOU'S LOOT, he was frowning so much, he could taste his eyebrows.

Then he saw the sign...

LOU'S MILK – FRESH TODAY
DON'T BELIEVE US? TRY SOME!

…and everything suddenly made sense.

And yet, it *didn't*.

"Milk?" Roger said, pointing at the sign.

"That's what it says," replied the old lady standing at the front of the queue, swinging an umbrella, even though it hadn't rained for a good few decades. "I've been here since the moon was over there," she said, pointing toward a sunny and cloudless patch of sky. "If he's winding me up, I'll cut his throat while he sleeps. I've been waiting for this moment for twenty years. My rice puddin' ain't ever been the same, not with using the well-water. Like I said, he'd better not be playing silly fuckers."

"But…*milk*?" Roger said, pointing once again to the sign. "Doesn't that strike you as a little bit odd?"

The old lady nodded and sucked in her cheeks. It was amazing, Roger thought, how the geriatric population could swallow their own faces due to their lack of teeth. "It's more than a *little* bit odd," she said. "It's off the chart ridiculous! There hasn't been any milk around these parts for years, nor *cows*, for that matter. I don't know where he's got it from, and I don't care, so long as he's got it. My rice puddin' ain't ever been the same, not—"

"With using the well-water, yes you said."

"*Did* I?" She looked confused now, as if Roger Fox had just told her a tale of the World Wide Web, God rest its soul.

"Yes. Look, can you do me a favour?" Roger said, rifling around in his trouser pocket for anything that could be considered currency. He found a plastic button, two strands of green cotton, and a nice, white rock he'd discovered at the mine the previous day. He was pretty sure the thread was useless – though not useless enough to throw away – and so stuffed it back from whence it came. The rock and the button, he held out for the old woman to inspect. "Will you buy me a bottle of this…this *milk*, and leave it with Roy at the Barrel? I can pick it up on my way home, only I'm in a bit of a rush."

The woman smiled, all pink gums and hairy tongue. "Malnutrition was it?" she said.

"Excuse me?"

"What your last slave died of. Was it malnutrition?" But she took the proffered button and rock anyway. "What do you want? Semi-skimmed? Pasteurised? Full fat? Gold Top?"

"I think we're overestimating Lou here," Roger said. "If he's got milk, that'll be fine. And you won't forget to leave it with Roy at The Barrel?"

"Probably," said the old woman, which wasn't what Roger wanted to hear.

"Was that probably you'll forget, or probably you won't?" He was getting later by the second, which tends to happen.

"Yes," the old woman said, which was no answer at all. "Now scram, before I change my mind." And with that, she waved her umbrella. Roger half-expected to turn into a frog.

He thanked the old lady and continued his commute. If Lou *did* have milk – and Roger would be on the fence until he saw it in person – and Roger was to turn up after work that evening with a bottle of the stuff, his entire family would treat him like a hero. A modern-day Saint. Like Bono, only less annoying and carrying a bottle of milk.

*

Inside LOU'S LOOT, Lou paced frantically from one side of the store to the other. At some point in the last hour, he had stopped lactating, and not a moment too soon, as far as he was concerned. For a moment there, he'd wondered if it was ever going to stop.

"They're *queuing*!" Freda Decker excitedly said. She was staring out through the one-inch square of door that wasn't covered with a flier or an ancient brown newspaper. "They're queuing all the way up the street, Lou!"

Lou sighed. He would have been excited, but his nipples felt like they'd been chewed upon by a pair of tigers. "How many?" he said. "At a guess?"

"At a guess?" Freda said, gazing for a moment back out onto the street. "I'd say half of them."

"Half of the *town*!?" Lou said, exasperated. It wasn't that he hadn't produced enough for half the town (he was operating at a one bottle per customer policy, and if they didn't like it, they could lump it), it was that he'd never had so many people lining up to get in to his shop.

"This is amazing," said his mother. "We haven't been this busy since you made bushy tails for those rats and sold them as squashed squirrels."

Was this any different? He'd tricked people then, and now he was going to sell them milk that had, up until last night, been sloshing around inside of him. Surely, there was some law against that. And if not, there damn well *ought* to be.

Lou carried through the final crate of milk and set it down on the counter. At some point during the morning, they had run out of empty bottles. The crate on the counter was therefore filled with a mish-mash of vases, urns, and jars, all topped up with the finest Lou's Milk your unwanted jewellery, bric-a-brac and I.O.Us could buy.

Freda Decker had, somewhat cleverly, decided that the brand needed a logo, and that logo was a drop of milk seeping from the corner of a pair of lips. It wasn't the most appealing image to ever grace a beverage, but it was either *that* or a pair of hairy breasts, and Lou had to draw a line somewhere. Happy with the logo, Freda had spent the rest of the morning hand-drawing labels while Lou had continued to milk himself dry. It was, and always would be, a cottage industry, but that suited Lou just fine as he only had one pair of titties to go around.

"Is that all of it?" asked his mother. "You're not going to suddenly start pissing milk all over the floor?"

Lou shook his head. The fact of the matter was, he didn't have a clue how long this respite would last. But one thing was for sure: there was more milk brewing inside of him. He could feel it. He could hear it as he walked, sloshing and swilling around, could feel it bouncing from rib to rib. He was a walking, talking milk-factory. Would he be able to control his nipples once the milk was ready? Would it just gush from him, an uncontrollable torrent, the way it had for most of the night? Would his secret come out sooner rather than later?

"Mother, I'm absolutely terrified," Lou said. "What if people don't like it? What if milk's just not as great as it used to be? I don't know if I can take that sort of rejection."

"Hey!" his mother said. She marched across the store and took him by the arms; for a dying woman, she sure did have a tight grip. "I don't want to hear it," she said, stoic as ever. "I've tasted it. It's like heaven. And now that we've figured out how to get the hairs out of it, it's going to taste even better. You've got to have faith, Lou. Do you think Albert Einstein got nervous when he invented gravity?"

Lou thought about correcting her, but decided against it.

"No, that's right. He threw some numbers up on his blackboard and told everyone who didn't believe him to go fuck themselves. That's what *we're* going to do, Lou. Sure, these pricks are going to be a bit sceptical at first. They're going to want to know where it's coming from. But what are we going to tell them?"

"We have a milk-well," Lou said, shaking his head even as the words passed his lips.

"That's *right*," said his mother. "We have a milk-well, and people are going to want to see that milk-well, and what are we going to tell those nosey bastards?"

"That it's invisible to everyone but us," Lou said. And to think they'd spent the best part of the night trying to concoct feasible explanations, and that was what they had settled on.

"Yes, we have an invisible milk-well," his mother said. "If they don't believe us, well, we'll blacklist them from the milk. I'm pretty sure they'll come around once they start hearing how sweet the stuff is…how it tastes of honey and summer and, on a really good batch, Chinese five spice."

"I threw that batch out," Lou said.

"What did you do *that* for?" She looked and sounded mortified. "I could have had that. It was alright. I don't know what it is about your milk, son, but it makes me feel alive again. I feel…like I've been *reborn*!"

Lou rolled his eyes. Now his unnatural tit milk had medicinal properties. Who would've thought it?

"Are you ready to open up?" Freda Decker could hardly contain herself. Lou, on the other hand, suddenly felt very exposed, as if he'd forgotten to put his trousers on that morning.

"Ready," he said.

Though he wasn't.

Not in the slightest.

"Then let's sell this shit-heap town some *Lou's Milk*."

And that, Lou thought, was a sentence he thought he'd never hear for as long as he lived.

14

The doors slowly opened, and people filed in through them in an orderly fashion, muttering pardons and excuse mes to anyone they accidentally clattered into. Each customer only picked up one bottle of Lou's Milk before queuing once again to pay for it. And, in an ideal world, that was how it *should* have happened.

But this was *not* an ideal world; it was barely even a world.

As Freda Decker turned the final key in its lock, she was knocked from her feet by an old lady, eager to get in and get her milk. "My rice puddin' ain't been the same without it!" she squawked as she flew past on a sea of excited bodies.

"Now, everyone," Lou said, taking up position behind the counter, where there was less chance of being trampled. "There's plenty for everyone, so let's just behave like human beings, shall we?"

The bodies continued to force themselves into the shop, even though it was quickly becoming cramped. Entire aisles were destroyed in an instant; tools and knick-knacks, Lou's livelihood, clattered to the ground in a raucous din. Freda Decker picked herself up and put a faulty piano between herself and the crazed milk-seekers, but it wasn't long before one of them leapt up onto the piano lid and began shouting. "Where's the milk!? Where's the fucking milk!?" whilst drooling and slathering like a thirsty bloodhound.

A single gunshot from somewhere in the room managed to settle things down. People stopped fighting and screaming and turned their attention to the store's proprietor, who appeared to be holding an antique pistol. Smoke was drifting from its barrel in long, thin tendrils, and the smell of cordite in the air was only marginally better than the stench of fifty grimy and perspiring bodies.

"Wow, I'm surprised it went off," said one man.

"That makes two of us," Lou replied. "Now look. I have the milk here. If you could all just form an orderly queue, I'll be happy to exchange a bottle for something of equal value."

"What do we want!?" the old woman said, in the hope of starting a chant, but nobody joined in, so she went back to swinging her umbrella.

With a queue (of sorts) running down the middle of the store, Lou felt much better. Everything was a mess, but that didn't matter right now. What mattered was that he got everyone served and out of his fucking face as quickly, and efficiently, as possible. It wasn't long before the tricky questions started to come. In fact, it was the first customer, the little old lady with the umbrella and the bubblegum-pink gums, that started it.

"What I want to know," she said, turning the bottle over and over in her hand, "is where it comes from." She was at the very front of the queue, and the customers within earshot were listening, trying to ascertain what was being said.

Lou glanced across to his mother, who was sipping milk (he wished she wouldn't) through a straw. She nodded: *Go ahead...just like was talked about.*

"Well, Mrs Warbrown," Lou said. "That's an awful question. Might I suggest something less offensive? Ask me how old I am, or if I've ever had sexual urges toward my dying mother."

But Mrs Warbrown was having none of it. "First of all, you're fifty, and yes, you lie awake some nights masturbating and hoping she's in the next room doing the very same thing. Now tell me, where the fuck is this milk from?"

Lou snatched the milk from the old biddy's hand and said, "How very rude! I'll have you know I'm forty-nine!" He wasn't – he was fifty, but he'd spent the last year in denial. "Do you really want to know where this milk comes from? Do you? DO YOU!!!"

Mrs Warbrown nodded. "'s why I asked," she said. "And don't give me any nonsense about invisible milkwells. I wasn't born yesterday, you know."

Completely thrown, Lou did some stammering. In fact, Lou did a *lot* of stammering, hoping to buy himself some time, hoping that when he did manage to finish his sentence, something feasible came out. This wasn't in the script, and the people in the queue behind Mrs Warbrown were growing increasingly frustrated.

"Look," Lou said. "It's *milk*. It's white and milky and it's made of milk. If you, or ANYONE ELSE HERE" – he raised his voice so that those present could hear – "DON'T BELIEVE ME, AND PERSIST WITH YOUR RIDICULOUS LINE OF QUESTIONING, THEN KINDLY LEAVE THE SHOP IN THE EXACT OPPOSITE TO THE MANNER IN WHICH YOU ENTERED." He lowered his voice again and used it specifically on Mrs Warbrown. "Now. Do you want to make that rice pudding of yours, or do you want to walk out of here empty-handed?"

Lou could feel his mother's eyes boring into him. She was angry at him for not sticking to the plan, but it had been a stupid one to begin with and Lou, for one, was glad he didn't have to pretend they had an invisible milkwell somewhere downstairs.

"I'll take the one bottle," Mrs Warbrown said, snatching it out of Lou's sweaty hand. "And in exchange,

I offer you this tin brooch." She unpinned the object from her lapel and slapped it down on the counter.

While they were being pleasant, Lou decided to play along. "I accept this tin brooch, and invite you to use the door, and please don't let it hit you in the derriere on the way out."

Mrs Warbrown, now cradling the milk bottle as if it was her firstborn, bid Lou a terrible day before accepting his invite to use the door. "Whatever you do," she told the line of people as she walked along it, "don't ask where it comes from."

It wasn't until she reached The Barrel that she remembered the miner and the promise she'd made to buy him a bottle of milk. "Oh, fucksticks!" she said, but it was too late to go back now, and there was not a chance on earth she was joining the back of the queue. At her age, every second of life counted, and she was damned if she was going to waste several thousand of them standing in a queue for the second time that morning.

"Oi, Roy!" she said to the barkeep smoking in the pub's doorway. "Some idiot's going to come to you later on for a bottle of milk. Give him these, will you." And she handed him a plastic button and a white rock.

"Will do," Roy said, pocketing the items. "But won't he be disappointed?"

"Very," she said.

Before he had a chance to ask what was going on at LOU'S LOOT, the woman was gone, scurrying down the

103

road with an umbrella under one arm and a bottle of white fluid under the other. It looked strangely like...

Milk.

But no, that was impossible. What were the odds that Lou had started selling silk *and* milk on the same day? Unless...

"Oh," Roy said, upon realising his mistake. "Oh," he said again, for one just didn't seem to be enough.

15

It was just before noon when Smalling and Harkness arrived at Kellerman's office in a state of utter shock. At first, Kellerman thought one of them had figured out the meaning of life, but then he saw the bottle Smalling was holding and pointing at as if it had said something offensive.

"Please tell me," Kellerman said as he regarded the bottle with a mixture of disgust and suspicion, "that you haven't taken to bottling up your semen in order to bury it like some spunky time-capsule for future generations to dig up and marvel over." Because in that moment, such a ridiculous thing was far more plausible than the alternative.

"It's *milk*!" Smalling said, shaking his head and sweating profusely. "Lou's Milk. He's selling it right now from his store. Got a lot of it, too."

Kellerman, frowning, snatched the bottle from his subordinate's hand. "What are you babbling on about?"

he said. "Milk is as rare as rocking-horse shit. Everyone knows tha…" He trailed off as he read the label sellotaped to the bottle.

LOU'S MILK
TASTE IT, LOVE IT, BUY SOME MORE

Kellerman couldn't believe it. Didn't believe it, not for one minute. "That little scoundrel," he said, gritting his teeth. "And I thought I was the villain of this piece."

"What?" Harkness said.

"He's bottling something *white* up and selling it as milk," said Kellerman. "He's tricking the whole town into buying it and making a killing in the process." A small part of the mayor secretly admired the deceitful fat bastard, but it was a very small part. The rest of him was just plain annoyed.

"But why would he *do* that?" Smalling said. "I mean, the stuff would have to *taste* exactly like milk in order for him to get away with it. It looks just like milk—"

"Only with little hairs in it," Harkness added.

"Yeah, milk with little hairs in it," Smalling said. "So if it looks like milk, and tastes like milk, wouldn't that, in fact, make it milk, or an acceptable substitute?"

Kellerman had to give his minion credit, but decided not to. "That's not the point," he said, uncorking the bottle and giving its contents a little sniff. "This is false advertising. It…" It did smell like milk. Very rich and creamy, with just a hint of honey. Its sweetness was extremely pleasant, but when you were surrounded by people who had been walking around in the same clothes for two decades, a sugary fart smelt like a gift from the gods.

Kellerman tentatively put the bottle to his lips and took a small sip.

"That was very brave of you, sir," Smalling said, for he would never have had the bollocks to do such a thing. But like the first person to eat a chilli-pepper, and the first lunatic to taser themselves, Kellerman, it seemed, would live to tell the tale.

"That," he said, pointing to the bottle in his hand, "is milk."

"What gave it away, sir?" Harkness said.

"Don't get sarcastic with me, you bald-headed buffoon," Kellerman said. "Not only is it milk, but it's probably the best milk I have ever tasted in all my life." He pulled a small hair from his mouth, which had got trapped between his front teeth. Then, he upended the bottle and swallowed the lot.

His henchmen could do nothing but watch, and occasionally heave.

When he was done, Kellerman wiped his dripping chin with the sleeve of his suit. "I don't believe it," he said. "That sonofabitch has got milk from somewhere. He's selling this to Joe public, is he?"

Smalling and Harkness nodded in unison, but it was Smalling that spoke. "Only one bottle per customer," he said. "Something to do with stock levels and replenishing, whatever that means."

"It means," Kellerman said, licking at the spout of the bottle with a darting, serpentine tongue, "that we have to speak with Mr Decker, find out where he got this from, and whether he will be getting more. If not, then we're going to have to confiscate the lot. It's been a long time since I had a bowl of Honey-Nut Cheerios, and this has given me a right yearning for them. Since cereal is no longer on the menu, I'm going to throw together a bowl of acorns, and I would like a bottle of Lou's Milk to go with them."

"You want us to go back to the store?" Harkness said. "But it was one bottle per customer?"

"There are, are there not," Kellerman said, "two of you?"

Harkness did a quick headcount, then nodded.

"Then get back to the store and pick up another bottle, and if Lou gives you any of his mouth, give it a little slap and then confiscate every drop of milk you can find in that place. Comprende?"

Neither Smalling nor Harkness knew what that meant, but they nodded anyway. "Do you want us to take your empty back?" Smalling said, gesturing to the vacant bottle in Kellerman's hand. "Lou said he needed the bottles."

Reluctantly, Kellerman handed the empty bottle over to his minion. Part of him wondered whether he would ever see it again; it was a very sad moment. "Any luck finding the girl?" he said, as an aside. The whole milk thing had thrown him, and for a moment he almost forgot that the shaven gorillas had waltzed into his office without Zee Fox, yet again.

"We're getting close," Harkness said. By close, he meant nowhere near, for the girl had seemingly fallen from the face of the earth. "We should have her by the end of today. In fact, we were hoping that Lou's Milk might draw her out. You know what the people around here are like, sir. One sniff of a bargain, and the next thing you know everyone's running around in the buff, screaming obscenities at the top of their voices."

Kellerman nodded. "You have until the end of the day," he said, pulling a handgun from his waistband. "I want the girl, and I want the milk. If I don't have both, I'm going to shoot one of you in the face."

"Which one?" Smalling asked, as unruffled as you like.

"Does it *matter*?" Kellerman said.

"Well, sir," Harkness chimed in. "It matters to the one about to get a new hole in his head."

Kellerman returned the gun to his waistband. "It'll be a surprise," he said. "Hell, it might be both of you, so just make sure I get the milk and the Fox girl before sundown." And with that, he shoo-ed them away, like recalcitrant kittens.

When they were gone, Kellerman settled into his leather chair and lit a new cigar. It didn't even matter that one of his snowflake moray eels was giving him the evil eye. He wasn't in the mood for silly fish games.

"Milk," he said, licking his lips.

It would change Oilhaven forever.

If only he knew, as he sat there smoking and *not* engaging in staring competitions with his fish, how true that was.

16

The town of Oilhaven, in full swing, was an absolute nightmare. El Oscuro didn't know how people could live like this. Day in, day out, mining for dirt that might or might not eventually turn into something more valuable; living in alleyways without any clothes (freaky, even by Los Pendejos standards); avoiding haggard old prostitutes like the plague. And they said that the small communities had it *good*, that they were living the dream, but El Oscuro wouldn't have swapped what he had for what *they* had, not in a million years. Being a bandit had its disadvantages, but he would rather spend the rest of his life on the run, picking the pockets of these small communities, than settle down in one.

The sun was unbearable, hanging over Oilhaven like a giant ball of ejaculating fire (which was, according to various encyclopaedias and reference books, pretty much what it was). People didn't so much walk through the streets as ooze. Sand and dirt covered everything. El Oscuro and his boys (and girl) had only been outside for five minutes and already they were plastered in grime.

They were used to it, though. It was part and parcel of living in a post-apocalyptic world. If you ventured outside in your best white clothes…well then you were an idiot. Those days were gone forever. The Goths had found the transition a lot easier than most.

"So what's the plan?" Blink asked, surveying the street intently. "Knock off a few establishments? Couple of home invasions? One or two wallet-swipes, then back to The Barrel for a cheeky cocktail?" Sand and grit had affixed itself to his eyeballs, covering the whites completely. It was quite unnerving to look at.

El Oscuro, sitting atop Mordecai, sipped from an opaque water bottle. The reason for its opaqueness was twofold. Firstly, it kept the liquid contained within just that little bit cooler, and secondly, you couldn't see the liquid contained within, or its unnatural colour, which tended to put a lot of people off.

"We're going to keep a low profile," El Oscuro said. "Try to fit in. You're all familiar with the chameleon? Adapt to your surroundings; make yourself less noticeable."

"Says the man sitting on the only horse in town," said Red, shaking her head. "Do you honestly think there is anything here for us? These people are worse off than *we* are. I don't know about you, but I'm starting to feel really guilty. It comes to something when one of your town's most prominent figures is a naked alleyway dweller."

"Don't feel guilty," El Oscuro said. "There is more to this place than meets the eye."

"Like *what*?" Samuel said, sidling up to the horse. "It's pitiful. I think we should go back, dig up the bikes, and be on our way."

El Oscuro shook his head. "You really *think* this is it. That this place is just full of oily bodies and worthless mineshafts?" He grinned. "Why do you think these people put themselves down those mines every day? Huh? It's because there is somebody in charge, somebody powerful, somebody that likes all the trappings of a luxury lifestyle and knows how to maintain it. When The Event hit, do you remember what people were saying? That they would never have to work again for as long as they managed to survive? Then what happened? People came in and took over. Before you had a chance to say 'momentary respite', everyone was back to work. Granted, money was useless and people were working for scraps of food and accommodation, but the same rules applied. These places – places like Oilhaven and the countless other backwoods towns we've stumbled across – are governed by one man. The fattest cat of all; and that's the fucker we're going to focus on."

Blink, Samuel, Thumbs, and Red all stopped walking at the same time, and it was a few seconds before El Oscuro realised he was talking to himself. He turned Mordecai around and cantered back to the flabbergasted bandits.

"You're going after the leader of this shithole?" Red said. "The guy at the top, the one in charge, the head honcho, and other things to that effect?"

El Oscuro nodded. "It's the only way to make this pit-stop worth our while," he said. "Or would you rather start pickpocketing these defenceless poor bastards, stealing their buttons and clothes, leaving them worse off than they already are?"

Red considered this for a moment, and came to the conclusion that they already had more buttons than they would ever spend. "Okay, so suppose we find out who's in charge here. We're just going to attack, take everything they own, and leave them dying in a pool of their own blood and vomit."

El Oscuro smiled. "It gives me an erection when you put it like that."

"I'm in," Samuel said.

"Me too," said Thumbs. "Be nice to get a good haul for a change."

"Count me in," Blink said. "But can we get some eye-drops first? I can't see a fucking thing."

Red shrugged. "What the hell," she said. "Let's make this one a good one."

"That's my girl," El Oscuro said. "Now if one of you wouldn't mind holding Blink's hand until we get to the store, that would be fantastic."

*

The last customer left empty-handed and extremely angry. That was the trouble with being at the back of the queue; there was always a small chance that by the time you were at the *front* of the queue, there would be nothing left to buy. Lou had been called every name under the sun by that disappointed customer, but it was nothing he hadn't been called before. Except Cunty-Bollocks – that was a new one.

Piled up behind the counter, various gems and valuables sat atop a tray. It was a sight to behold; more currency than the store had seen in years. And yet there was something inherently wrong with it. Lou felt terrible, that he was somehow deceiving the 'haveners by selling them milk from his own teats, that in a week or so, there would be a knock on the door and he would be hauled off to Oilhaven Gaol – which wasn't really a jail, but a rock with an axe leaning against it.

"Well, that was intense," his mother said as she set about locking the door. "You did well, son. *Really* well. I thought you were going to lose it there for a while, but you managed to keep it together. Pity the invisible milk-well lie never really got off the ground, but hey-ho…we sold the effing lot."

Lou stroked his fat breasts, for they were sore and it was only a matter of time before they started leaking again. "Why do I feel so bad?" he said. "Why do I feel like I've just sold the whole town a clapped-out Ford?"

Freda Decker walked the length of the store and placed her son's face between her sweaty, wrinkly palms.

"You cancel that shit right now," she said, smooshing his face together as if it were made of dough. "You have just gifted them something remarkable, and they are going to thank you for every ounce that they swallow."

"Couldyouletgoofmyfashe?" Lou said, and she did. His mother was right; he had done nothing wrong. They were getting exactly what they paid for: Lou's Milk. There was no false advertising; he wasn't bottling up the well-water, slapping a picture of a spring on it, and selling it as fucking *Volvic*.

It really *was* Lou's Milk, straight from the nipple. This was no worse than selling dead rats as squashed squirrels, or cheese-graters as backscratchers. This was real milk, and he was making it.

"You're *right*," he told his mother, who was frantically counting out buttons and brooches, occasionally stopping to whoop and applaud. "I'm pretty sure they're going to love it. It does taste good, doesn't it?"

"Good?" his mother said, still counting. "If God had a penis, I'm pretty sure that's what it would taste like."

Lou frowned at that analogy. His mother always had an odd way with words, which was why he preferred her when she was silent and dying.

Just then there came a loud and desperate knock on the door. "Mr Decker?" said a frenzied, deep voice. "Lou?"

It was the local, and only, priest, Reverend Schmidt. Nice fella, if not a little tactile.

Lou walked across the room and, after turning the key in the lock, opened the door. A pair of filthy hands latched onto him almost immediately, bunching up his shirt. "You have to give me another bottle!" said the reverend. "I have to have more."

Lou couldn't help but notice the white stain around the clergyman's lips, and the way his eyes protruded from their sockets, all bloodshot and manic. "Reverend, there *is* no more," Lou said, easing the grotty, trembling hands from his collar. "I will be taking delivery of another batch tomorrow, but until then—"

"Tomorrow!?" The reverend looked apt to explode. "I can't wait until *tomorrow*! You have to get more *now*. It's the most delightful thing I've ever had on my tongue, and I'm a clergyman, if you get my drift?"

Unfortunately, Lou got his drift just fine. "That's all well and good," he said, "but there will be no more Lou's Milk until tomorrow. I'm sorry."

"You're *sorry*?" said the reverend. "Sorry that you tease us with this miraculous elixir? Sorry that you dangled such a tasty carrot in front of us and then snatched it away?" He took a step back and regarded Lou with what looked like pure hatred. "I'll pray for you, Lou Decker. I'll ask the Lord to forgive you, and in the meantime, if you could put a bottle aside for me when your delivery comes in…"

"Will do," Lou said, easing the door shut on the clergyman, who was still banging on about carrots and potions.

"You *see?*" Freda said from across the room, where she was drinking Lou's Milk from her own personal stash. "They can't get enough of it."

Lou sighed deeply. Getting people hooked was not what he'd intended. All he had wanted was to provide a service, a product that they would enjoy. When the local Catholics started having withdrawals, something was very wrong...

A knock on the door stopped Lou in his tracks, not that he was going anywhere.

"I told you, Rev," Lou called through the door. "There will be no more milk until tomorrow." *Honestly,* he thought. *The nerve of some peop—*

"Hello?" a voice that didn't belong to Reverend Schmidt said. "Is there anyone in there?"

Lou sighed again. It was becoming quite a habit. "We're closed for the rest of the day," he said, stroking at his tender nipples, which were showing fresh signs of leakage. "Come back tomorrow."

There was a slight pause, and then Lou heard whisperings, which meant there was more than one person out there – or one incredibly crazy one.

"I believe you are the only store in Oilhaven," said the voice. There was a slight accent there that Lou couldn't quite put his finger on; it sounded Spanish, by way of Hawaii. "Is that correct?"

"That is bang on correct," Lou said.

"Then it is imperative that you open up," said the voice. "You see, our friend, he suffers from a rather odd defect called *lagopthalmos* and we're in dire need of lubrication."

Lou frowned, as did his mother. "That sounds nasty," he said, pressing his head against the locked door. "What, if I may ask, is in need of lubricating?" The body was made up of many parts, but there were only a couple which required such treatment. Lou wasn't about to let a bunch of people in so that they might lubricate their friend right there in the middle of the store. Not only would it be embarrassing (for all parties) but there was the small matter of hygiene to consider. Yes, the place was dusty as hell, and yes, the post-apocalyptic winds were forever bringing in disease and radiation from the streets, but there was no sense in adding to it.

"It's his *eyes*," said the voice. "He doesn't blink."

"Tell him how sore it gets," added another voice.

"Oh, it gets *very* sore," said the first voice. "Like rolling a hedgehog around in his irises."

Lou caught a glimpse of the callers through the tiny gap in the door. There was at least three of them; maybe more off to the side, and they were all unfamiliar to him. One of them was female, blonde, pretty – if you liked that sort of thing. The one with the wide-eyes (and presumably the one in need of…*lubricating*) gawped toward the door. It was as if he believed the door was in fact the one doing the talking, and not the person standing on the other side of it.

"I will open the door on one condition," Lou said, placing a hand on the key. "You are to wait right where you are until I have located suitable lubrication for your goggle-eyed friend, and you are to pay me in advance. Is that acceptable to you?"

"Sounds fine," the lead speaker said. "Do you accept silver cutlery, only we've got an odd spoon here?"

Silver cutlery? That was one of Lou's favourite things in the world, after his vast array of claytex vaginas. "That will do just fine," he said, turning the key in its lock and easing the door open just a crack. The silver spoon was thrust upon him almost immediately, and so he took it with eagerness. "Wait here. I've got some motorcycle chain lube here somewhere." And off he went, in search of something that would either relieve that poor man of his discomfort, or melt his eyes in their sockets. He didn't care much which.

Upon returning to the door, chain lube in hand, Lou said, "It does say to avoid contact with the eyes, but I think that's just the standard warning they put on these things. You should be alright, so long as you don't get any on your skin." He handed the can over. "Now, if you would all kindly piss off, I've got lots to do and…heeeeeeey, do I know you from somewhere?" He was talking, of course, to Samuel, who had been doing everything in his power not to make eye-contact with the proprietor. "You look awfully familiar."

"No, sir," Samuel said, still avoiding the storekeeper's gaze. "We're not from around here, and we only arrived this morning." He was sweating like Mel Gibson at a Bar Mitzvah, but that could have been the sun's doing, and nothing at all to do with his nerves, or the fact that he'd lost them all.

Lou squinted. "Yeah, you look just like a guy that tried to rob me yesterday. A little thinner, maybe, and not as cocky. You look a lot more *haunted* than he did, but apart from that, it's uncanny."

Samuel shook his head and giggled anxiously.

"Some people say he has one of those faces," interrupted the lead speaker.

"What? A face that looks like other people's faces?" Lou was confused, at both what was being said and his apparent willingness to persist with the conversation at all.

"No, one of those faces you could just slap over and over," the blonde girl added. Something told Lou that, for a little thing, she had quite a nasty bite.

"What's this sign mean?" asked one of the group. "Milk? Why would you be telling people that you've got milk for sale?"

"Because I *have*," Lou said, somewhat defensively. "I mean, I *did* have. Now I just have empty bottles and dependent customers, at least until tomorrow."

"Wait a gosh-darn minute," said the one at the front, the one with the Hawaiian-Spanish inflection. "You're telling us you've got milk. That you had milk here earlier today."

Lou nodded. How many times did he have to go through all this? "Yes, gen-u-ine milk, as fresh as the day it was bottled."

The group did various glancings amongst themselves, before the one without any thumbs (Lou couldn't help but notice) said, "That must have been what that fucking priest was babbling on about."

"Yes," Lou said. "Now, if you really don't mind, I've got thousands of things to—"

"Okay," said the leader. "One more question and we'll leave you in peace."

Lou dry-swallowed. "Shoot."

"Where can we find the person in charge of this godforsaken town?"

And so Lou told them, quite gladly, of Kellerman's whereabouts before slamming the door shut in their faces.

He turned to find his mother, slurping voraciously from a saucer. "You ready to make another batch?" she asked, her mouth thick and gloopy with her son's milk.

Lou glanced down at his sodden shirt. "You know what?" he said, flicking one nipple and then the other. "I think I am."

17

On the outskirts of town, in a small cave that only she knew about, Zee Fox settled down with a thick book and a glass of murky water. According to her mother, it was best to keep her distance from Oilhaven until Kellerman had stopped looking for her, and this quiet, secluded cave on the edge of town afforded her the sanctuary she needed, at least for the time being.

The book she was about to plunge into was by legendary homemaker and amateur cook, Mrs Beeton. Between its pages were recipes for homemade remedies, broths, tips and cheats on how to fold sheets, and various other guidelines that, should she follow them to the letter, would make her the most knowledgeable girl in Oilhaven, and the most sought after. Come to think of it, that was the exact opposite to what she wanted, but it didn't hurt to learn a little every now and then, so long as you didn't go around flaunting it.

"An hour and forty-five minutes to boil pasta?" Zee said, reading what was quite obviously a mistake. In fact, it wasn't the first mistake she had come across. There was a very good chance that Mrs Beeton had spent a lot of her earnings from previous books on crack cocaine, and had written this one whilst under the influence.

Still, Zee persisted. Where else was she going to learn about level teaspoons and ounce-to-kilo conversions?

The cave was well-shaded, protected from the overwhelming heat and inexorable sunshine, and sitting there upon a rounded rock – she had avoided the jagged rocks ever since one had almost impregnated her – it was quite easy to forget where she was, or that she was in hiding and that the rest of the town was going about its business somewhere behind her.

That was until somewhere between the chapter on starch and the chapter on middle-class etiquette, when something caught the corner of Zee's eye. Just a flicker, a light shape as something shifted in her peripheral vision, but it was enough to cause her to lower the book.

There, walking naked across the mouth of the cave, was an old lady. In her hand, an umbrella went over and over, as if she was trying to take off and just couldn't quite get the momentum up to do so.

Zee froze, the way people do when faced with something creepy and incongruous. Even if she wanted to move, she wasn't sure that she could. Paralysis had set in, rendered her limbs ineffectual. What made things worse was the fact that her machete – her chosen weapon of survival to use on bandits, rapists, coyotes, and anyone that looked like they might be trouble – was leaning against the cave wall a few feet to her left. She hadn't anticipated an altercation, and hopefully there wouldn't be one, but all of a sudden she wished the machete was in her hand. Now all she could do was watch, and hope that the old lady went away.

She was singing, now. Zee could hear her tiny, shrill voice as she struggled to hit the right key. Not that it mattered. It wasn't as if Zee was going to stand up and complain. *"No, that's not how it goes. You're in C when you should be in G#. Go home, put some clothes on, and come see me when you've figured it out."*

The song, if you could call it that, was about rice pudding, and as the woman sang, it became increasingly clear that she was not of sound mind (though the lack of suitable clothing had been a good indication).

Still frozen, Zee allowed her head to move across the mouth of the cave, to follow the warbling old biddy as she pranced and danced and swung her bountiful hips, all the time singing about rice pudding and how it was the bee's knees, etc. etc.

Just when Zee thought the song was over, off she went again with another verse. On several occasions, the old woman peered into the darkness of the cave, as if she could sense there was somebody watching her but didn't quite have the balls to go looking. Her eyes mustn't have adjusted to the darkness the way Zee's had, otherwise she would have seen the girl sitting atop the smooth rock, staring out incredulously, and that, Zee thought, would have been the end of that...

"Yes, yes, rice pudding," the old woman said. "Delicious it was. Thick and creamy, and hardly any lumps."

Zee had no idea what the woman was rambling on about, or why she was doing so in the buff. Surely someone had seen her walking through town like that? Surely someone would have tried to intervene, throw a blanket over her, do *something*!

Apparently not.

"All thick and drippy, it was, not watery, no, no, no!"

Zee felt sorry for the old dear, who was clearly out of her superannuated mind. *If I ever get like that*, she thought, *I want someone to put a steel bolt through my brain.*

Just then, the book – *Mrs Beeton's Book of Household Management* – slipped from Zee's lap and landed on the cave floor with a thump. Dust and sand flew up into the air, and Zee, panicking, reached down for the book, forgetting for a moment about the old lady and her confused ramblings.

"I *knew* there was someone there," said the old lady as she stepped into the gloom. "Oh, I *see* you now. I see you very well, indeed."

Zee didn't know what to do, but standing seemed to be a good idea. After managing that without too much trouble, she said, "Are you okay? Do you need me to escort you home?"

The old lady cackled. "*Home?* Why would I want to go *home?*"

"I'm assuming that's where your clothes are," Zee said. "And, no offence intended, I'm almost positive that you look better with them on."

"Have you tasted the milk?" said the old lady, prodding at Zee with her umbrella.

It's worse than I thought, Zee thought. "There is no milk," she said. "Hasn't been for a very long time. Do you have any family in Oilhaven? Someone that will take you off my hands for free?"

"But there *is* milk, dear. There is lots of it, and it rescued my rice puddin'." She allowed the umbrella to fall to the floor of the cave before cupping her hands together. Then, leaning forward, she belched, vomiting something thick and uneven into them. It was all Zee could do not to scream. "Go on, love," the old lady said. "'elp yourself."

Zee gagged but managed to compose herself. Was it this poor old lady's fault that she was lost, that she was confused, that she had just upchucked into her own cupped hands? It would have taken a right old meanie to simply walk away and leave the befuddled biddy to her own devices.

Zee picked up the heavy tome she had been reading and dropped it into her rucksack. She was meant to be avoiding town like the plague, but things had changed. This old lady needed her help, and...

"The milk," said the old lady, grinning wildly. "You have to try the *milk*. It's sooooo creaaaaaaaamy!"

And then something bizarre happened, something that could only be described as a waking nightmare, one that Zee would not recover from for quite some time.

The old lady's expression changed from one of joy to one of utter horror. Something white and gloopy spilled from her wide open maw as her face contorted, stretching first one way, and then the other. Violent tremors wracked through her entire body as she dropped to her knees, coughing up more of that terrible white stuff.

"Oh my god!" Zee said. "What can I do? What do I do to help?" As far as she was concerned, this was something the old lady suffered from regularly, something for which she took pills, or rubbed lotion on, or got used to with minimal fuss. And then she remembered her little brother and his exploits from the previous day, how he had fallen ill and had spent the majority of the day with his head buried in a bucket. Maybe that was what this was.

But no. Clint's face hadn't contorted like that, as if a thousand restless worms squirmed beneath its surface. That was like nothing Zee had ever seen before.

"The *miiiiiiilllllk*!" the old lady said, but it was no longer her own voice. To Zee, it sounded like three or four people talking at once.

"I don't know…what to do!" Zee said, hooking her arms beneath the elderly lady's and hoisting her to her feet. The feel of her clammy, wrinkled flesh made Zee gag again. "*Tell* me what I can do!"

The old lady stopped wriggling for a moment; long enough to regain her footing. Zee couldn't see the woman's face, since she was holding her up from behind, but she could hear the long, languorous breaths emanating from her goo-drenched face, and she knew that something very bad was about to happen.

And it did.

The old lady (though nothing of the sort anymore) snapped her head around one-hundred-and-eighty degrees, like an owl only evil and wrinkly. Her tongue darted in and out of her puckered old mouth, but it was black, long and bovine. White slime dripped from it, stretched down onto Zee's arm, causing her to let go.

The old lady stumbled forwards a few steps before composing herself. Her distended belly rolled, as if she was about to give birth to not one, but *many*, aberrations. Her head snapped back into its rightful position just as that terrible tongue leapt from her mouth and snatched the umbrella up from the cave floor.

Zee, no longer paralysed, lunged for her machete, and would have made it had an umbrella not smacked into the back of her head, sending her sprawling.

The old lady/evil creature roared triumphantly, but Zee wasn't beating around the bush. She dragged herself forwards and, in one swoop, gathered the machete up. The monster groaned, clearly not pleased with the sudden shift in impetus.

"What the fuck *are* you?" Zee said, turning to face the beast, which now had an extra set of arms hanging from its anus. They propelled it forwards, pushing up from the ground with giant, hairy knuckles. One swing of the machete, though, and the monster backed off.

"*Miiiiiiiiiilllllk!*" the thing hissed, circling Zee, prowling like a lion – an extremely wrinkly and bloated lion that had been shaved haphazardly and left to fend for its self. Every time its mouth opened, thick white liquid leached out. Zee could smell it – an odd combination of death and honey and brimstone and earth – as it splattered onto the cave floor. Whatever the liquid was, it had no right pouring from a previously-normal old lady's disfigured face.

It lunged again, this time managing to penetrate what Zee liked to think of as her 'safe zone'. Acting fast, Zee brought the machete up, whipped it through the air so quick that it was invisible to the naked human eye.

The beast drew back, shrieking like a cornered fox, and then a thin line appeared along her chest, running up through the gelatinous mountains that were her mutilated breasts. At first it was a red line, no thicker than a pubic hair, but then it opened up more, and the woman-thing screeched as she realised she was, in fact, coming apart.

"Oh!" Zee said, for she hadn't meant to split the thing in half. "Oh, fuck!"

But it was no use; the damage had been done. Zee's blade had sliced through the beast as if it were made of butter, or mallow, and now all she could do was stand and watch as the thing's left side and its right side parted company for the foreseeable future.

The haggard old face of the thing twisted into something even *more* unsettling, something so far from human that Zee dared not look at it for too long, lest she go completely bonkers. And then its body snapped apart; blood and white liquid sprayed out, coating the walls of the cave, combining to make an almost rosy pink. It was a colour that didn't suit the environment. *Maybe someday*, Zee though, *a camp drifter would stumble upon the cave and make it his own, but until then…*

Zee took a step back as the thing teetered forwards on fleshy, perpetually-warping legs. It was hard to believe that, just a moment ago, a naked old lady had stood there, singing about rice pudding and swinging an umbrella. It was so hard, in fact, that Zee refused to believe it. She couldn't live with herself, knowing that she had ended the life of some insane old biddy. It was much easier pretending this thing, this *monster*, had been a monster all along, masquerading as an old lady with an umbrella and a terrible singing voice.

"I'm so sorry!" Zee whined as the thing toppled backwards, its innards flying up into the air before slapping back down again with a meaty thud. It gargled, it choked, it farted, and it hissed, and Zee heaved as the stench of the thing filled her nostrils. There was nothing sweet or honeyed about it now. It was like licking shit off the back of a decaying dormouse.

Three minutes later – though it could have been a lot less – the geriatric ladybeast stopped twitching and gargling and fell still.

Zee exhaled and lowered the machete, watching as the thick, pink slime pouring from the creature's wounds blossomed outwards, surrounding the dead thing like a fancy aura.

Another minute passed, and it was then that Zee decided to end her voluntary exile.

She ran as quickly as her legs could carry her, leaving her rucksack, along with *Mrs Beeton's Book of Household Management*, precisely where it had fallen.

Who needed to know how to darn socks, anyway?

18

An old boiler, rusty but not cracked, lying in the store's basement, was the perfect receptacle in which to shoot one's surplus bodily fluid. It was half-filled with Lou's Milk when both nipples decided to take a little break. *And not before time*, Lou thought, breathless and tender. He drained off what remained in his ducts before pulling his shirt back on, being careful not to set the little buggers off again.

"It's amazing, isn't it?" said his mother. She was sitting in the corner of the room on a dusty, old rocking-chair that would have buckled under a normal person's weight.

"What?" Lou said, leaning, for a moment, against the vast vat he was in the process of filling. "The fact that I'm pissing enough milk to nourish the whole town, or the fact that I haven't gone crazy yet?

"No," Freda said, smiling thinly. "I was just thinking about how many years we've been here. How long this store has been running. All those years you've been in charge…and only *now* have we started stocking something really profitable."

Lou shrugged. What was she saying? That she resented him for not going through this ridiculous metamorphosis before now? Any other time he would have argued with her, but he simply wasn't in the mood. Too much craziness rolled around in his head; too many questions that, if he was really lucky, would remain unanswered, for did he really want to know what was happening to him? Why he had suddenly started to spout milk? Of course he didn't, because the answer could not be a good one. He was either dying, or malfunctioning, and neither of those would help him sleep better at night. No, it was best to remain aloof, unknowing, and just hope that his titties weren't going to be the death of him.

"I remember when you were a little boy," said his mother. Her beatific expression suggested this was going to be a long story, one filled with tales of yappy dogs and weekends on the beach. It came as quite a shock to Lou, then, when she said, "You were a right little shithead."

"Thanks, mother," Lou replied, ignoring the urge to pace across the room and kick the ancient rocking-chair from beneath her.

"No, I didn't mean it like that," she said, before swallowing down the remnants of her mug. She had been drinking the milk nonstop, or thereabouts. Lou just hoped it didn't extend her life-cycle too much. "What I meant was, you were always fighting, never one to be controlled or dictated to. Me and your ol' father used to call you Tonka. It was the way you were built, see. Like a Tonka truck. Course, you never had much luck with the girls, but that didn't mean you were without your admirers."

"*Who?*" Lou said, genuinely intrigued. If there had been an admirer – a single *one* – surely he would have known about her. He'd gone through his entire life feeling utterly repellent, and this new ability wasn't doing much to change that, but it would have been nice to settle down…wife, two kids, dog, cockatiel…maybe a bungalow somewhere – less rooms to clean, and much easier to shift the TV aerial…

"That ginger boy at the end of our street," his mother said. "What was his name again? Barry? Bobby?"

"*Bandy*," Lou said. "Bandy *Borkenstein* was my secret admirer?"

His mother visibly recoiled, as if she'd been slapped across the face by an invisible man wielding an invisible kipper. "Lou Decker! You could have done a *lot* worse than Bandy Borkenstein. Besides, he looked lovely in that spotty dress he used to wear."

"Why are you doing this?" Lou said. He didn't have many memories from before The Event, and there was a perfectly good reason why that was: they were all shit.

"Just trying to make conversation," she said. "Thought it might help with your lactating; something to take your mind off how *gross* it actually is." She held up her empty mug. "One for the road?"

Reluctantly, Lou took the mug and filled it from the vat. He was halfway across the room when his mother groaned and clutched at her stomach.

"Oooooooh," she said, sucking air in through her toothless gums. "Ooooooh, second thoughts, I might give that one a miss."

Lou shook his head. "I *told* you to slow down. We don't know how safe this stuff is, and you've been knocking it back like Keith Richards at his own wake."

Freda Decker stopped rocking and eased herself up from the chair. "Nothing a good shit won't heal," she said, staggering forwards a few steps. "But maybe we need to put something on the bottle. A little disclaimer…"

"Don't drink more than one gallon in every hour?" Lou said. "Unlike *you*, the 'haveners don't have unlimited access to Lou's…to *my* milk. From now on, you're on strict rations. Can't have you dying on us, can we, not before this new venture gets off the ground?"

She moaned again; Lou didn't think this one was ever going to end. It was more like a plaintive keen than a human complaint, the kind one might hear out in the desert late at night, the kind that usually meant you were about to be chased, or eaten, or both. Whatever was wrong with her, it would take a lot more than a forced shit to put it right.

"I don't feel too good, Lou," she said, stumbling across the room as if someone had tied her shoelaces together when she wasn't looking. "I feel…something's not *right*…my innards are giving me some right gyp…"

Lou had spent the last thirty years listening to her various complaints, the myriad afflictions affecting her, keeping her bedridden and bedraggled and, frankly, he wasn't going to honour this one with anything more than a 'told you so' and a 'don't forget to flush'.

Just then, a foul smell filled the room. It was the kind of smell that, even if you had been out on the street when you passed it, would have followed you to the end of your journey.

Freda Decker regarded her son with something akin to fear. He had never seen an expression like that painted upon his ailing mother's face, and he didn't like it one bit. Perhaps…just perhaps…

"Mother?" he said, trying not to inhale one ounce of the malodorous stench permeating the basement.

She looked back at him in silence, her eyes wide and watery, her bottom lip quivering in much the same way a young girl's might if you were to sequester her favourite doll.

"Mom?"

" _ "

Lou didn't know what was happening before it had already happened, by which time he'd lost the ability to react.

His mother came at him like a bull in a china shop, only now it wasn't his mother. It was a shifting, transmutating mass of flesh, held together only by snapping bones and sinew. White fluid geysered from her gummy maw, coating Lou from head to toe in less than a second. Its vile warmth reminded him of the time he'd slept out under the stars for the very first time.

Had Bandy Borkenstein been with him that night? Masturbating in his sleeping bag whilst Lou peacefully slept, unaware that he was being simultaneously watched and violated?

"Miiiiiilllllllk!" Freda screeched in a hundred different voices, none of them her own. She caught Lou by the throat and picked him up, as if he was no more cumbersome than a broomstick. It was then that Lou saw his mother's eyes – two milky-white pits devoid of any life, any sign that she was in control.

"*Grghhhgergh!*" Lou said, which was about all he could manage with his crazed mother's desiccated hand wrapped around his throat, squeezing the life from him ever-so-slowly.

She drew back her hand and tossed Lou to the side. He crashed into the wall and was followed on his way to ground by a selection of useless power-tools that had been hanging there since the world had ended all those years ago.

Lou wasted no time – the floor was nice, spacious, and relatively clean, but you wouldn't want to live there – and quickly scrambled to his feet. He turned to face his mother, half-expecting her to be rushing him again, only now she *wasn't*.

Something had caught her eye. Something far more important than brutally assaulting her son.

"*Miiiiiillllk!*" she snarled, moving slowly toward the half-filled vat. Her saggy breasts spilled up over her blouse and began to stretch upwards, as if reaching for the basement ceiling. Little nubs pushed outwards next to her gigantic areola, and it wasn't long before Lou realised what he was looking at.

Fingers.

Her droopy breasts had grown hands.

Why of course they have, Lou thought, making himself as small as possible. He was on the verge of insanity; it was like staring into some stygian abyss. It would be much easier allowing the madness to consume him than fighting back. But fight back he did; he wasn't ready to die just yet, and especially not at the hands of this atrocity.

The mother-beast loomed over the vat as its breast-hands scooped up the milk from within. It slurped and growled and made generally uncouth sounds as the milk was fed into the unnaturally wide hole in its face.

There was, Lou realised, nothing of his mother left in the creature standing before him. No sign that she had ever been there.

He had to act fast.

Unfortunately, he was paralysed with fear, and it took a helluva lot just to make his feet comply. Eventually – though not as quietly as he'd intended – his legs were moving, and he raced up the basement stairs, tripping only seven or eight times as he went. His nipples screamed out in agony, and Lou knew he needed to calm down, lest he start producing again.

He reached the top of the stairs and paused for just a moment to listen to the mother-beast's insatiable groans. Part of him wanted to run away, to put as much distance between himself and the store as possible; another part wanted to slam the trapdoor, confining the thing that used to be his mother to the basement, at least until he had a chance to figure out what to do.

Neither of those options were the right ones.

Lunging across the room, Lou had only one thing in mind. He grabbed the duel pistols from beneath the counter, said, "Fuck, fuck, fuck, fuck, fuck!" and made his way back down to the basement, to where the mother-beast lurked.

*

Descending, down, down, steps, mind that one (it's a bit creaky). Lou tried to regulate his breathing, keep the noise to an absolute minimum, but as a fifty-year-old man who seldom exercised, it was easier said than done.

The basement was quiet. Not 'you could hear a pin drop' quiet, but creaky old basements rarely are. The mother-beast – whatever the *hell* it was – was nowhere to be seen. But it was down there somewhere, hiding in the shadows, waiting for Lou to return.

Did it know about the pistols? Was it hiding, anticipating the right time to attack, thusly snatching the antique guns from the petrified man nervously wielding them? Lou had hoped the thing wasn't that smart – his mother hadn't exactly been the sharpest tool in the drawer – but if it was *hiding*, it had at least a soupcon of intelligence about it, which put them on pretty much a level playing field.

Three steps from the bottom…two…

One…

Lou slowly, carefully, made his way through the basement, listening out for any noises that weren't his own – wheezing, rattling, occasionally trouser-coughing. Other than his own noises, he couldn't discern a thing.

The vat, previously half-filled with his milk, was now empty but for a centimetre of lumpy bile and coarse hair at the very bottom. The mother-beast had devoured the lot, and in such a short space of time. That giant, inhuman hole in the centre of its face sure did have its advantages.

The basement stank of piss and milk and shit and vomit, as if the creature hadn't been able to control its bodily functions. Lou fought back the urge to vomit, knowing that if he did, the mother-beast would attack. It is a known fact that vomiting with one's eyes open is a scientific impossibility, like pissing in a busy urinal, or eating Oreos without becoming hopelessly addicted. If Lou's eyes should close for just a moment, no matter how brief, the beast would lunge from the darkness and despatch him.

He was the fly; his mother was the spider, and this was her web. And it was thoughts like that which made Lou realise he should have run for the hills while he had had the chance.

A noise, somewhere behind, made Lou turn. He was about to level the pistols into the darkness when something slammed into him from the right, knocking him from his feet.

"Miiiiiiiiillllllllk!" the thing hissed, its rancid breath slamming into the side of Lou's face like a freight train. The mother-beast was bearing down on him, grabbing at him with four hands (Lou tried not to think about the new growths), flipping him over, and yet not killing him.

It knows, Lou thought. *It knows I'm the milk-maker.*

As the creature unceremoniously rolled him around the basement floor like a Vileda supermop, Lou fumbled with the one pistol he'd managed to keep a hold of. There was a good chance it wouldn't work, but he had to try, he had to do something…

"Suck on this, you milky bastard!" he said, rolling onto his back. The mother-beast's gigantic forehead crumpled up, folded over like an accordion as it frowned. For just a second, Lou thought he saw something in its eyes, something human in those cloudy cataracts that suggested his mother might not be lost forever.

He wasn't taking any chances.

He pulled the trigger.

The mother-beast's head snapped back as the ancient bullet tore through its skull. A shower of milk and blood rained down on Lou, who closed his mouth tightly, lest he ingest the disgusting drizzle. The thing that had birthed him, that had brought him up and forged him into the man he was today, slumped to the side, spilling grey matter and cream across the basement floor. Its breast-hands shrivelled up and turned black, like those antediluvian mummies people used to dig up.

The thing was heavy – much heavier than it had been as a dying old lady – but Lou managed to ease it off after a few minutes of struggling.

He stared down at the body, the thing that should not be, and a tear crept from the corner of his eye.

A milk tear.

"Well, that was a fucking nightmare," he said, stowing the antique pistol in the waistband of his slacks. She had been possessed, infected by a demon; that was the only explanation he had.

But then he saw the vat, all rusty and barren in the middle of the basement, and something terrible occurred to him.

"Shit," he said as milk began to, once again, seep from his nipples. "Shit, shit, fucking shit!"

19

El Oscuro parked the horse and tethered it to a sign that said OILHAVEN – WHERE DREAMS COME TRUE...OCCASIONALLY. He climbed down, joining the rest of Los Pendejos on the sandy road.

"You sure this is the place?" Red said, surveying the two storey building they found themselves standing before. It didn't look like much, but it was fancier than the rest of the edifices in town, inasmuch as it had glass windows (none of which had been put through by rocks or planks of wood) and a steel door that suggested the person who lived there did not like to be interrupted. Someone – some brave soul – had graffitied the word *cockbasher* on the door, which was, El Oscuro opined, the usual attitude shown toward small-town authority.

"This is the place," El Oscuro said. "This mayor, Kellerman, is probably up there right now, fiddling taxes and counting whatever passes for currency in this shit-forsaken town."

Blink stepped forwards, examining the steel door carefully. He could see a lot better now that the grit and filth had been removed from his eyes, which were stinging a little, but it had mentioned possible side-effects on the side of the can, and unbearable agony had been one of them. "So what?" he said. "We're just going to go up there and rob the man?"

El Oscuro laughed. Thumbs, Samuel, and Red joined in, but if you were to ask them why, they would have told you they hadn't got the foggiest. "Is that how we operate, Blink?" he said. "Heavy-handed, shoot first ask questions later?"

Blink shrugged. That was *usually* how it went down.

"No, we're going to play this one cool," El Oscuro said, giving the steel door a gentle nudge. It was locked, which made perfect sense. What was the point of having a steel door if you were just going to leave it hanging on its hinges all day long? You could do that with a wooden door. In fact, you might as well not have a door at all...

"By *cool*," Thumbs said, "you mean we're going to stand out here and talk about what we would do if we had half a chance?"

There were times when El Oscuro wished he was a one-man operation, and this was one of them. "My dear idiot," he said, shaking his head, "we are going to make this man, this Kellerman, believe that we are here to offer him a service. In doing so, we will gain his trust, and therefore, access to his assets." He smiled. Not bad for a plan he'd just fabricated on the spot. It sounded almost...*feasible.*

"I don't mean to burst your bubble," Red said, "but what services could we possibly have to offer a man who clearly has his shit together? I mean, people don't just become mayor of a town willy-nilly. He's obviously got folks doing his dirty work for him already."

"Ah," El Oscuro said, wishing, all of a sudden, that he'd thought that far ahead. "Yes, but...but what we are going to offer him is something he can't get in this town. Something that only *we* can provide."

"I think I've got herpes," Samuel said, scratching at his balls. "But he can get that in this town. All he needs is an appointment with Madam Sneve."

"Keep your herpes to yourself, Samuel," El Oscuro said. "We're going to make this Kellerman geezer an offer he can't refuse."

The bandits did scratchings of the head, and glancings at one another, hoping that someone could explain what the hell their leader was babbling on about. When no-one did, El Oscuro sighed as hard as he could – he almost ruptured his spleen – and said:

"We're going to tell him we know where to get e-lec-tricity from."

There was a pause as four bandits tried to get their head around El Oscuro's plan, and the myriad flaws that came with it.

"Electricity?" Red said, incredulously. "That's your plan, is it?"

"She's right," Thumbs said, wiping grease from the side of his head with the stump of his right hand. "There hasn't been a sighting of electricity for over two decades."

El Oscuro shrugged. He would have left it at that had he been in the company of geniuses. Unfortunately he wasn't. "*He* doesn't know that," he finally said. "If we tell him we know there's a place not far from here that's got light and power, all rigged up to the mains, that's going to set his little noggin to thinking."

"But what's to stop him from sending out his scouts?" Samuel said. "Surely he'll just dispatch a reccy, and what happens when they come back empty-handed? They ain't gonna be too happy being sent on a wild goose chase to some fictional electric town in the middle of the desert."

"Ahhh," El Oscuro said, tapping the side of his nose with a grimy digit. "That's why we're not going to *tell* him where this fictional town is. We'll have the upper hand, no offense, Thumbs."

"None taken," Thumbs said.

"We'll offer to rig this place up, just like the fictional town we've just come from. We've got the know-how, you see. We've got detailed drawings of how they did it, and since Samuel and Blink here used to be trained electricians, it'll be a walk in the park, so long as the funds are in place for us to do the work."

"That's all well and good," Samuel said, "but we're not trained electricians. In fact, I've never even *seen* a light bulb in action."

"Yeah, what is e-lec-tric?" said Blink.

"Look, it's not as if you're going to have to pass a *test*," El Oscuro said. "You don't even need to know what electric *is*, Blink. All you need to do is pretend you know how to get it, and Robert's your auntie's husband…"

There was another pause, in which cogs could be heard turning, albeit very slowly. El Oscuro needed them all to understand what was about to happen before they made contact with Kellerman, but standing out there in the scorching heat, pissing sweat by the bucketload, was starting to take its toll.

"Dave," Thumbs said. So unexpected was his 'Dave' that El Oscuro started.

"What?"

"Dave," Thumbs reiterated. "That was my auntie's husband's name. He was a right bastard, used to knock her about something silly, but he did buy me a fish-tank once…so, swings and roundabouts, really."

El Oscuro stood, slack-jawed, for a relatively long time, before saying, "Look. Can we just act like professionals for one minute?" Nobody spoke, which was as good as a *yes* as he was going to get. "Right. Now, just let me do the talking, and everything'll be fine. Like the contractors of yesteryear, we're about to become very rich, so let's not fuck it up."

"You might want to cover up your weapon," Red said, pointing to the samurai sword hanging from his waist. "If this guy's in charge around here, he might take offense to us waltzing into his office tooled up."

"Ah, good thinking," El Oscuro said, draping a pair of dirty, well-worn pants over the end of the sword. As disguises went, it wasn't the best. In fact, it looked like a samurai sword with a pair of paints hanging off it, but you worked with what you had.

Stepping up to the steel door, El Oscuro took a deep breath, immediately wishing he hadn't. Once he'd finished coughing and spluttering, he banged three times with the ball of his fist. The door rattled, like an epileptic rat in a discarded tin-can, and then the noise tapered off altogether.

"We'll just give him a few minutes," El Oscuro said. "He's probably a very busy man."

*

Kellerman's feet weren't even touching the ground anymore; the sign of a very arduous and violent shit. Every now and then he would allow himself to relax, if only to catch his breath, but it wasn't long before the next wave hit him, and up went his feet again, and that strange eggplant hue returned to his face with a vengeance.

When will it end? he asked himself, or God, or anyone with access to his thoughts that might have been listening in. He had been laboriously defecating ever since Smalling and Harkness left, and yet whenever he checked, there was nothing in the bowl beneath him but a strange, white liquid. He'd considered the idea that he was laying phantom turds – the ghosts of poos that had somehow died inside him – but it seemed a little far-fetched, even by Oilhaven standards.

"Owowowowow!" he said, but again there was nothing solid emerging; the sound of a liquid hitting the bowl was slightly disconcerting. The whole experience brought back memories of a time before The Event, when something called Vinda-loo was readily available. At least with a vindaloo, you knew you were in for trouble the following morning. This anal assault had caught him completely off guard, and he had a damn good idea who and what was responsible.

The *milk*. It had to be, for that was the only thing he'd had that deviated from his normal diet of bread and squirrel. And if it *was* the milk – and it looked that way – then Lou Decker was in for a nasty surprise when Kellerman caught up with him.

Just then, someone banged on the door – three times, because once is never enough and five is taking the piss. Kellerman eased his feet to the ground and tried to breathe, but the smell – a sickly-sweet stench that seemed intent on rendering him unconscious – made breathing an impossibility. Still, the colour returned to his cheeks, and after a few moments he felt a little better.

He wiped, using the three envelopes he'd lined up beforehand, and slowly stood, holding onto the wall for support. He had been there for quite a while, and his legs were buzzing with pins and needles; the last thing he needed was to fall, hit his head off the side of the lavatory, or worse, the *inside*. Once the feeling returned to his lower half, he yanked up his suit trousers and pulled the chain hanging from the ceiling next to him.

The milky faeces disappeared, and Kellerman felt a lot better for it. Maybe, he thought, it *wasn't* Lou's Milk that had caused his sudden discomfort. Maybe he just wasn't used to such richness, such pure dairy. It had been so long since he'd had anything remotely milky or cheesy; perhaps he needed to simply become accustomed to it again.

Whatever it was, it seemed to have passed for the time being. Kellerman, whistling like a tin-kettle, made his way to the front door, but not before picking up a shotgun that had been leaning against the toilet door. His favourite Remington – a 10 gauge semi-automatic in camouflage finish. Anyone foolish enough to argue with it deserved the huge hole it left in their face; although he had not yet fired it at anything other than coyotes and hares, and on those occasions he'd missed by quite a margin. In truth, he wasn't the greatest shot, but more often than not, just holding a gun was enough to deter the wrong kind of people. Statistically speaking, you were more likely to get shot by a passing meteor than you were a bullet, but that was only because there were far more meteors out there than there were bullets. Not to mention that the number of people with the weapons to fire said bullets had depleted, meaning you were far better off buying a good telescope than a Kevlar vest.

Kellerman reached the door and glanced out through the peephole, where five fisheye-lensed faces gawped back at him, their grins seemingly wider than their faces. One of them was an extremely pretty woman, not that such things bothered the mayor any longer. Besides, out of all of them, it was she that looked the most menacing, despite the smile.

"Yes?" Kellerman said. It was strange answering his own door. Perhaps things would be different once the Fox girl was under his employ. Yes, she looked the type that could answer a door at the drop of a hat...

"We're here on behalf of...of...*Oscuro* Contracting," the one at the front said, tilting his head. "We need to speak with the mayor urgently."

There was something about the way the man said *urgently* that Kellerman didn't like. Nothing was *urgent* any more. There was nothing you could do today that you couldn't put off until tomorrow, and that was a fact.

"The mayor isn't available," Kellerman said. "But if you tell me what's so urgent, I can pass on a message." *I'll pass on the message,* he thought. *I'll pass it on to my boys, along with five warrants. You like banging on fucking doors? Let's see how you cope down at the gaol, you fucking—*

148

"We're trained electric-icians," said one of the callers, pressing his face so close to the door that Kellerman could only see one giant eye. It appeared to be caked with dirt and oil.

"Shhhhh!" the one at the front said, pulling the one with the big eye back into line. "What he means," he went on, "is that we've recently discovered something. Something that will change your little town forever."

"Is it bleach?" Kellerman said. "Because we tried that already. Didn't seem to make a difference."

"No, not bleach," said the head caller. "When was the last time you read a book by bulb-light? When was the last time you put your food into a small box that went *ding!* and then came out all lovely and warm, at least on the outside? When was the last time—"

"You're not Jehova's Witnesses, are you?" Kellerman said. "Because we don't tolerate that sort of nonsense in Oilhaven. In fact, we had the last pair hung, drawn, and quartered before setting fire to the remains. Then we took it in turns to wee on them. It was a great night..."

"Not for the Jehova's Witnesses," said the leader.

"Indeed," Kellerman said. He'd completely lost his train of thought.

"What we're hoping to sell to you today is a vision. One of power. Of growth. Of a return to some normality. I'm talking, of course, about volts."

"Votes?" Kellerman said, frowning needlessly. "I'm not interested. I get plenty of those, year-in, year-out.

Fortunately, I'm the only one to ever run for office. Strange that."

"Not votes," said the woman, who was not as pretty as Kellerman had first thought. In fact she was *hideous*, in a lovely way. "Volts, as in Ohms."

"But we've already *got* homes," Kellerman said, growing tired of all this nonsense. "Most people are happy with the ones they have, and the ones that aren't, well they make do or I toss them out into the desert."

"Not *homes*!" the leader said, huffing exasperatingly. "Ohms! As in Watts!"

"What?"

"Watts!"

"What Watts?"

"Hasn't this joke run its course yet?" the lead caller said. "Look, we're here to offer you an opportunity. Now, we can shout it through the door, no problem, but there are a lot of people gathering down here, pointing things at us and, if I'm being completely honest, making me very nervous, so why don't you just let us in and we can talk in private? We think that you will want to hear what we have to say."

Kellerman stared out through the peephole, the shotgun growing heavy in his hand. "Oh, alright," he said. "But at the first mention of God, loft-insulation, or raccoon adoption, I'm going to shoot you where you sit."

He unlocked the door just as his stomach started to roll once more.

Not now, he thought. *Please not now…*

20

The Barrel was heaving by the time Roger Fox arrived. Covered in filth and grime so thick that you couldn't see the man beneath, he stepped up to the bar and beckoned Roy, the landlord. "Hello, Roy," he said, trying not to touch anything. The bar wasn't exactly spotless — nowhere was, not anymore — but he didn't want to make it worse with a flick of the wrist or a misplaced elbow. "I was wondering. Did a little old lady with an umbrella leave something here for me?"

Roy stared him up and down, and then said, "Is that you, Roger? For fuck's sake, I didn't recognise you under all that filth. What can I get you?"

Roger smiled. "The *thing?*" he said. "The *thing* the old lady said she would leave here for me to pick up?"

"Oh," Roy said, grasping what the miner was getting at. "That's right. Little old lady, umbrella, mad as a box of frogs, came by this morning, early, wanted me to give you these." And with that, he reached into his trouser pocket and produced...

"That's my rock!" Roger said, baffled. "And my plastic button."

"And now I'm giving them back to you," said the barkeep. "Enjoy."

"What about the milk?" Roger said, snatching the button and the rock from the man standing on the other side of the bar.

"Oh, not bloody *you* as well," Roy said, shaking his head. "All day I've had people coming in here, yapping about Lou's Milk." He put on a whiny voice for the next part and, to be quite frank, it warranted one. " *'Oh, it's lovely'. 'It tastes just like heaven'. 'I hope he gets some more tomorrow'.*" His voice returned to normal, he said, "If you ask me, no good will come of that milk. Nobody's stopped to think where it's all coming from. I mean, I've heard a lot of rumours today – some bullshit about an invisible well; some more bullshit about a cow from another dimension – but if you ask me, Lou Decker has sold his soul to the devil, and I, for one, won't be touching a drop of the stuff."

Roger was about to speak when there came a growl from the far end of the bar. Both he and the barkeep turned to find Reverend Schmidt, nursing a large scotch (99% water), batting it from side to side as if he were a cat and his glass a dead mouse.

"It's not the devil's work," said the clergyman, turning his attention to Roger and Roy. "You have no idea what you're talking about. Unless you've tasted it – and Lord, have I tasted it – you should keep your opinions to yourself, you pair of clueless cunts."

Now, Reverend Schmidt was a devout Catholic, the kind of clergyman with all the faith in the world for himself, and some spare for those around him. He hadn't missed a sermon in over forty years, even in the weeks following The Event, when there wasn't even a church in Oilhaven, just a pile of rubble and a battered old cross.

If you were to ask anyone what they thought of him, words such as wonderful, nice, affable, and delightful would come back at you. In Oilhaven, perhaps even the world, there was no better man left standing.

So to hear him call two 'haveners 'clueless cunts' came as quite a shock to anyone within earshot, and there were plenty. A card-game in the corner came to a complete halt as three of its players toppled back off their chairs. One of them, a man by the name Derringer (no relation), was so shocked that he went into cardiac arrest and was carried out by his friend, who was, until that point, having a very nice afternoon.

"You've *tried* the milk?" Roger said, forgetting, for a moment, that he had just been called a clueless cunt. Besides, there was no point in arguing with religious men. They had God on their side; Roger had a pudgy bartender and an ashtray full of acorns on his.

"*Tried* it?" said Schmidt. "Oh, I've *tried* it. And I won't have a bad word said against it." He sipped at his scotch and hissed as the burn reached his stomach. There wasn't actually enough alcohol for a burn, but old habits die hard. "Look at this," he said, holding up a hand, which was shaking so much that you had to really look just to see it was still there. As he lowered it, he said, "I'm hooked on the stuff. I'm counting down the hours until tomorrow, until Lou gets more." He wasn't going to tell them that he had plans to pop in on his way to the church later, just in case an order had arrived early; it didn't seem important, and they didn't seem to understand, judging by the way they were looking at him. It was as if he'd just told them a recipe for dog-shit sandwiches. He gave them both a gregarious nod before returning to his drink

"See?" Roy whispered, so only Roger Fox could hear. "Nothing good can come of it."

Roger tried to conceal his disappointment (Rita and the kids would have loved just a taste of Lou's Milk) with a forced smile, but he looked as if he was trying to push something terrible from his body, and so soon stopped. "So he's getting more tomorrow?" he said, mainly to Schmidt, who seemed to know more about it than Roy.

But something was not right with the reverend, hadn't been for some time, if his cursing was anything to go by. He looked pallid, bilious, not quite with it, and when he next spoke, there was something in his voice that suggested he wasn't the same man that had given countless sermons and never missed one. "It's mine," he said, a whisper at first, but repeated over and over until it became an unnerving roar. "*It's mine! It's mine! It's mine!*" He stood, back-kicking the stool he'd been sitting upon so hard that it flew across the room and shattered against the wall. As splintered wood rained down, the reverend leapt into the air and came crashing down on the bar, as if he weighed twice – nay, thrice – the amount he had a second ago.

"He's paying for that chair," the barkeep told Roger. To Schmidt, he said, "Walter, either you *calm* down or I'm going to have to ask you to leave." That was the thing about Roy; he was fair to those he knew, offered them second chances, and in some cases, third, fourth, and fifth, depending on how desperate he was for the custom. There were, in fact, seven people drinking in there at that very moment who were barred for life.

"You know," Roger said, taking a tentative step away from the bar and scrutinising the maniacal clergyman as he stalked along the countertop. "I don't think that's the reverend."

"What makes you say that?" asked Roy, spit-polishing a glass before placing it on its shelf.

"The way his head's doing that weird thing, for starters," Roger said, pointing at the anomalous way in which the reverend's noggin pulsated, as if something was fighting to break out of it.

"Now that you *mention* it," Roy said, also taking a step back, "that is a bit freaky, even from a clergyman."

Kicking empty glasses and bowl of acorns aside, Reverend Schmidt rushed across the bar. His body and head bloated and drained, bloated and drained, as if he was being inflated by some imperceptible force. His eyes lost all colour – except white – and his lower jaw hung listlessly, as if it had become detached from the rest of his skull.

"Yeah, there's something very *not* right about Walter," Roy said, reaching under the bar for his baseball bat. Roger scrambled back, toppling over a table and the three people sitting around it.

"Hey!"

"Watch it!"

"Is this your rock and button?"

But Roger didn't hang around down there on the floor of The Barrel. He struggled to his feet just in time to see Roy administer the first clobbering.

"This…is…my…pub…" he said, punctuating each word with a swing of the bat. The reverend took the blows as if they were nothing but a hindrance; blood and…something *else*, something sickeningly creamy, sprayed from his nose and mouth as the bat made contact.

People were screaming, now. Running from The Barrel, leaving their watered-down drinks where they sat. After a few seconds, there were only four people left in the room (including the malfunctioning clergyman), and for the life of him, Roger Fox couldn't fathom why he was one of them.

"Tiny!" Roy said, rushing around the bar. "Finish him off for me, would you? There's a good chap!"

The big man cracked his knuckles and took a step toward Schmidt, who had now taken on the appearance of a hippopotamus. If it wasn't for the moustache and the torn clothes dangling from its distended body, the similitudes would have been uncanny.

It rolled off the counter, somehow managing to land on its huge, mutating feet. For a second, Roger thought he saw fear in the eyes of the man about to take it on.

"I don't know where to hit it!" said Tiny, ducking this way and that, as if competing in some strange 1920s bareknuckle bout.

Roy, now behind his bodyguard but still holding the bat, said, "Just hit it all over. Something's bound to knock it out."

Roger Fox had seen a lot of fights in his time. Usually, disgruntled miners went at one another over something or other, but down there, where it was so dark it wasn't considered odd for one's shadow to get laid off, people seldom landed punches on their intended targets. Broken hands were the number one injury for miners in Oilhaven, because rock walls are incredibly hard, and nowhere near as malleable as a human face.

So, yes, he had seen a lot of fights, but nothing quite like this.

The reverend lunged for Tiny, swinging a giant fist through the air. Tiny dodged to the right, and not a moment too soon. The fist slammed into the wall, knocking the dartboard from its rightful place and revealing a relatively clean patch compared to the rest of the wall.

Tiny kicked at the beast with a huge, lumbering foot, and connected with its god knows what. The whole thing shook, as if made of jelly, and it screeched and cursed in so many different voices, it was impossible to tell whether there were words in there or not.

"Hit it again!" Roy said, swinging the baseball bat for effect.

Roger was rooted to the spot. Sure he could run, but it wasn't every day you saw a clergyman turn into a monster…at least, not *anymore*. This was something he could tell his kids, his *grand*kids (if his kids ever met kids they weren't related to), and he wasn't about to scamper now, when it was about to get good.

The clergy-monster hissed and growled as Tiny began to pummel it with fist after fist. At some point during the trouncing, the creature's moustache fell off and shrivelled up like a dehydrated pomegranate, leaving nothing of Schmidt to see in its angry and wounded countenance.

"Yeah! You like that!? You fucking demon! You fucking like that!?" Tiny was really getting into it, and for a moment, Roger Fox almost felt *sorry* for it, whatever *it* was. "You like that!? Oh, I bet you like that, you filthy fucking hippo!" *Punch, punch, kick, kick, headbutt…*

And it was the headbutt that broke the camel's back, so to speak, as the clergy-beast reared up onto its hind legs and spewed forth a torrent of white liquid, coating Tiny from head to toe in an instant.

A strange stench washed over the room, far worse than anything either the miner or the barkeep had smelt before. It was like dirty socks, filled with edam, left out in the sun for three days, then pooped on. In other words, not the kind of smell you'd want caught at the back of your throat.

Tiny turned, the white liquid dripping from him in thick globules, and for some reason, as if it already knew the fight was over, the creature stepped back, forfeiting its best opportunity for attack.

There was really no need…

Tendrils of white smoke began to curl up and away from the drenched giant, accompanied by a gentle hissing noise, the kind that suggested something was cooking.

And then Tiny's mouth fell open and he screamed. Pain racked through his body as his skin began to melt. For some reason – Roger couldn't figure it out at that point – Tiny began to pull at his flesh, which only made things worse. Thick clumps of meat slapped onto the pub floor, still hissing and dissolving where they landed. Tiny dropped to his knees, which were nothing but bone and liquefying sinew by that point anyway. Roger Fox was grateful when the poor man's vocal chords had dissolved, for he was making a right fucking row.

Roy, frozen to the spot as if Medusa had just popped in for a cheeky half, said, "No! Not *Tiny*!"

The rest of the landlord's favourite giant fell apart with an almighty squelch, proving that, yes, *yes* Tiny. There was just a puddle of viscera and white gloop where he had stood a moment before. It would take one helluva recovery for the poor man to get up again.

The clergy-beast roared, filling the room with an unsavoury stench, and then it turned on Roger and Roy, not quite sure which one it was going to destroy first.

Roy did the first thing that came to mind; he took a step back and pointed a tremulous finger at Roger Fox. *This one! Take no notice of the dirt, he's much tastier than me!*

A thousand-and-one thoughts tore through Roger's mind as death stared him square the face. It was true what they said; life really did flash before your eyes in the moments before death. *It wasn't a bad life*, he thought, gulping audibly. Kids, missus – the only one in town not averse to putting out, once in a while – nice house, if not a little open plan. There were far worse off out there. Such a shame it was all going to come to an abrupt, and painful, end.

"Miiiiiiiillllllk!" the clergy-beast bellowed, and then it was galloping toward Roger Fox, its long, black tongue flapping up and down as it loped.

"Shit, shit shit, shit, SHIIIIIIT!" Roger Fox said, shutting his eyes. He'd had some truly awful days in his life, but this one was up there with the worst of them. Still, if he was going to die, he was damn well going to do it with his eyes closed. He wasn't a complete masochist.

Just then, something whooshed past Roger's head. He felt the wind from it, heard it whistle as it coasted by. He opened his eyes just as a sharp stake thumped into the clergy-beast's grotesque face. The creature roared in agony and, more importantly, stopped careering toward Roger. Dazed and wondering what the fuck had just happened, the beast staggered back, knocking several tables aside before slamming into the bar. Its roar developed into a shrill squeal as it thrashed and writhed, trying to remove the projectile from its head.

But it was buried deep, and the creature seemed to be somewhat lacking when it came to opposable thumbs.

Roy, sensing an opportunity, barrelled forwards, the baseball bat raised high. "This is for Tiny!" he snarled, and brought the bat down as true as possible. The clergy-beast whined as the thick, wooden stake was pushed deeper into its head. There was an audible crunch and, pretty soon after, the clergy-beast decided to give up the ghost and allow the inevitable death to steal it away.

Breathless, sobbing, Roy of The Barrel allowed the bat to fall from his grasp. Only then did he look up to see the person who had come to their aid.

"I knew this place was lively," said the naked alleyway man, "but where the fuck did you get an albino rhino from?"

21

"Run that by me again," Kellerman said, tapping the tube of fish-food until the flakes sprinkled out and landed in the water of his tank. "It sounded as if you were telling me you, I mean *we*, could bring electricity back to Oilhaven." He sniggered. "Which, of course, is impossible."

El Oscuro took a sip from the glass the mayor had handed him, not anticipating that the liquid contained within was genuine, undiluted alcohol. "Holy shit," he croaked. "This is *real* whiskey."

Climbing down the stepladder leaning against his aquarium, Kellerman said, "Not only that, but it's one of only three bottles remaining from that year. You should consider yourself privileged."

The other bandits, who *hadn't* been handed a glass, scowled at their leader. He saw their reproachful glances and smirked, licking the side of his glass with mock pleasure.

"What are you doing?" Kellerman said, sneaking up on El Oscuro like a miming ninja.

"Er, nothing," said the bandit, taking another sip from the glass. "So, yes, where was I? Oh, yeah, electricity! Not impossible. In fact, we saw it with our very own eyes, and managed to get some blueprints down before we were chased out of town by their sheriff."

"Sheriff, huh?" Kellerman said, thoughtfully. "What was his name, this *sheriff?*"

All of a sudden, the whiskey left a bad taste in El Oscuro's mouth. "I didn't get his name," he said. "But he was definitely a sheriff. He had the badge and bad attitude to prove it."

"Sounds about right," Kellerman said, pouring himself a large whiskey. By now, those without glasses were practically drooling. "So, you think you know how to rig this place up, just like the old days? No more diesel generators? No more batteries?"

El Oscuro nodded. "That's exactly what I'm saying," he said. "We come from a very long line of professional electricians. Blink over there, he was the guy who wired up The White House. And *Samuel*...well, let's just say the

Queen of England would have been pissing in the dark if it wasn't for him."

Kellerman frowned, which was never a good sign as far as the bandits were concerned. "If you're all professional electricians," he said, "then how come you haven't been able to figure this out until now? Until you stumbled upon this mystery town north of here?"

"That," El Oscuro said, "is a damn good question, and one I would love for my colleague and wife, Red, to answer for you."

Red, who was blonder than any woman Kellerman had seen in the last twenty years, was slightly taken aback by being thrust into the limelight. Also, she made a mental note to kick El Oscuro very hard in the nut-sack when they got out of there.

"Well, until *now*," Red said, slightly flustered, "we haven't come across the equipment needed to complete the work. But this fiction…I mean, *mystery* town has everything we need. Once we get the go-ahead, we'll strip that place clean in the middle of the night and get it all transported here. You get your electric, we get our contract. It's a win-win situation if ever I heard one."

Kellerman nodded. He liked the cut of this woman's jib. "Okay, so say I might be interested," he said. "What do you need from me?"

El Oscuro puffed out his cheeks and pretended to do some figures in his head. He was, of course, doing nothing of the sort. In fact, while everyone else thought he was doing math, he was really thinking about how hard Red was going to kick him in the nut-sack when they got out of there. "Do you have any bullion?" he said. "Jewellery? Silver? Brass?"

"Actually, I have a rather fine selection of silver…" But that was as far as Kellerman got before doubling over, pain coursing through every inch of him, as if a family of poisonous ants were using his arteries as a nest.

"You alright, mate?" Thumbs asked.

"Of *course* he's not alright," Blink said, pointing at the folded over mayor. "People don't just do that for the fun of it."

"I'm…I'm okay," Kellerman lied, clutching at his stomach. *I was doing so well*, he thought. *So, so well…*

"You don't *look* okay," Red opined.

"If the man says he's okay," El Oscuro said, nonchalantly sipping at his whiskey – his incredible, wonderful whisky – "then he's okay. Ain't that right, Mr Kellerman?"

But Kellerman could no longer speak, for his tongue was twice the size it had been a second ago.

"He's going to fart," Blink said. "I've seen that look before, and it's usually followed up with a colossal guff."

"Are you going to fart, Mr Kellerman?" Red said, taking a step away from the obviously pained man. "Because, I know things pretty much went out the window after The Event with regards to general etiquette, but there is a lady present, and—"

Kellerman's head snapped back at the exact same time the colour drained from his eyes.

"This is gonna be some fart," Samuel said.

The mayor, in that moment, seemed to grow several inches. His suit expanded outwards as muscles rippled beneath. Audible tearing sounds filled the room. Even the fish turned away, reluctant to watch what happened next.

"What's happening to hi…" was all Samuel managed before his head was knocked from his shoulders by a giant, black tail, which seemed to be poking out of Kellerman's arsehole. Blood spurted from the stump of the freshly decapitated bandit's neck, pattering down onto the luxurious, cream carpet like rain on a tin roof. By the time the body crumpled lifelessly to the floor, pandemonium had ensued.

"Weapons!" El Oscuro shouted, tearing the pants from the end of his sword.

"What is it!?" Red screeched, pulling out a small knife.

"Is Samuel dead!?" asked Blink, who wasn't exactly firing on all cylinders at the best of times, let alone when he was faced with a grotesque monster.

Kellerman had grown to twice his original size. His tail – a dragon-like appendage replete with scales and spines – whipped around the room, searching for its next victim. From the mayor's hands, claws sprouted out, tearing at the carpet beneath as if it had said something to offend him.

Thumbs rushed for the door, but the tail got there first, slamming it shut before knocking the digitless bandit across the room with one formidable swing.

"Lop its fucking head off!" Red screeched, forcing herself as far into a corner as she could possibly get. If she was to turn around in that moment, she would have found herself face-to-face with a rather solemn looking angelfish.

El Oscuro lunged forwards, swinging the sword as if he knew what he was doing. The truth of the matter was, he'd never really had to use it before. All of his moves he'd learned from *Shogun Assassin* and *Lone Wolf and Cub*, classic Japanese films he'd owned as a youngster. The only thing he'd ever killed with it was a rat that had crept up on him one night in the desert, and even that had been a fluke.

"*Mmmmmmk!*" the giant ball of scales and claws groaned. "*Mmmmmmmmmmk!*"

"What the fuck does it want!?" Red yelled from the corner of the room.

"It wants *mmmmmmmmmmk!*" Thumbs said. "Does anyone have any *mmmmmmk!?*"

There were shakings of heads as they determined, between them, that *mmmmmmk* was not readily available.

Blink was about to make a run for the door when a clawed hand, seemingly from nowhere, latched onto his ankle. "Ah! Get it off! It's got me!"

"Calm down!" El Oscuro said. "You'll make it angry!"

Although, knocking someone's head from their shoulders could have been considered quite a curmudgeonly thing to do.

Blink tried to stamp on the thing. "Fuck! You! Fuck! You!" *On the bright side*, he thought, his inner-monologue a lot calmer than his outer, *we never had any electricity to begin with, so the joke's on you, motherfucker!* But then his ankle snapped to one side, the bone revealing itself like a peeled banana, and any inner smugness he'd felt was quickly washed away, replaced only by pain of the highest order.

"Kill the fucking thing!" Thumbs said. "I'd do it myself, but I've only got this butter-knife."

Blink toppled backwards, his busted ankle flapping about as if independent to the rest of him. It was all he could do to remain conscious. Luckily, he didn't have to suffer for long, as something appeared above him. A giant, dark mass, seeping white liquid from its pores. Those milky-white eyes gazing down at him, evilly. Those thin, sneering lips – like a well-healed scar – curling up ever-so-slightly, as if the thing was thoroughly enjoying itself. And then there were fists; two huge fists, and they were brought down with such force that, for just a moment, Blink's eyes shut. It was the first time ever, and he didn't even have time to celebrate as the fists continued all the way through his face and smashed into the carpet beneath.

"Shit!" El Oscuro said, dancing around at the far side of the room. "We have to stop it!"

"You don't say," Red sneered. She was looking for a way in, a way past all the flailing appendages and general grossness. "You're the one with the sword."

El Oscuro glanced down at the samurai sword in his hand, then tossed it in the general direction of his female counterpart. It landed next to her feet. "Not anymore," he said. "Now cut its fucking head off before it kills all of us!"

Red reached down and grabbed the sword. It felt good in her hands, as if they were old friends, reunited at last.

"Red!" Thumbs yelled. He was cornered by the creature, then it tails lashed out so fast it was barely visible, pinning him up against the gigantic aquarium, his legs dangling as if he was a marionette version of himself.

"Miiiiiiilllllk!" the beast hissed, and then its arm shot forwards, destroying Thumbs' head completely and shattering the glass behind. Water spilled out into the office, along with fish and various tank ornaments (divers, castles, treasure chests, the usual bullshit). The beast stood firm, but Red and El Oscuro were knocked from their feet by the surging water. One thought ran through Red's mind:

There are people drinking piss out there and dying of thirst, and he's got (had) his own personal SeaWorld™ (other aquatic-based theme parks are available).

After slamming into a filing-cabinet – W-Z, according to its label – Red clambered to her feet and splashed around on the spot for a few seconds until she regained her bearings.

The monster (she had no other word for it) was advancing on El Oscuro, who was doing an extremely good impression of a pleading, sobbing bandit. It was pitiful, really, but enough of Los Pendejos had died already that day. It was time to put an end to this thing before it claimed two more.

She whistled, and it was a very manly whistle, as if she had, at some point or other, spent time on a construction site. "Oi! Shit-breath!"

The creature's head snapped in her direction, its milk-white eyes boring into her. She could almost feel the hatred, which was fine, because she wasn't going to be sending *it* a Christmas card, either.

El Oscuro relaxed a little against the wall. The thing was no longer interested in him.

It wanted Red. The woman with the sword and the builder's whistle.

"That's right," Red said, satisfied that she had its full attention. What she was going to do next, well, that was anyone's guess, but she imagined it would involve lots of running and hoping for the best.

The creature leapt for her, its hulking mass bulging and contorting as it flew through the air like an obese superhero. Red, not fancying the look of it, dodged to the right and almost slipped on a floundering hatchetfish. There were fish all around, all thrashing and flailing as the life drained from their bodies. The bastard beast's deathcount was now three bandits, twenty-two tetras, four angelfish, a dozen gobies, the hatchetfish she'd almost slipped on, and a dozen others that no doubt had silly names, like Blackwater Turdfish, and Hamster-brained Pencilfish.

Red took a few steps back as the creature took a few forwards. It was a silly game, really, but them's the rules.

"You killed Thumbs!" she gasped. "And Blink, and Samuel!" She didn't know why she was telling it all this, for it already knew. It had been there when the killing took place. "I will avenge my friends," she said, with newfound vigour. "I will send you back to whatever hell spawned you!" And with that, she leapt into the air, the sword raised high, her hopes even higher.

The monster that had once been a well-dressed and not unsightly mayor did the same. If this were a film, they would have been moving in slow-motion, slipping through the air with a certain grace, almost balletic. The camera would be panning around, capturing them from every available angle. Even the floundering fish would have been moving in slo-mo; if you looked really closely, you could see one of them mouthing the words: *Is anyone going to even try to save us?*

However, this was no Hollywood blockbuster. This was real life, and in real life, things are a lot uglier than any movie, which was why the creature's jowls were flapping, why drool was trailing behind it as it swam through the air like a mongoloid walrus, why Red's hair was painted to her face, covering her eyes, instead of flapping about her like in some pre-apocalytic shampoo commercial. Why her sword was a damn sight heavier than it should have been and, subsequently, pointed at anything *but* the approaching monster. If this were a movie, it was safe to say that it would have been a box-office flop.

But then, as if some affluent producer had decided to throw some money at it – *"Hey, if it worked for Transformers…"* – Red's hair parted enough for her to see through, and she found the strength to raise the sword. What she couldn't figure out, though, was why everything was still moving in slow-motion.

"Stab it in the fucking eye!" El Oscuro called from the edge of the room, where he was cowering behind a leather swivel-chair, wielding a catfish as if it were loaded.

But Red didn't hear him. She was focused. Wholly intent on getting this right. She had been in the air now for, whew, almost thirty seconds, which must have been a record, even by the Wachowski's standards. Then…

They were engaged.

The creature's tail whipped through the air, knocking Red slightly off-balance, but she had been prepared for it and brought the sword up at just the right moment, slicing a stripe through the beast's trailing appendage. It let out a shrill scream as it landed on the opposite side of the room.

Red landed, too, albeit with a lot less grace and a lot more fish and water. She fought her way to her feet and growled at the creature, which was evolving again. Its flesh squirmed, its bones cracked, its tail disappeared and was replaced by a piece of…

"Holy shit!" El Oscuro said, his eyes wide enough to be seventy percent outside his face. "Red, get out of there!"

She saw the sparking cable protruding from the beast's arse. "How is that even possible?" she gasped, but it was not the time for questions. It was the time for avoiding electrocution.

The cable slammed into the water just as Red dove out of it. A burning smell filled the room as the beast's new tail fizzled and sparked, and the water coating the office floor began to boil.

El Oscuro, leader of Los Pendejos, shook violently as the power surged through him, blackened his flesh, singed his hairs, and did absolutely nothing good for his complexion. There was a certain irony to his death – he'd come here to offer Kellerman electricity, not the other way around – that was not lost on him, even though his tongue had melted, and he could feel his own innards poaching.

Red landed on Kellerman's crowded desk, knocking papers and various writing implements to the floor. A squirming angelfish was the unfortunate recipient of an eyeful of paperclips, but that was the least of Red's concerns.

In the corner of the room, El Oscuro exploded as if someone had told him that fifteen sticks of lit dynamite in the arsehole was a great way to lose a few pounds. Body parts rained down around the office, and several dying fish vomited partly-digested flakes all over their own fins.

"No!" Red screamed. "Noooooooooo!"

The beast's cable-tail came around in a wide arc, still fizzing and crackling. As the only light in the room, it was almost psychedelic. But Red wasn't as entranced as the creature had hoped, and dropped down onto her haunches, the samurai sword shining and flashing in her hands.

The sole survivor of Los Pendejos launched herself into the air, knowing that it would be the final time; that any error in judgement would see her join the rest of her crew in Bandit Hell, where everyone had those pockets that were stitched shut at the top, and every purse and wallet was filled with polystyrene peanuts.

"*Miiiiiiiilllllllk!*" the beast roared, aiming its sparking tail at the airborne woman, but she slipped past it – just – and brought the blade down on the back of the monster's neck.

There was an audible squelch – yes, this Hollywood producer had had the sense to employ a decent foley artist – as the creature's head was severed from its thick neck. Though not entirely.

Red landed in the water next to the beast's right hoof, and wasted no time in putting as much distance between herself and the screeching monster as possible. Across the room there was an alcove, slightly raised up, filled with clean suits. Kellerman was nothing if not professional. She thumped into the recess, yanking trousers and jackets down on top of her.

She was out of the water.

And not a moment too soon as…

The beast roared and, losing control of itself, slammed its tail into the water. There was a loud bang and then the smell of burnt crumpets and singed flesh filled the room. Red watched through a pair of suspenders as the giant beast thrashed and fried. Sparks leapt up into the air and came down, landing on the glistening surface of the office floor like glow-worms.

Affording herself a smile, Red took a deep breath. The creature's head – attached by only sinew – fell from its neck and landed in the boiling water with a splash. After that, the rest of it quickly followed, for heads are relatively important when it comes to survival – unless you're a chicken, in which case, run free, you headless bastard!

For fifteen minutes – she counted it in her head – Red sat in that nook, coming to terms with the fact that, for the first time in twenty years, she was very alone, that things would be different from now on, that demons – *despite* what she had been led to believe – were very real, and right here in Oilhaven.

That no matter what happened, she had a week's supply of cooked fish to look forward to.

She dropped the remains of an angelfish into the puddle beyond the alcove and licked her lips. It had been a long time since she'd eaten something so substantial in one sitting, which would explain why she was feeling a little queasy.

Hopefully it had nothing to do with the water in which the fish had been kept, or the strange, milky fluid coursing through it now.

Well-fed and re-energised, Red climbed from the niche and headed for the door.

"Let's find out what the fuck is going on around here," she said, hoping that at least one person had an inkling, lest she go completely mental.

22

Lou covered the dead monster in the basement with a sheet. It seemed only right, since said monster had brought him up to be a decent chap, taught him right from wrong, tied his shoelaces for him, sang him to sleep, made his bed, made his breakfast, thrown his breakfast out when he'd grown tired of it (Weetabix™. Other horrible cereals are available). She had been a good mother to him, a real mother, the kind of mother that never revealed how hurt she was, how dismal her life was. It was only in the later years, those awful years following The Event, that she had given up entirely, confining herself to her room, believing herself to by dying.

In the end, death hadn't crept in the way Lou imagined it would. There was no way he could have foreseen what was going to happen, that there was something wrong with his milk.

"It's not your fault," he told himself, but deep down, he knew it was. He had had his doubts about the milk – why the hell was he *producing* it, for a start? – and yet he had sold it anyway, and now…now his mother was dead, and there were god knows how many 'haveners about to have a really bad day.

A loud bang on the door upstairs startled him. He wasn't in the mood for disgruntled customers or…

Maybe one of them had turned – mutated – come back to finish the job his own mother had started. Maybe the whole town were mutants, out for his blood, royally pissed off that Lou's Milk was about as good for you as an acid bath.

"I won't answer it," he mumbled. "Knock all you like, I won't answer it."

There came a second bang, and once again Lou's heartbeat quickened, proving that you could fool the same person twice if they were stupid enough. "You'd better open up, Lou!" said a voice. "We wouldn't want to have to break and enter!"

"Smalling." Lou growled. Just what he didn't need; Kellerman's destructive duo. Couldn't a guy mourn in peace anymore?

Lou made sure that the mother-beast was covered over before heading up the basement steps and into the store. Smalling and Harkness had no reason to go into the basement, but he wasn't taking any chances.

"What do you want?" Lou said, through the door. "I'm in the middle of something."

There were whisperings and murmerings, and then one of them, Harkness, Lou thought, said, "Put the claytex vagina down and let us the fuck in. We're here on official Kellerman business."

Aren't you always? Lou thought. Was there any other kind of business?

Sighing, Lou unlocked the door and walked across the room to the counter. The shorn gorillas let themselves in and followed.

"So what can I do for you?" Lou said. "More specifically, what does Kellerman want now? It seems like only yesterday that you came in and robbed me blind. Surely it's not been a month already."

Harkness sniggered, though it was less than jovial. "You're a funny man, Lou," he said. "Probably best if you don't try to piss us off too much, not if you enjoy wearing your teeth in your jaw." He crunched his knuckles so hard that Lou felt the pain. "We're here for more milk."

Lou shook his head. "It's off the menu," he said. "There won't be any more. The invisible well has dried up, so to speak."

"That's not good enough," said Smalling as he glanced around the room. "Now, Lou, you know how much Kellerman hates being told no, and he is under the impression that this milk is readily available. Do you want me to go back to him and let him know that you made a mistake? That there is no more? That you lied to the people of Oilhaven, and to *him*, our founder and mayor?"

Lou was about to speak, to tell them they could pass on whatever message they wanted to Kellerman, but it wouldn't change the fact that there would be no more Lou's Milk, when Harkness suddenly leaned in and sniffed the damp patch spreading around Lou's left nipple.

Lou slapped a hand to his chest, covering the blossoming dampness. "It's nothing," he said. "I had a little accident bottling up earlier. Got some of the damn stuff on my shirt."

Harkness frowned so hard that you could have fit a deck of cards in the crevices of his forehead. "Wait a...I think...but that's not possible, is...?"

"No, it's not possible," Lou said. "Whatever it is that you're thinking, it's just not possible, so don't even try to convince yourself that it is."

Smalling, catching on a few seconds behind his hulking counterpart, said, "Oh! You mean...but milk doesn't come...man can't do that, can...?"

"No, they can't," Lou said, but by now both of his nipples were pouring. His shirt was drenched; the milk pattered on the floor beneath, a terrible drumroll of betrayal. "It's not what it looks like. I can...I can explain!"

Smalling shook his head. "It's *you*!" he said. "*You're* the invisible cow!"

"I fucking *knew* something was wrong about that milk," Harkness added, gagging. "Too many hairs and lumps for my liking. Eurgh, and to think I almost drank some." He spat on the floor, clearly disgusted by the notion.

"Don't be silly," Lou said, but he could see no way out, now. He was wasting his time trying to explain. Might as well bite the proverbial bullet and get it over with. "Yes, okay, I'm lactating, but there's something you should know about the milk. It's not right."

"You can bleeding well say *that* again," Smalling said. "It's coming out of a man's tit. Of course it's not right. You should be put down. I've never heard anything so absurd in all my life. Of course, we're going to have to tell Kellerman, and he ain't going to be pleased about it."

"Did he drink it?" Lou asked. "Please tell me he didn't drink it."

"What *else* was he going to do with it?" said Harkness. "If he'd known it had been forced from a fat man's wobbly breasticles, he might not have been so eager."

Oh, shit! Lou thought. Kellerman had polished off a bottle of the stuff. Would that be enough to affect him? His mother had been knocking it back by the gallon. Perhaps it would be okay; maybe you needed a lot of it in your system before anything happened. Maybe, just maybe, there was a light at the end of the tunnel for Lou.

"We need to destroy as much of that first batch as possible," Lou said. "It's *poisonous*." It wasn't, of course, not in the 'fall about the floor, clutching your chest and gargling' sense, but he didn't want to panic the 'haveners by informing them there was a good chance they would soon turn into stinking, drooling, defecating monsters.

"Poisonous?" Smalling said, his brow furrowed. "Shit! *Kellerman*!"

The follically-challenged henchmen turned and rushed for the door, which they became wedged in as they both tried to pass through it at the same time. The Event had changed a lot of things, but slapstick, apparently, lived on.

<h2 style="text-align:center">23</h2>

"Mom!" Zee Fox screeched as she landed on the kitchen floor with a thump. One of these days, she would use the door, and to hell with who saw her.

"What on *earth*...?" Rita rushed into the kitchen, a snot-faced Clint under one arm and a terrified-looking Tom hanging from her leg, like a libidinous mongrel. "Zee, what are you *doing* here? You shouldn't *be* here! You should be...anywhere *else*!"

Zee stood and dusted herself down. "Something *terrible* has happened," she gasped. Visions of the crazed geriatric monster flooded her head once again. She shuddered. It would be a long time before she trusted an old person again.

Rita placed Clint on the kitchen floor, where he swayed back and forth for a few seconds before deciding he would be much better off unconscious. He lay down, curled up into a ball, and began to snooze. "Awwww," said his mother, smiling slightly. Then, to Zee, she said, "What do you mean 'something terrible'? Oh, Zee, you're not pregnant are you? You haven't married a coyote, have you? You aren't up the duff with a coyote baby?"

Zee shook her head and tried to find the words to answer her mother. "I've only been gone a couple of hours," she said. "What do you think I get up to when I'm not here?" She paused, then said, "On second thoughts, don't answer that."

"So what is it?" asked Rita. "And why is your machete covered in white goo? Oh, no! You didn't let a pack of horny coyote masturbate over your sword, did you?"

"Mother, you frighten me sometimes," Zee said. "If you'll just shut up for a moment, I'll *tell* you what happened."

"She got into a fight with an old lady," Tom said, releasing his mother's leg.

Zee didn't know what to say; how had her little brother known that? Was he a precog? Was he possessed of strange and amazing powers?

"Don't be silly, Thomas Fox," Rita chided. "Your sister's not a biddy-beater, are you?"

Zee was still flabbergasted by her brother's accuracy. He was a witch! A warlock! A psychic psycho!

"She's got rice-pudding on her shoe," Tom said, pointing at the lumpy, white residue stuck to his sister's foot. He wasn't a warlock, after all. "And blood on her hand. I might only be eight, but I'm not stupid."

Rita Fox's face dropped another few inches. "Is it true, Zee?" she said. "Have you been attacking the elderly?"

"That's what I'm trying to tell you!" Zee said, her patience fast running out. "I was up in the cave, keeping my head down, learning how to get red wine stains out of suede, when all of a sudden, that old lady from town attacked me."

"What old lady?" Rita said. "Mrs Warbrown?"

Zee nodded. "That's her. The one with the umbrella."

"Oh, come on," said her mother, incredulous. "You're telling me that Mrs Warbrown, the town's oldest survivor, and winner of the best crocheted blanket for the last twenty years running, *attacked* you!"

"It wasn't her!" Zee said. "I mean, it was *her*, but she wasn't in control. It was as if she had been possessed by a demon. She…she changed shape, Mom. She grew, and she almost killed me!"

"Yes, of *course* she did, dear," said her mother. "Was this before or after she flew across the desert on a carpet made of pubic hair?"

"I'm telling the truth!" Zee said. "She attacked me, and I had no choice but to take her down."

"She killed the little old lady," Tom said, grinning and shaking his head. He liked nothing more than seeing his sister in trouble, and she was definitely in trouble with this one.

"You *killed* Mrs Warbrown?" Rita put her hands on her hips, as if Zee had just told her she'd done nothing more illegal than steal a battery from LOU'S LOOT. "The only woman in Oilhaven with a decent rice pudding recipe?"

Zee wished people would stop babbling on about fucking rice pudding. It was driving her insane. "It was either her or me," she said, wiping her machete blade on the kitchen curtains.

"This is some kind of sick joke," Rita said. "And it's not funny. Go to your room, and I don't want to see your face again today. Do you understand, missy?"

Just then, the front door swung open so hard, it splintered on its hinges. Zee brought the machete up, ready to stave off the mutant hordes. On the floor, Clint Fox slept like a baby, albeit a very poorly one.

"Close the fucking door!" Roger Fox said as he stormed across the room. Behind him, a naked man and Roy of The Barrel bickered over something or other. Zee heard the words 'giant' and 'dead' and figured they were here for her, for what she had done to Mrs Warbrown. In all honesty, it was the worst lynch-mob she'd ever seen. They didn't even have flaming torches or spitting wenches.

Rita rushed toward the door and eased it shut. "Roger!" she said. "What's going on? Why is Roy here, and why is there a dangling schlong in my kitchen?" She pointed at the naked alleyway man's shrivelled joint. In his defence, he had just *killed* a man. If it had gone the

183

other way – and he'd suddenly found himself the proud owner of a throbbing erection – he would have had to question his own mental state.

"Something's going on out there," Roger said, glaring out through the glassless kitchen window. "Reverend Schmidt's dead. Mickey over there staked him."

Mickey – Naked Alleyway Man – nervously smiled. "Don't say it like *that*," he said. "Say it like, 'We were about to get devoured by a horrible mutant, when Mickey over there rescued us'. It sounds so much better."

"And now there are *more* of them out there. Skulking in the shadows, evolving into things more hideous than they already are. Honestly, it's like fucking England out there, only without all the bicycles and monarchs."

"Roy?" Rita Fox said, turning on the barkeep so suddenly that he took an involuntary step back. "What is my husband going on about? Please, talk some sense."

Roy didn't know if he was qualified to 'talk some sense', and so he did the next best thing. He told the truth. "It's like the man said. There are monsters out there. Hideous fucking monsters with six legs and fifteen eyes and heads twice the size as they should be. I ain't never seen nothing like it, but I know what I saw, and it ain't fucking right. It ain't right at all."

Rita Fox sighed. "Thanks for that, Roy," she said, clearly still unconvinced. She pinched the bridge of her aquiline nose between thumb and forefinger. "Why am I suddenly surrounded by lunatics?" she asked herself. "Must be something in the water."

"It ain't the water!" Roger said, grabbing his wife by the arms and shaking her so hard that her skirt almost fell down. "It's the milk! It's Lou's Milk!"

Rita suddenly wished Oilhaven had a psychologist, for this had to be a group hallucination. "Roger, there is no *milk*," she said. "There hasn't been milk for years, and not around these parts."

"There *is* milk!" Roger said, shaking his wife once again. She clung on to her skirt for dear life. There was already one too many bottomless people in the room. "Lou's selling it over at his store by the bucket-load. I almost got a bottle this morning, but the silly old bitch I gave currency to forgot to pick it up."

Zee nodded. Everything suddenly made sense, or as much sense as it was ever going to. "This old lady wouldn't have happened to be carrying an umbrella, would she? Liked to talk about rice pudding a lot?"

"That's the one," Roger said. "How did you *know* that?"

"I hacked her up with my machete," Zee said, as calm as you like. "I tried telling mother, but apparently, she's the voice of reason around these parts. In which case, I didn't hack the mutated old hag up, and you guys are clearly on some sort of psychedelic drug." To her mother, she said, "Or, you could be completely wrong, and Oilhaven is going down the pan faster than a curried shit."

Rita Fox – voice of reason – shook her head. "None of this makes sense," she said. "Milk doesn't grow on trees. It grows in cows, and when was the last time you saw a cow around here?"

"There are rumours," Roy said, settling himself down at the kitchen table, "that Lou has an invisible milk-well."

"Well, that's bullshit," Mickey said, towelling at the sweat beneath his armpits with a dusty rag he'd found in the corner. It had a little picture of a sailboat on it – very cute.

"I agree with the naked man," Rita said, even though he was removing perspiration from his body with one of Clint's tee-shirts. "Invisible things seldom exist, and I, for one, won't believe in one until I see it with my own eyes."

"Look!" Roger said, slamming both hands down on the kitchen table. "It doesn't *matter* where it's coming from. What matters is that it's turning everyone into grotesque mutants. There are hundreds of them out there. Lou must have sold a bottle to half the fucking town. Those who didn't drink it are either dead, dying, or soon to be one or the other. Who knows what those monster are capable of, or what they want from us, but I'll bet it's not a cucumber sandwich and a nice chat about the weather." He straightened up, rubbing his now-sore hands (stupid rock-hard table) on the seat of his trousers. "Now, we've got two choices. We can either stand here, wait for those creatures to figure out we're in here, and accept that our days are numbered. Or, we can barricade the hell out of this place; make it as impossible to penetrate as we can, at least until we figure out what the fuck's going on out there."

Zee waved her machete around a little. "Or we can fight *back*," she said. "They might be big, they might be ugly, but they're pretty damn clumsy. If we find enough weapons, we might—"

A sudden explosion that sounded as if it were just outside rocked the house. Everyone dove for cover as the blast echoed around the room. Fifteen miles away, seven crows sitting atop an unused telephone cable glanced at one another bewilderedly before flying away.

"What the hell was that?" Rita Fox gasped. Despite the blast, everything remained in its place, apart from little Clint, who had rolled over onto his back and yet continued to snore.

"I have no idea," Roger Fox said, scrambling to his feet. He made his way across the room and opened the front door a fraction. "Erm, you remember those houses that used to be over the road?" he said.

Everyone nodded.

"Yes, the McKenzies live in one, and Terrence Brown in the other," Rita said. "Of *course* we remember them, Roger. They've been there since we moved in." She clicked her tongue, as if to say, *What are you like, crazy husband of mine*.

Still gazing out through the crack in the door, Roger said, "Well, at least we've got a better view of their back gardens, now."

"You mean…?" Rita said, trailing off for dramatic effect.

"That's *exactly* what I mean," Roger said. And then he added, "Oh, shit!"

"Oh shit!?" said Rita.

Roger slammed the door shut and pressed himself against it. "Indeed."

"What's going on, Dad?" Zee said. The machete in her hand, in that moment, felt about as useful as a Swiss-army knife, one with toenail clippers, toothpicks, miniature saws, everything *except* a decent blade.

"You remember the McKenzies?" Roger said, closing his eyes momentarily. He took a deep breath.

"Roger, this game is *awful*," said his wife. "Of *course* we remember the McKenzies. Bruce and Bonnie are a lovely couple." She paused, slapped a hand to her wide open mouth. "They're dead, aren't they?" she said.

"Not quite," Roger said, bracing himself just in time as something thumped into the door, knocking him forward a couple of inches. He managed to push back just enough to keep the door from swinging open. "They're now fucking mutants and they want to come in."

The door rattled and shook in its frame. Roy, who was a portly man and just the type of guy you would put in front of something to prevent it from opening, scrambled across the room and joined Roger at the door.

"This can't be happening!" Rita screeched. "We've known them for decades. Neither of them would hurt a fly." Bonnie McKenzie was her favourite babysitter, and the Fox's only real break from parenthood. If she was, as her husband had so delicately put it, a fucking mutant, who was going to look after the boys next time she and Roger fancied a date or a dirty weekend in the desert?

The door, already damaged from Roger's panicked entrance not too long ago, creaked and groaned as both sides pushed against it. A small crack appeared, and through it came a large, fleshy tentacle.

Rita screamed. "Look out!"

The tentacle stretched all the way across the room, seemingly reaching for *her*, swinging this way and that as it undulated and squelched.

Mickey latched onto it, lugging it away from the cowering Rita. As it thrashed and jerked, dragging the naked alleyway dweller around the room like a fireman struggling to contain a recalcitrant hose, Rita began to cry.

"She was such a great babysitter! What's happened to her!? Why does she have tentacles!?"

"I...told...you..." Roger said, gritting his discoloured teeth so hard that one of them popped from his jaw, bounced off Clint's snoozing face, and rattled its way along the floor. "These things...are *mutants*..." A giant hand forced its way through a new fissure in the door. Pretty soon, there would be more cracks and holes than there was wood.

"Three plastic buttons and a bag of acorns," Rita said. "That's all she used to charge for six hours watching the kids. So cheap…so charitable…and now she's trying to kill us! Oh, Lord! Oh, what a fucking nightmare! Tom, go hide in your cupboard—"

"But, Moooooooom—"

"Don't you 'But, Moooooooom' me, Thomas Fox. There are mutants outside, now go and hide."

Tom, reluctant but resigned, ran from the room.

"A little help over here!" Mickey said. He'd managed to pin the struggling tentacle to the floor with one knee. "I can't hold it all day."

"That makes two of us!" Roger Fox said, head-butting the oversize hand reaching for him, but inflicting minimal damage.

Zee leapt across the room, bringing the machete around in a wide arc. The blade thunked into the tentacle just behind Mickey. It didn't go all the way through – it was made of much stronger stuff than Mrs Warbrown's neck, that was for sure. Over by the door, something screeched in a hundred voices.

"Saw through it!" Mickey yelled, struggling to hold on to the flailing appendage. "Think of yourself as a construction worker!"

"But now's not the time for a cup of tea and a read through of a skin mag," Zee said. "Oh, you mean a *decent* construction worker?" She nodded, then set to work on the tentacle, dragging the machete's blade through it over and over, back and forth, back and forth. Outside, the neighbour-beast continued to scream, still striving to get in.

"She *never* gave them bad food before bed," Rita said, shaking her head, "and she was always happy to hold on to them for an extra few hours if we were running late."

"Darling!" Roger said, snapping the wrist of the giant hand as it reached for him. "Now's not the time!" She was clearly in shock, and it would have been unfair to tell her to pull herself together, given the sudden change of circumstances.

"Are you through yet!?" Mickey said, punching the end of the tentacle as if it were a speedball. The trouble with speedballs, though, is that they keep bouncing back, and this one was no different.

"Almost!" Zee said, hacking at the fleshy meat of the thing as violently as she possibly could. White fluid had formed in a pool beneath the squirming appendage; it sprayed out of the wound, coating Zee's knees and hands. She kept her mouth shut throughout. It was best to, at least until they figured out whether the infection could spread through bodily-fluids. "Aaaaaaaaaannnnnd it's off!" she said as the last coarse sinew was severed.

"Then why is this thing still fucking moving?" Mickey said, dodging and weaving as the tentacle slapped him repeatedly across the face.

The rest of the appendage – that which was still attached to the beast outside – left the room through the same crack in the door it had used to enter. Zee climbed to her feet and ran across to help her father, who was having an awful time of it thanks to the four hands that had now punched their way through the wood.

"*Duck*, Dad!" Zee said.

"What?"

But Zee was already swinging, aiming for the wrist of the arm that had Roy Clamp around the throat. Roy was making noises like, 'Grghhh' and 'cherck', which were never a good sign.

Roger Fox managed to shift his head across just enough to avoid the blade. It thumped into the thick, black wrist belonging to the hand that was squeezing the life out of the landlord, and then wedged itself in the door. Roy Clamp fell forward, grabbing at his throat, pulling the severed hand away and throwing it as far and hard across the room as he could. It landed in a bucket of sick, which was, Roy thought, an odd ornament to have knocking around the place.

"I can't hold the door on my own!" Roger yelled. "The...the mutants...they're too strong!"

He looked up to find his wife standing in front of the kitchen table. Gone was the fear that had affected her only a few moments ago. She had the look of a woman intent on only one thing.

Keeping the mutants out of her damn kitchen...

"Roger," she said, with more coolness than she had any right to. "When I say so, I want you to let the door open."

That'll be easy, Roger thought. He was already fighting a losing battle. "And then what!?" If they were going to die in the next thirty seconds, it would be nice to know they had had a plan, and that it had just gone sideways.

But Rita Fox *did* have a plan. She also had a small kitchen knife in one hand and a corkscrew in the other. The corkscrew was probably the more dangerous of the two weapons. "We're going to take the McKenzies down."

Roy Clamp positioned himself in front of the door once again. The colour had returned to his cheeks. "We are not going to let those fucking monsters in here," he said. "It's *suicide!*" But Zee had already scooped Clint up into her arms and stuffed him away behind the sofa, out of harm's reach – providing the mutants didn't look behind the sofa.

"Actually," Mickey said, stroking at his pubic hair as if no-one else was in the room. Rita was a little uncomfortable with it, but she appeared to be the only one. "If we don't do *something*, more of those things are going to come. We won't have a hope in hell of keeping them out. If we let just the two in and barricade the door, we've got a lot more chance of surviving the afternoon."

"*If* we kill the two giant mutants," Zee said.

"*Hey!*" Rita said. "That woman looked after you as a child and she *never* touched you inappropriately. Show some respect!"

Zee shrugged. "Yeah, but we're still going to chop her to *bits*, aren't we?"

"Damn *right* we are," said Rita. "Now, on the count of three—"

"You can't be serious!" Roy said. "We let those things in here, we're *all* dead!"

"If we don't let them in and take care of them," Roger said, finally coming to his wife's defence (it seemed only right...plus she was wielding the corkscrew as if she meant business), "we'll be outnumbered. Five against two isn't bad odds."

A cloven hoof smashed through the door between Roy Clamp's legs. An inch or two higher and Roy would have had to consider changing his name to Roberta. Outside, something roared, and then another something, and in the distance, several other somethings concurred.

"Okay, we're doing this," Roy said. "No need to count to three, either. Let's get it over with." And with that, he stepped aside and took up the stance of a boxer in those times before gloves were considered useful.

Roger Fox took a deep breath...

Closed his eyes (and then opened them again, for they were pretty useful tools to someone about to go into battle)...

And stepped aside...

24

Bonnie McKenzie was the first through the door, barrelling into the room on thick, black tentacles. Her face – now somewhere between her navel and breasts (eyebrows?) – was so badly malformed and utterly hideous that it was hard to believe she had once been a capable and friendly childminder with great rates and good morals.

A second later, Bruce McKenzie came through the door, and was comparatively less mutated than his wife. In fact, if it wasn't for the hairless testicles hanging from his nose and the strange noise he was making (like an angry sea-lion), you wouldn't have noticed the difference.

Roger slammed the door shut; things were about to get very messy, indeed.

Bonnie must have recognised Rita Fox, or sensed she was the biggest threat in the room in that moment, for it was her that she lunged for first. Dark tentacles seemed to fill the room between the two women, and Rita suddenly found herself wishing she'd spent more time in the cutlery drawer instead of grabbing the first things that came to hand.

Zee swung the machete at the ever-expanding creature. There was so much of it to hit that it was sod's law that she would miss entirely. It was like trying to kill a jar of eels with a safety-pin.

"You *bitch!*" Rita screamed at the onrushing beast. She raised the corkscrew and the knife simultaneously, leaving herself hopelessly exposed to the ferocious tentacles whipping through the air. The first hit her in the side of the head, knocking her off balance and causing her to drop the small knife. The second – and this one was the stinker – caught her in the midriff, knocking the wind from her. As she doubled over, she saw her husband in the corner of the room, sitting on top of Bruce McKenzie while the Bruce-monster kicked and writhed, changing shape as if it was the easiest thing in the world. Every time Roger got it in a headlock, the creature simply grew a new head and sucked in the old one. It was, Rita thought – a terribly unfair advantage.

"Mom! Look out!" Zee yelled as she saw the giant arm forming in the air above her mother's head. Rita looked up, fear etched upon her face, and realised she didn't have time to react. The fist of the thing came down, and would have annihilated (or at least *squashed*) Rita Fox, had it not been for the naked alleyway man, who had wedged himself between the giant arm and the floor and was unwilling to step aside, judging from the stoic expression upon his countenance.

"She's a fucking feisty one!" Mickey said, wondering why it was always him left swinging from the giant mutant's angry appendage.

Rita, spotting the milky-white eyes on the main body of the beast, said, "I never really liked you, Bonnie! We only used you 'cos you were fucking cheap!" And with that, she lunged forward, the corkscrew gripped firmly in her palm, only the coiling stainless steel protruding between her third and fourth knuckle, the same way people repel rapists with now-defunct car keys.

The babysitter-monster's eye squirted thick, viscous cream as the corkscrew plunged into it. There was an audible squelch – like wellington-boots in a muddy field – followed almost immediately by a plaintive shriek.

"Yeah, that's for complaining about the kids when one of them shit the bed!" She pulled the corkscrew out and rammed it, hard, into the other eye. As she twisted, more white gunk tricked down the creature's belly-face. A tongue – thick and black, like something you would find lining a giant's shoe – darted out and lapped up the escaping fluid. "And that's for the time you refused to read Clint a bedtime story because you didn't like the protagonist." She pulled the corkscrew out and held it over her head in both hands, as if she was about to slam it down into the beast's forehead. "I mean…who doesn't like Peter Rabbit? What kind of sick bitch roots for Mr McGregor?" She brought the corkscrew down as hard as she could, embedding it between the thing's seeping eyes.

Bonnie the Babysitter-Beast thrashed violently back and forth, side to side, swinging its tentacles around the room, screaming in a hundred different voices, none of them English. Utterly blind, Mickey knew he could release the monster's writhing arm without worrying too much about reprisal. He dove to the right, did a little roll, and landed against the skirting. It was, of course, all completely unnecessary, but if this were a film, with a decent budget and a good male lead (Jason Statham, Karl Urban, Jet Li, Kelly McGillis), such acrobatics would be expected by the baying audience.

The creature staggered backwards, white liquid now geysering from both eyes. It was time to put the thing out of its misery, and Zee was more than happy to step up to the plate.

"And this is for that time you caught me flicking my bean and told me it would fall off if I wasn't careful!" She leapt up into the air, bringing the machete over the top. And then it sliced straight down the middle of the creature. One gushing eye went one way, the other went another. The babysitter beast was now, thanks to Zee's blade, *two* babysitter beasts, neither of them functional, both of them already shrivelling up and dying. Zee landed in front of the withering monster, her machete dripping with viscera and white goo. "It *never* fell off," she said, wiping her blade on the kitchen tablecloth. "It just got *stronger*."

"Am I the only one here who thinks that is way too much information from a seventeen-year-old girl?" Mickey said. He was back on his feet, admiring the pile of dead beast and trying not to vomit.

"Yes, Zee," said her mother. "Jeez, I'm your mother; I don't need to hear that kind of thing. Now, go help your father. He appears to be in a spot of bother."

The spot of bother that her father was in was, in fact, a *lot* of bother. The Bruce-monster had managed to get to its feet, and had subsequently cornered both Roger Fox and Roy Clamp who were pushing at one another, each hoping that the creature picked the other. In truth, the Bruce-monster was too confused to do anything.

"I've got kids!" Roger told the barkeep. "They need me. Sacrifice yourself!"

Roy Clamp pushed back at Roger. "I've got a pub to run! This town will go down the Swanee without it, and since I'm the only licensee, and therefore the only man legally able to sell booze in this district, you should sacrifice yourself for the good of the 'haveners!"

The creature was about to make his final decision – the one on the right was the fatter of the two, but the one on the left didn't look as sweaty – when there was an almighty whoosh, and then everything was upside-down for a moment...then the right way up...upside-down...right way...floor...

"How do you like them apples?" Zee said, placing a foot on the severed head. To her left, the headless body crumpled to the floor like Charlie Sheen at an all-you-can-snort buffet. Then, for the Bruce-monster, everything went dark, which was a shame, really, as he was just starting to enjoy himself.

Roger and Roy stared down at the creature, watching as it dried up like a year-old avocado.

"I was just buying some time," Roy said, patting Roger on the back. "I was never going to let anything bad happen to you."

"Yeah," Roger said, coyly. "I saw my daughter with the machete, and I thought it was the best way to confuse the monster until she lopped its head off." He kicked the severed head across the room, where it disappeared behind the sofa. "Worked a treat, really."

"Isn't your *son* behind that sofa?" Roy asked.

"Ah," said Roger. "Can somebody move the detached monster head away from my sleeping son? I'm going to start barricading the doors and windows. If we can just hold on long enough, I'm sure all this nonsense will blow over."

"Yes," Rita Fox said, slumping to the floor and examining the ooze-covered corkscrew as if it were a new species of slug. "If I remember correctly, you said the exact same thing the day after The Event."

And in that moment, Roger Fox hated his wife as much as he hated the dead creatures strewn across his living-room floor.

25

"What the fuck *is* that thing?" Harkness yelled as the colossal mutant came a-stomping toward them like something that had escaped from one of Clive Barker's nightmares. It had four tree-trunk sized legs, and was as white as snow, but its face was discernibly human, and appeared to be grinning at them from atop the long, broad stalk that was its neck.

Whatever it was, it was running away from the explosion that had just rocked the street and was now barrelling toward the rooted henchmen, screaming something like, "*Mike*! Or *meek*! Or..."

"Isn't that Terrence Brown?" Smalling said, recognising the face of the creature as it approached.

"Oh, yeah," said Harkness. "I recognise those bushy eyebrows anywhere. Why's he so big and angry all of a sudden?"

There were, Smalling thought, far more important questions than that, such as a) Why did he look like something that would be born if a giraffe and a panda got it on? b) Why was he screaming *Miiiiike*, or *Meeeeeek*, or whatever the hell it was? And c) Why were they just standing there like a couple of simpletons, waiting for the thing to slam into them at forty miles an hour?

"RUN!" Smalling said, heeding his own advice before Harkness had a chance to get out the gates.

The beast was a few houses back, snarling and farting as it careened after the fleeing duo. The unbearable heat didn't seem to be affecting it, not in the same way it affected Harkness and Smalling, who had only been running for three seconds and were already struggling for breath and looking for the nearest shade.

Weapons, Smalling thought, would have been very useful right then. As Kellerman's enforcers, you would have thought they would have at least carried guns, but the truth of the matter was that guns were as rare as alcohol, tobacco, and hen's teeth. Only those at the top possessed anything more formidable than a dagger, and even then there was the small issue of ammunition, and the lack thereof.

"Is it gone?" Harkness wheezed as they turned the corner onto Coleridge Street.

Smalling glanced across his shoulder, saw the surging beast, and said, "It's not a fucking wasp. I don't think it's going to just give up because we're running away."

"What's that smell?" said Harkness, as the scent of something pungent and unholy and completely alien stung at his nostrils. A second later, the Terrence-monster's head pushed between them, snapping at their shoulders, and for a moment, the stench worsened. The henchmen picked up the pace; Harkness was sobbing as he ran.

"It's the thing's *breath*!" Smalling gasped, trying to swallow down the bile that had risen in his throat. "That's what Hell smells like!"

"We're gonna die!" Harkness said, his bottom lip quivering like an upset child's. "I know it, we're going to…"

A sharp slap across the face cut him off mid-sentence. "We're not going to die!" Smalling said. "We're just going to keep on running until we either lose it, or it loses interest."

"But I'm tired," Harkness said. "I don't think I can…"

Another slap, this one hard enough to leave a red print on Harkness's cheek. "You can, and you *will*," Smalling said. "Would you rather just lie down? Wait for what's left of Terrence Brown to bugger you senseless? Huh? Is that what you want, or do you want to keep running? To keep running until we get the better of it?"

"How…" Harkness panted, "did…you…manage to say…all that…without…losing your…breath…?"

Smalling smiled. "I don't know," he said. "Something to do with keeping the plot moving forwards, I guess. Now keep up. We could be at this for quite some time."

A screech from behind caused both men to falter momentarily. Smalling turned around, not sure what he would find, but *what* he found was one of the most amazing things he had ever laid witness to in all his life.

They stopped running – not a moment too soon, as far as Harkness was concerned – and watched as the drama unfolded.

"Is that a woman?" Harkness said, doubled-over, gasping for air.

"Yes, that is a woman sitting on a horse," Smalling said. "Can't get anything past you, can we?"

The woman had in her hand a large sword – Japanese, Smalling thought, but he had been wrong before, which was why he no longer purchased goods from hooded figures in back-alleys in the dead of night.

"Blimey! She's good with that, ain't she?" said Harkness. "Like that Warrior Princess, Xena, I've heard stories about. Hey, you don't think it's *her*, do you? You don't think it's Xena?"

"You're *right*," Smalling said, shaking his head, still enthralled by the cat-and-mouse battle taking place just fifty feet away. "I *don't* think it's Xena. I also don't think it's the fabled Buffy, or the legendary Cynthia Rothrock." He, too, had heard the stories, the bedtime tales of vampire slayers and blonde-haired assassins, but that's all they were. Myths, legends of a time long forgotten. Whoever this woman was, she was very, very real.

"Maybe it's Chun-Li!" Harkness said, hopeful.

"It's not fucking Chun-Li," Smalling rebuked. "Can we just watch, see what happens? Huh? You're starting to get right on my tits."

The woman, sword raised high, blonde hair flowing behind her like in those ancient, pre-Event commercials for shampoo and conditioner, manipulated the horse like a pro. Clearly, the poor horse wanted to be somewhere else, but the woman...oh, how she manoeuvred that reluctant mount.

The giant anomaly didn't seem to know what to do. Its cries of *Miiiike! Miiiike!* were now followed by question marks. It danced from side to side, looking for a way past the brave woman and her, let's face it, less than noble steed. Each time it moved in to attack, the sword came close to slashing the stalk that was its neck.

"Three gold earrings says the chick gets it," Smalling said. He didn't *want* that to happen, but like any good gambler, you backed the one you didn't want to win. That way, whatever the outcome, you had something to be pleased about.

"You're on," said Harkness, finally recovered from the sprint around town. "That thing is going to eat her up and spit her out."

They shook hands, lit thrice-smoked roll-ups, and turned to watch the battle unfold.

*

Red swung the sword once more, knocking the beast's head aside with its tsuba. An inch higher and the blade would have ripped through its face, but the thing was fast – a lot faster than one might expect from such a hefty creature – and she was just grateful that she'd made contact at all.

The horse bucked beneath her. "No, Mordecai!" she screeched. "Steady!" But Mordecai was having none of it. *Steady* was something he did when he was in the shade, or drinking water from a river with nary a dead body in sight; it was not something he did when being attacked by an outsized human/giraffe/panda hybrid.

"Mordecai!" Red yelled, swinging for the creature. This time, she made contact; the blade slit a thin line on the beast's right cheek, through which blood and white goo began to push, like a gelatinous Play-Doh factory. The creature shrilly cried and staggered back on four unsteady legs (two of which were still wearing dungarees).

Red would have celebrated the mini-victory had it not been for the fact that Mordecai, El Oscuro's wondrous horse from Ohio, was no longer beneath her. For a second there was only empty space, a gap between her ass and the sand, and then she hit the ground, biting the end of her tongue off in the process. Thick, bitter blood filled her mouth and she whimpered as pain tore through her entire body.

Mordecai settled at the side of the road, whinnying and snorting, shifting nervously from one hoof to the next, as if he knew how much trouble he was in when the bandido caught up to him. The right thing to do, the horse thought, was hope that the giant mutant monster finished her off, thusly removing the threat of any punishment she would surely administer for dropping her on her ass so unceremoniously.

Red picked herself up, spat blood into the sand, and turned to face the creature, which was still reeling from the attack on its face. "Why aren't they *helping*?" she said, turning to face the two bald idiots she'd rescued. They were watching from a safe distance. "Why aren't you *helping*?"

Both men shrugged, then one of them said, "You're the one with the sword. If it helps, we can distract it by running away…"

She turned back to the creature, now slowly prowling toward her, almost feline, its expression one of sheer discontent, its gash spraying pink goo. It was too late to outrun the thing, which meant that she had no choice but to engage it. *Perhaps*, she thought, *I could communicate with the human part of it, try to make it see sense.* It was worth a shot, for the thing had, earlier that day, been walking around, doing human things, saying human stuff, generally being human. In there, somewhere, there had to be something, some retained memory, a switch that could be flicked. It was just a matter of finding it…

"Hey, hey hey!" Red said, holding her hands out in a placatory manner. The fact that there was a samurai sword in one of them probably didn't help matters.

"Look, whatever your name is...you're *not* a monster...you're *not* some savage beast that just wants to kill for the sake of killing...you're a human being, or at least you *were*...but something's happened to you...something terrible, and until we figure out how to fix it...I guess what I'm trying to say is...there's no need for anyone to die here today...enough people have already perished, good and bad, and...I don't know about you, but I...I don't want to be one of the dead folk..."

"Is she *talking* to it?" Smalling asked Harkness as the mysterious woman's words reached him on the breeze.

"Why?" Harkness said. "Why would she do that? She's wasting valuable slashing time."

"You were probably just a nice old man until today, weren't you...?" Red said, circling the huge creature. It matched her step for step. "Just minding your own business...eking out an existence...here...in the hottest damn town left on the face of this godforsaken earth...and then boom!...you wind up a savage mutant...but that's not the end for you...it doesn't have to be...I can help you...but you have to *not* kill me...you're human...and humans have the right to make choices...don't make the wrong choice..."

"What did she say?" Harkness asked, waggling a finger around in his sweat- and wax-filled ear.

"She said," Smalling replied, " *'Don't bake the long voice.'* " He shook his head. "I think she's mental. The bet's off."

Red didn't know how much – if any – of what she was saying was registering with the mutant, but she thought she saw something in its cloudy, colourless eyes; some sort of comprehension. Either that or the beast had wind and was fighting to hold it in.

"See, you're not such a bad guy," Red said, lowering her guard for just a moment, but a lot of things can happen in a moment, and this was the order they happened it:

One: The monster lunged forward, its wide open maw drooling like a thirsty bloodhound on a hot day.

Two: Red, realising how foolish she had been, dropped down onto her haunches.

Three: The creature farted and belched at the exact same time, proving the wind theory correct.

Four: Red gagged and spluttered as the stench enveloped her, but she managed to dig the pommel of the sword into the sand and ease the blade forward.

Five: Mordecai whined and grunted, and even shut his eyes, for the tension was fucking ridiculous.

Six: The beast snarled as it came down upon the nonsense-talking woman, but not before something shivved it in the chest.

Seven: Red screamed as the full weight of the monster landed on top of her, but the sand beneath was soft.

Eight: One of the bald men did a little dance, as if he had just won something of incalculable value. Then, he stopped dancing, as if remembering that any bets placed were null and void, as denoted by their colleague, under the belief that one of the runners was, in fact, a few cards short of a full deck.

Nine: The beast went, "Cor blimey, guv'nor, that really smarts," only in mutant-speak, which Red wasn't very good with.

Ten: Mordecai peered through his hooves and tried to think happy thoughts.

Eleven: The mutant began to shrivel up as the life drained from it.

Twelve: Red could breathe again, and managed to pull herself away from the dying creature, taking the sword that had penetrated its heart with her, just in case...

She stood for a moment in absolute silence, staring down at the mutant as its flesh contracted and its bones snapped in on themselves. In a strange way, she felt sorry for the thing. Despite her best efforts to communicate with it, it had tried to kill her. These things couldn't be saved, couldn't be convinced that killing was wrong, couldn't be tamed like some circus bear.

They had one purpose and one purpose only; to destroy as many humans as they could.

"Whew," one of the bald men said as he sidled up alongside Red. "That was a close one, huh? I liked the way you tried to distract it. You're really something. Hey, you wouldn't happen to be Xena: Warrior Princess, would you?"

The punch knocked Harkness from his feet. Smalling, sensing she had plenty in reserve, took a step back and held his hands up, as if the sword in her hand was capable of firing rounds as well as being impossibly bloody sharp.

"Someone tell me what the *fuck* is going on around here," Red said. "Before I really start to lose my fucking temper."

26

Abigail Sneve limped across the street, a beatific smile stretched across her face, her loins suitably oiled, thanks to the reluctant bandit from the night before. She'd had better – of course she had – but she'd had a lot worse, and in this day and age, you took what God gave you. You took it, and you fornicated with it, because when you've been around the block a few hundred times, and you've got a face that would make Rocky Dennis choke on his cornflakes, good sex is hard to find.

Along the street she moved, unaware that she was being watched, that something was sticking to the shadows, remaining out of sight, at least for now. It could smell her – a strange mix that was as nauseating as it was intriguing. What was she? Why did she smell different to the others? Why was she limping?

"There once was a whore from Kilkenny," Abigail sang in a tuneless voice. "Who charged two fucks for a penny. For half of that sum, you could bugger her bum, an economy practised by many." She cackled. Her toothless grin only served to intrigue her unseen watcher more, for it had never seen such terrible dental work, or lack thereof.

"There once was a whore on the dock. From dusk until dawn she sucked cock. 'Til one day it's said, she gave so much head, she exploded and whitewashed the block." Another witch-like cackle, as if these limericks were new to her, and not something she had been singing since childhood. Her mother had used to sing them to her in the crib as a way of coaxing her into the trade, and it had worked. Abigail Sneve had not matched her mother's numbers, but her mother hadn't had to work through an apocalypse like she had.

Abigail stepped into The Barrel, thirstier than a world Ryvita-eating champion (other snacks made of cardboard are available). She had never seen the place so empty, and so…untidy.

"Roooooy!" she screeched, perching herself at the bar and tossing an acorn from the bowl into her puckered old mouth. "Y'all better get out here and serve me fast. Had a hot date last night, with lots of licking and a-slurpin, and my mouth's drier than a popcorn fart."

An uneasy silence answered her. After a few seconds of rattling her long, desiccated fingers on the counter, she decided to try again.

"Roy Clamp, don't make me come back there. Now, I've got plenty of currency, and I would like to spend it on booze, or what passes for booze in this here establishment, so why don't you drag your fat ass out here before I take my business elsewhere." There was, of course, nowhere else to take her business, since Roy's rival pub, *The Green Hen*, had collapsed a little over a dozen years ago. Some said it was an insurance job, but insurance didn't mean shit in a post-apocalyptic world. A lot of people believed *The Green Hen*'s sudden demise to be the work of one Roy Clamp, jealous licensee, arson expert, threat-slinger, and general angry man, though where they got that idea from was anyone's guess.

"What the fuck is going on around here?" Abigail mumbled, standing. "Tiny! Are you here, you big clumsy ogre!?"

No reply.

"Well, *alright*," the whore said, moving around the bar like a spider trying to climb out of the bath. "I guess I'm just gonna have to help myself to all this free alcohol, then, ain't I?" She poured herself a large scotch – absolutely *no* water, which was unheard of in The Barrel – and touched it to her lips. "Mmmmm. This is how scotch should be drunk," she said, savouring the smell, enjoying the sting as it reached her nostrils. "Without the H2O." She coughed and spluttered for a moment, licking the rim of the glass with her hairy tongue. "Okay, I'm going to drink this now. If you want to stop me, you'd better come out…"

Nothing.

"Down the hatch it goes, and don't say I didn't warn ya." And with that, she swallowed the contents of the glass in one thirsty gulp. Slamming the empty down onto the counter as loudly as possible, she said, "Well, I guess one just isn't enough for today. I might just pour me another freebie. And who knows what'll happen then. Heck, I might even take this bottle over to the corner and drink the whole damn thing…for free…without paying…gratis…"

She glanced around, expecting someone to step out and reproach her for being such a cheeky hooker, but they didn't. The pub was completely deserted, and while that would have excited some people, it was terribly unsettling to Abigail, who had never known such an incident, and she'd been drinking in The Barrel since day dot.

"Roy?" she said, placing both the bottle and the empty glass down onto the dusty counter. "Say something if you're there." *It's not a séance, you dumb bitch*, she told herself. "Roy, if you are under duress, knock once for yes, or twice for no." *What if his legs are tied together? Huh? What if he can't knock, idiot?* "Roy, if you have been kidnapped, don't say a word."

Silence.

"Holy fuck!" gasped Abigail. "Roy's been kidnapped." This was not how she had envisioned her day. A couple of drinks, followed by a couple of games of poker, then home for a bit more how's your father with the shy bandit – that was how she had planned it, which just went to show that there was very little use for a calendar or Filofax after the apocalypse.

She pointed herself at the door, and was about to limp toward it when something big and dark walked across the front of the building, casting the room into darkness not once, not twice, but three times, thanks to the trio of windows lining the façade.

Abigail swallowed (which was also her nickname the first year on the game) and took a dainty step back. Part of her wanted to scream out for help, but something told her that it would be a bad idea, that there was something going on here today a little different to the norm.

The room went dark once again as the windows were blocked by the giant shape. Abigail whimpered and slapped a hand to her lips to prevent anything more substantial from falling out.

It's an elephant, that's all…a lost elephant…in the middle of the desert…lost…fuck…

Stumbling along the edge of the bar, Abigail couldn't take her eyes off the door, and the thing just beyond it. There was a back way out of The Barrel, and she had used it on many occasions, when ashamed punters stole her away in the dead of the night, desperate for a little action, and yet not so desperate for the whole town to know that they had crossed Abigail Sneve's palm with silver, and various other stuffs (of a much sticker nature).

Walking backwards, Abigail's foot came up against something heavy and yet malleable. She tripped, almost went arse over saggy tit, and only just managed to stabilise herself thanks to the overturned table in the gangway.

"!" she said, which was more than she'd anticipated. Staring up at her from the semi-adhesive floor was a dead something or other. "Reverend?" she whispered. "Is that you?" It certainly looked like him, albeit a lot bigger, and with some sort of wooden stake buried in his forehead. "If you are under duress, knock once for…"

The door flung open, cutting Abigail off mid-sentence. Sunlight flooded the room. Sand danced along the floorboards on a barely noticeable breeze, and Abigail's heart leapt up into her mouth, choking her scream.

She managed a step back, where her feet found something smelly and gooey and not at all nice to tread in, and then she went down like a sack of spuds, hitting the floor with a meaty thud and cracking her head a good one in the process.

Stars…

Beautiful stars…

Her vision filled up with them, but Abigail was abundantly aware that she was no longer alone in the deserted pub. In fact, referring to it as a deserted pub, now, was like calling it a lived-in ghost town.

Somewhere down by her feet, something snarled. Abigail could feel its warm breath – could smell what it had for breakfast, too – as it hovered above her.

Stay…very…still…

In the months following The Event, Abigail Sneve had made a decent living from hijacking refugees as they fled the surrounding towns in search of survivors. She would lie down in the middle of the street and pretend to be dead, and then when people came to help, she would threaten them with anything from a sloppy kiss to full-on sexual intercourse. She'd made quite a lot of money out of it, and had got real good at lying still for extended periods of time.

But that was a very long time ago. Since then, she'd been infected with more STDs than your average high school sorority. Not a second went by when she wasn't subconsciously raking at herself, scratching at itches that would never go away, trying to figure out whether it was her warts, her crabs, or her thrush giving her gyp. It was like a ticking timebomb down there, and unfortunately for Abigail Sneve, she would be there when it finally blew.

"Oh, fuck it!" Abigail said, climbing to her feet and aggressively scrubbing at her crotch. "You want a piece of me? I'm your worst fucking night…" She trailed off, as she realised that she was not, by any stretch of the imagination, the worst nightmare of the thing standing before her.

If anything, *it* was *hers.*

A morbidly obese grizzly – thirty-plus stone of unbridled terror, with a thick coating of black fur and claws sharper than a wolverine – snarled at her. She thought about snarling back, but quickly realised she was out of her depth.

"Nice puppy," she whimpered. "You don't want to hurt little old Abigail, now, do you?"

The beast roared, beat at its chest like that mythical ape from Skull Island. In other words, *Yes, I do want to hurt little old Abigail, and I'd be ever so grateful if she would shut up and let me do the killin'.*

"Now, now…" Abigail took a step back. Her legs – a pair of veiny stork legs jutting out from a far-too-short-for-her-age skirt – trembled, and she had to fight to remain on her feet. "I've got *diseases*," she said. "One drop of my blood might be enough to drop you like a pickled cabbage. I know I don't look like much, but I'm telling you, I'm more polluted than the Thames."

The creature, for a moment, looked uncertain. Not because it understood what she was saying (all it heard was eat me, *eat me, eat me!*) but because it had spotted the fallen creature a few feet away.

The clergy-monster.

One of its own.

Had this woman, this vile looking thing with stringy legs, hair-lip, and a hole in her face where there should have been a second eye, taken down the priest-beast on her own? Was there something special about her? In other words, was she some sort of geriatric ninja? The grizzly-monster had seen no-one else enter the pub, and there didn't appear to be anyone around now, other than the woman standing in front of it. To be honest, she made the mutant very nervous indeed.

"Look," Abigail said, backing away just a little more. She was almost at the window. She could feel the sunlight boring into her neck, its magnificent power augmented by the glass. "I don't know what's going on here, but you're obviously…" What was it? Really? It looked like a fat bear, but there was something about it – something almost human. "You're obviously pissed off for some reason or other. Hey, we all have bad days." This was one of hers. "So, why don't we make a deal, huh? I'm going to leave now. Forget that I ever laid eye on you, and you can go ahead and get out of town before Kellerman and his goons have a chance to mount you and hang you on the big man's office wall." One more step back. The creature remained still across the room, huffing and growling as it tried to fathom just what was going on, and what it was going to do next.

As a young whore, Abigail had found herself backed into many a corner. Punters didn't like to have their jewellery removed while they slept post-coitus. They often woke up during said theft – she wasn't the stealthiest of dollymops – and not many of them believed her when she said 'I was just going to give it a polish, me lovely'.

This – being backed into a corner by an angry, hulking monster – reminded her of that. The only difference here, though, was that she hadn't taken anything from the grizzly-beast. But the way it was scrutinizing her, you would have thought she had stripped it of everything it possessed and then slapped it across the fizzog.

"Okay," Abigail said. "I'm going to take your silence as an acceptance of my offer. Try not to savage anyone else on your way out of town. I'll be off, then…" She edged along the wall, slowly, not taking her eyes off the grizzly-beast. "You wouldn't happen to know what happened to Roy, would you? Little fat fella, stands on the other side of the bar…"

The grizzly-beast straightened up, roaring once again, beating at its chest hard enough to send coarse, black hairs across the room. And then it dropped to all fours and began bounding toward her.

Abigail screamed.

The grizzly-beast roared.

An unbiased onlooker would have been hard pressed to tell you which was scarier.

28

"We need to get back to Lou's," Smalling said. "He's responsible for all this. Maybe he knows how to stop it."

"What do you mean, he's responsible?" Red said. "What, like, he's some sort of mad scientist? Like Dr Moreau? These things are his genetically-enhanced creations?"

"He's leaking titty-milk," Harkness said, still nursing his face, which was now completely swollen on one side, as if he was plagued with abscesses.

"What?" was all that Red could manage, and she asked it of Smalling, for he seemed to be the most senior of the two men.

"He's telling the truth," Smalling said, slapping a mosquito against his neck. "The guy's been selling his own titty milk to the 'haveners, but there must have been something wrong with it."

"I'll say," Red agreed. "So you think this milk has been turning the townsfolk into savage mutants? Is that what you're telling me?" It was as good an explanation as any. She'd seen first-hand what these things were, how they went from human to monster in ten seconds flat. If she hadn't witnessed it with her own two eyes, though, she would have told this pair of slapheaded misfits to go bother someone else.

"If we can get back to Lou's, we can at least hunker down until we figure out what to do," Smalling said. "I mean, most of the town's food is there anyway. If we're going to get through this, that store is the best place to be. And I know damn well what he's got in that basement of his. I sure could use a drink or two right about now."

"What about *Kellerman*?" asked Harkness. "He's going to be pretty pissed off at us if we don't get back to the office and start protecting his ass."

Red pulled the horse to a halt. "Actually," she said through gritted teeth. "I wouldn't worry about that. Your boss turned into one of those things and killed the rest of my crew. I had to put him down."

"He drank the milk!" Harkness said, wiping a tear from his eye. "We gave him the milk and he…it's all our fault."

"Now, don't be like that," Red said. "You weren't to know that the milk would turn him into a raging walrus-beast, now, were you?"

Harkness nodded sorrowfully. Smalling patted him on the back. It was the most tender moment they had ever shared, and one that would not be repeated any time soon.

"Okay, so let's get to this store, talk to this Lou character, and see what we can do to put this shit right," Red said, tapping Mordecai with her heel. The horse cantered along once again. "Sound like a plan?"

"As good as any," Smalling said. "Let's just hope that—"

Suddenly, a window across the street erupted, and through it came a tiny, skinny woman wearing a short skirt, and what looked like a giant grizzly bear. They hit the sand at the same time, but it was the grizzly-beast that got to its feet first.

"Fuck!" Smalling said. "Is that Abigail the whore?"

Harkness squinted through the sunlight. "Nah, she was hairy, but not *that* hairy."

"Not that one," Smalling said. He jabbed a finger toward the tiny form climbing up from the sand. "Her!"

"Oh," Harkness said. "Yeah, that's Abigail. I'd know that limp anywhere. What's she doing fighting a giant grizzly?"

"That's *not* a bear," Red said, climbing down from Mordecai, who shuffled backwards, once again loath to get involved. "It's one of those *things*. A milk-mutant. And it's about to rip that poor woman's head clean off."

Abigail rocked back and forth on unsteady legs, one of which was twisted, broken in several places. A jagged shard of bone jutted out through the flesh. Blood sprayed out, raining down on the sand with a gentle pitter-patter. Mordecai vomited on his own hoof.

"You're messing with the wrong hooker!" Abigail said, adopting the only stance her legs would allow – the broken ankle posture. Her foot hung listlessly from the end of her leg as she waved it around, trying to confuse the beast. It hurt like hell, but it was also strangely hypnotic. The grizzly-monster, oddly, couldn't look away.

"What's she playing at?" Harkness said. "She's going to get herself killed."

"She's doing the broken ankle hypnosis manoeuvre," Red said. "She's trying to put the monster to sleep, and I think it's working. Look!"

The grizzly-beast followed the dangly, busted foot with its eyes, grunting softly. The more rotations the floppy appendage did, the sleepier the grizzly-beast appeared. It even yawned, a mouthful of razor-sharp teeth.

"Has this ever worked before?" Smalling asked. "Because I've never heard of it."

"Shhhhhh," Red said, mesmerised by the display. "Just keep watching. Any second now, that thing's going to fall asleep. That whore is a fucking genius."

"Yeah, because geniuses usually wind up selling their saggy tits and infected pussies for money," Harkness said.

"You're feeling very sleepy," Abigail sighed. "Picture yourself floating down a stream. You're in a large basket.

Just you and the water, and the trees either side of you."
She couldn't believe this was working. Hypnotised by a
broken foot; who would have thought it? "The water is
still. Ooh, look, there's a frog. 'Hello, you big grizzly
bastard,' says the frog. You ignore it, because talking
frogs aren't to be trusted."

"Is she talking about frogs?" Smalling said.

"I think so," Red replied. "Look, it's working. That's
all that matters. She's going to get out of there in one
piece."

"You've got a sword there," Harkness reminded the
bandido. "Pretty sure she would appreciate the help."

Red looked at the whore, at the swinging ankle, at the
giant grizzly-beast, and said, "No point interfering at this
point. If it makes a move for her, I say we take it down.
She seems to have it under control."

Harkness and Smalling shook their heads in unison.

"There's a waterfall ahead," Abigail continued. She
hadn't been expecting to encounter a waterfall, which
just went to show how ridiculously improvised this
whole thing was. At the mention of the word 'waterfall'
the grizzly-beast snorted. Even from twelve feet away,
Abigail could smell its breath – a harsh combination of
rancid cream and jellied eels. She gagged, but managed
to stifle it. "Your basket is not going anywhere near the
waterfall. It's floating toward the riverbank, where a
badger walks by smoking a pipe and reading a copy of
the Financial Times." See, totally unrehearsed. Her leg
was getting tired; not to mention very sore indeed. The

amount of blood she had lost was apparent, thanks to the circle of red sand between her and the monster.

Just then, something happened. The creature managed to blink itself out of its trance. Maybe it didn't like badgers, or fiscal newspapers, but whatever it was, the grizzly-beast was back, *compos mentis*, and judging by its expression, not best pleased at being duped by the old broken ankle hypnosis trick.

"Shit, she's fucked now!" Red said, unsheathing the samurai sword.

"Give her a chance," Harkness said. "She might beat the thing. She's a feisty one, is Abigail Sneve."

The grizzly-beast leapt forwards, bringing its giant paw around in a wide arc. Abigail shrieked, and somehow *continued* to shriek as her head flew from her body, somersaulted through the air, and landed at the feet of the gobsmacked onlookers. Smalling kicked the head away, for the blood squirting from the stump was making a right mess of his shoes.

The grizzly-beast dragged the headless body of the whore to the sand and began to drink from the geysering neck, lapping at the blood as if it was the best thing since blue Slurpees.

Harkness doubled over and unleashed a torrent of spew toward the sand. A disorientated scorpion looked up at just the wrong time, and instantly drowned in the bile.

The grizzly-monster had gnawed its way down to the whore's sagging breasts, but seemed to be keeping away from them, as if the flesh there was rotten. And maybe it was.

Red, with the sword held tightly in her grasp, said, "I can't watch this. It's fucking disgusting."

"Are you going to kill it?" Smalling whispered, hoping that she said yes, yes she would kill it, because then there was less chance it would kill *them*, either now or later.

"I'm going to try," said Red. "And I'd appreciate a little help this time. I almost got my ass handed to me back there while you and your buddy viewed from afar."

"Now, wait a minute…" Smalling said, about to explain that they had not been, as she so delicately put it, viewing from afar, but anticipating the right moment to get involved, when…

The beast groaned. It slumped back onto its haunches, meat falling from its mouth, blood seeping from the corner of its mouth. As if angered at its apparent ability to stomach anymore, it punched the savaged body aside. It landed face-down in the sand, or would have had it still possessed a face.

The plaintive whimper that came from the grizzly-beast was not what anyone would expect from such a large and brutal freak, but the day, in general, was an odd one. It seemed nothing was beyond the realm of possibility.

"Is it *injured?*" Smalling asked, helping the bilious Harkness to straighten up.

"It doesn't look well," Red said. "Maybe it ate too much."

"Please die, please die, please die," Harkness mumbled, over and over again.

The grizzly-beast howled at the sun, as if it had been wronged by the giant star. Before it had chance to finish its complaint, though, something popped, and then the creature was flying in every direction, in many pieces. White ichor and black fur fountained up into the sky before raining down again.

A huge paw flew through the air toward Red, but she saw it coming and managed to swing the sword up, slicing it into two. Both pieces flew past without making contact, but there was a dot of white goo on her shoulder that hadn't been there a moment ago, which she quickly wiped away with the heel of her hand.

Smalling and Harkness were over by Mordecai, all three of them trying to decide how quickly they could flee the godforsaken town, before they, too, succumbed to the milky disease, or the madness that now clawed at them like Lovecraftian elders returning from the abyss...

"So, I think it just exploded," Red said, perhaps a little more cheerily than she should have. "Just when I thought today couldn't get any more fucked up, too." She walked over to where the others stood, silently gazing toward the crater in the sand and the fur and milky goo surrounding it. "Did any of you see that coming?"

Smalling opened and shut his mouth a couple of times before anything came out. "I have to admit, that was one of the *last* things I thought would happen."

"And neither of you are, like, telekinetic, or anything?" Red said. "I mean, were either of you willing that to happen?"

"I was too busy trying not to shit myself to blow the fucking thing up," Harkness said.

"Yeah, we're really not telepathetic, or whatever it was you said," Smalling added. "Wait a minute…would we know…I mean, would we know if we—"

"Yeah, you're not," Red said, sheathing the sword and climbing up onto Mordecai. "Let's get the fuck out of here before more of those things come."

They continued along the street, only one destination in mind.

LOU'S LOOT.

Where answers awaited them, and failing that, a bottle of something to numb the pain of death.

29

"Will you put some clothes on?" Rita asked the naked man he stalked back and forth across the living-room, his tackle dancing like an epileptic vole. "I don't mind, personally, but I've got kids in the house, and they don't need to see that kind of thing."

Mickey covered himself up, suddenly embarrassed. "Sorry. I guess living nude for the last few decades has desensitised me to it."

"Why do you do it?" Zee asked. She was sitting in the corner, trying desperately not to look at anything below the man's waist, She hadn't got to the chapter on 'How to Polish a Penis' in *Mrs Beeton's Book of Household Management* yet, though she was sure the chapter existed.

"Why do I do *what*?" Mickey said, smiling. "Why do I live in the alleyway naked?"

Zee nodded. "Yeah. I mean, that's a little bit weird, isn't it? I get the homeless thing; there are loads of people living rough, but naked?"

"It's kinda like my thing," Mickey said. "Some people have guitars, others have dogs…"

"So it's how you stand out from the rest of the vagrants?" Roger Fox chimed in. "Why not just get a cat?"

"Luke Smith over on the corner of Bakewell Avenue has a cat."

"Well, it doesn't necessarily have to be a *cat*," Roger argued. "Another animal…*any* animal. Surely that's better than walking around with your trouser-snake out."

"I don't own trousers—"

"Snake, then. Just snake. You must get a lot of funny looks, being nude all the time, and all. Doesn't it bother you?"

Mickey shrugged. "The way I see it," he said, "it's hotter than hell out there. People are literally falling down dead in the street on a daily basis. I once watched a rat cook after falling asleep next to a chain-link fence. It was the easiest meal I've ever had. Didn't have to cube it, or anything."

"Ewwwww," Zee said, but part of her was secretly impressed with this naked vagabond. He had survived by adapting to his surroundings, worked with what he had available, and the fact that he walked around stark bollock naked without so much as batting an eyelid only made him more intriguing.

Mickey smiled. "I don't usually eat rats," he said. "Most days I just pick those mushrooms growing over by the McKenzie place."

"Not anymore you don't," Roy said from the tattered armchair he'd claimed as his own. "I don't think there will be anything growing over there for a very long time."

"You can always pop in here for something to eat," Rita Fox said. "I mean, if you put some pants on, or something. I've always got a pot of something stewing."

"Ah, mystery stew," Mickey said, laughing and licking his lips. "My favourite. I might take you up on that offer if we get out of this alive."

"Mommy?"

Rita turned around to find Clint standing in the doorway. He looked a little ashen, but at least he was speaking, now, and not fainting every few minutes. Could it be that he was on the mend?

Rita bent and gathered him up into her arms. "Oh, Clint!" she said, peppering his face and head with kisses. "How are you feeling?"

"I had the strangest dream," said the boy, "that a severed head thumped me in the face."

Roger Fox coughed. "Yes, well, it's good that you're feeling a little better," he said. "Go and sit with your brother, and try not to look at the naked man's willy."

Clint walked across the room, to where his brother sat playing with a pair of Tonka trucks. Tom handed one to the recovering boy and smiled. It was a sweet moment, but also one that required your presence to appreciate it.

"So what's the plan?" Zee said, happy now that the young of the family were out of earshot. Zee liked to count herself amongst the adults, even if she was the youngest girl in Oilhaven. At seventeen, she was old enough to drive (if she ever came across any abandoned vehicles) and old enough to marry (if she ever came across an abandoned husband she took a liking to), so, in her eyes, she should be treated with the same respect and sincerity as the other adults present.

"Go and sit with your brothers," Roger Fox said, which hadn't been what she'd expected, at all.

"No!" she said, which hadn't been what Roger had expected, either. They were locked in some strange battle, a game of *shock the family member*, where the rules were simple: render your opponent speechless.

"Zee," Roger said, after sucking most of the air from the room with one deep inhale. "What's going on out there, it isn't a game. It isn't some fantasy, like in those books you've always got your nose stuck in. It's really happening, and as your *father*, I'm asking you to leave it to the grown-ups to make the decisions. Now—"

"Fuck you!" There, she'd said it. At any other time, she would have regretted it almost immediately, but on this occasion she felt no remorse, no urge to follow it up with an instant apology. "I'm not some little girl, Dad, some naïve little princess that you can protect. Let me ask you a question…"

She could have asked as many questions as she wanted in that moment, for Roger Fox's face was frozen with shock. Rita Fox, too, was gobsmacked, but willing to see where this led. She wanted her daughter to be as strong as possible, and if standing up to both she and Roger was what it took, then so be it.

"How many of those things have *you* killed?" Zee folded her arms across her chest. It was the only way she could prevent them from shaking.

Roger faltered momentarily, then said, "Well, there was *Tiny*."

Mickey held is hand up, as if to ask teacher a question. "Mine," he said.

Roger shook his head. "Yes, but you couldn't have done it if Roy and I hadn't blindsided the thing."

"Still mine," Mickey said. "You don't gate-crash a barbecue and then take credit for the burgers."

"So you haven't, have you?" Zee said to her father. "Killed any." She knew she had him where she wanted him, and the silence that answered her question confirmed it. "Well, *I* have. I had to kill one of those fuckers. I didn't have anyone there to help me. It was just me and it, and I took it down, so don't talk down to me

231

like one of your buddies from the mine, okay? I'm as much a part of this shitforsaken town as you are, all of you, and if I have to, I'll fight to defend it." Though she really didn't want to, not if it could be avoided. "So...I'll ask again. What's the plan?"

Her father sat at the kitchen table, running sweaty fingers over the dust that had settled there in the past hour. "Okay," he said. "I guess we have to weigh up our options. We can stay here and hope that nothing tries to get in, that the cavalry is on its way, and that everything will sort itself out soon enough." He paused. Option two terrified him, but it made more sense than hanging around, hoping for something that might not happen. "Or," he said.

"Or?" Mickey replied.

"Or..." Roy added.

"Or what?" said Rita.

"Or we can get as tooled up as possible and head on over to Lou's. It's only a couple of streets away, and if we stick to the back alleys and yards, we might make it all the way without being spotted."

"Why in the hell would we want to do that?" Rita said. "It's that fat bastard's fault we're in this mess. Put me in a room with him for five fucking minutes and we'll see what happens."

"It's not Lou's fault," Roger said. "He wasn't to know that his product was contaminated, that in selling his milk to the unsuspecting public, he would turn them all into giant mutant monsters. Do you think he would have gone ahead and bottled it up if he'd known that?"

"I don't know," Rita said. "Remember the time he sold those rats as squirrels?"

Unfortunately, Roger remembered just fine. They hadn't realised what they were eating until the toilet brush fell off the rat's backside. "Yes, but that was harmless. Mostly. This is different. This is his *livelihood* we're talking about. Lou would never knowingly mutate his customers. He's a good man, and he works hard over there, making sure we all have everything we need and looking after his perpetually dying mother at the same time."

"He does have a lot of supplies over there," Roy added, which carried far more weight than Roger's argument. "How long can we eke out an existence here? I'm guessing your cupboards aren't fully stocked? It'll only be a matter of time before we have to go out there, anyway, to the well. I'm not keen on the idea of heading outside, either, but if we stay here, we might not get the chance to leave. We'll be weak, thirsty, hungry, unable to run." He sat up straight in the armchair. A spider ran from beneath it, which Mickey stamped on before crouching and forcing its mangled corpse into his mouth.

"Ewwww," Zee said, once again fascinated by the exposed hobo.

Chewing frantically, Mickey said, "You won't be saying that in a few days' time. It'll be all 'Hey Mickey! Catch me a spider, will you?'."

"I say we leave now," Zee said. "Before we're all scouring the skirting-boards for arachnids, like that creepy dude in Dracula."

Something bounced off the front door, causing it to rattle in its frame. Everyone jumped, except for the boys, who were far too busy crashing cars to notice.

"They're outside," Roger said. "Do you think they know we're in here?"

Another thud. This one from the MDF board covering the front window.

"Maybe they can smell their dead," Rita whispered, gesturing to the mangled bodies stacked against the far wall: the McKenzies. "We haven't been making much noise," she added. "I doubt if they could hear us in here."

"MIIIIIIILLLLLLLLK!" something bellowed from just beyond the door.

"Okay, everyone out the back window," Roger said. "Zee, you're a little bit transient. Do you know a quick way to Lou's from here? One that keeps us off the streets and away from those things?"

Zee had been waiting for this moment her entire life. "I know how we can get all the way to Lou's without our feet even touching the ground," she said. "All we need is some rope. I don't think the boys will make it across some of the gaps, not on their own."

A hammer-fist smashed through the door, putting a huge hole next to the ones already there. Everyone rushed into the kitchen. Rita snatched Clint and Tom up from the floor as she ran past, one under each arm. It was amazing the weight a woman could carry when the need arose – a trait they'd inherited from their shopaholic descendants.

Zee rifled through the large chest that was pushed up against the kitchen wall, found what she needed, and followed the rest of her family, the naked alleyway man, and Roy of The Barrel out through the back window.

Just as the barricade, the front door, the front window, and half of the building came down in one fell swoop, proving that post-apocalyptic architecture was nothing to write home about.

30

"Please stop! Please fucking stop! Gaaaahhhhh!" Lou stood in front of the giant vat, his shirt removed, his entire body coated with sweat and lumpy milk. He had been lactating for an entire hour, and it showed no sign of slowing down. The vat was full to the brim; pretty soon, he would have to simply accept the fact that not all of it could be contained, that he needed to make very good friends with the mop in the corner of the room.

"No use crying over spilt milk," Lou said, sob-laughing. Whoever came up with that little gem had obviously never filled a massive bucket with the stuff from his or her own tits. In less than twenty-four hours, Lou had grown sick and tired of the stuff, and the smell that came with it. How cows slept at night was beyond him.

The milk was now pouring over the sides of the vat, cascading down to the basement floor, pooling around the covered cadaver of the mother-beast. At the rate he was going, he would flood the place in less than an hour. In two hours, he would be swimming through the basement, and in three…well, he'd have to make his way upstairs, lest he drown in his own fucking cellar.

"To hell with it," Lou said, scrambling up the steps three at a time. For an aging fat man, it was amazing how quickly he moved.

Into the store he went, dropping the trapdoor as soon as his feet were clear. His nipples continued to spray milk everywhere, but no matter what he did, he couldn't stop it. He'd tried putting a hand over one breast, stifling it, holding it tight against the nipple, but that just caused the other one to pump out at twice the rate. And if he tried to shield both tits at the same time…well, it had almost blown both of his hands off. They were still sore now, thirty minutes after the incident, and he wouldn't be making the same mistake twice.

He dragged a tarpaulin out of one of the racks and stretched it out across the floor knocking three shelves over in the process. Tidiness was no longer something that concerned him. Stemming the flow of this milk, or storing it somewhere for now, just until he could get outside without being murdered to death by giant angry mutants, was of paramount importance.

After locating a ball of string, he tied the four corner of the tarp to racks and shelves, elevating the whole thing slightly, creating what was essentially a giant milk hammock.

"At least it'll keep the floor dry," he said, standing back and admiring his handiwork. It seemed like such a small thing, considering what had happened to his mother, what was going on outside, and that he was probably going to be dead by the end of the night.

The milk came thick and fast for the next fifteen minutes. The tarpaulin was already touching the floor in the middle. There had been a few minutes when the milk simply rolled and bounced about on the tarp, making something of a dairy trampoline, but that hadn't lasted.

Lou stroked at his tender nipples, easing the liquid out – not that it needed any coaxing. He was an uber-cow, the most productive dairy-human that had ever walked the face of the earth.

Not that it was something to be proud of. He wanted it to stop; the sooner the better.

A heavy thud at the door caused him to spin away from the tarpaulin. Milk spurted across the room, dripped down the still-rattling door.

It's one of them, he thought. *One of the milk-mutants, come to exact its revenge.*

"Lou, let us in!" said a voice, one that he recognised as belonging to Smalling...or Harkness, one or the other.

Lou relaxed slightly, turning his back on the door, aiming his spraying mammaries toward the tarpaulin. "What do you want?" he called. "I'm in the middle of something at the moment. Come back later, if you haven't been brutally murdered by the milk-mutants."

There was a slight pause, several mutterings, and then a female voice said, "Mr Decker, we've had a hell of a shitty day so far, and it's all your fault, so why don't you open the fucking door and I promise I won't cut you."

Lou's breasts stuttered momentarily. The woman – whoever she was – sounded like she meant business. But she was out there, and he was in here, and there was a locked door between them. "I have guns," he said. "They're old, but they work, and I have no problem shooting things." It was true. He had despatched his own mother (or what was left of her) with the antique pistols. He would take great pleasure in turning the guns on Kellerman's henchmen and their new female friend.

"We just need to get off the street, Lou," Smalling said. "There are…things out here. Big angry fucking things. Please, just let us in. We'll help you to barricade the store up properly. And just think, there will be four of us in there…"

"And?" Lou said.

"Well, if there are *four* of us," Smalling explained, "there's less chance that you'll be the next one to get butchered."

Lou made an O with his lips as he considered what the baldy was saying. But then he looked down at the tarpaulin, at the way it was filling up fast, at his sodden nipples, the hair there matted with milk and creamy globules. "I really wish I could help," he said, "but I can't get to the door right now. If you come back in about an hour, maybe t—"

A large blade, sharper than any he had ever encountered, came through between the door and its frame. There was an audible *chi-ching!* as the blade went down, slicing through the latch bolt in one quick movement. Then the door swung open and the three people that had, a moment ago, been on the other side of the fucking thing, came through it, breathless, fear etched onto their faces. Following them was a gasping horse.

Lou was about to object when the woman eased the door shut and, leaning against it, gawping at Lou and not knowing whether to be impressed or revolted, she said, "So you're the milkman, huh?"

Lou nodded. "I believe I *am*. But you have to believe me when I say, I didn't know any of this would happen…I…I just wanted to give the town what they wanted…"

Smalling and Harkness were carrying a piece of chain toward the door with the intention of securing it. When they were done, Smalling turned to the lactating storekeeper and grimaced. "How do we *stop* this, Lou?" he said.

"Well, I'd be lying if I said I knew," Lou said. "I've tried everything. Sellotape, nipple-clamps—"

"Not your *lactating*," Smalling said, though he did wonder where all that milk was coming from. Lou was relatively short, dumpy, the kind of guy you used to see hanging around bookies, smoking roll-yer-owns and drinking Red Stripe from a can. The milk on the tarp would have filled him twice over, which meant that he was producing it as quickly as he was leaking it. "I'm talking about the milk-mutants. How do we stop them? You said you have guns…"

"Forget about the guns," Lou said, only because he *wanted* them to forget about the guns. They were his…and his alone. If things were going to go south that night, he wanted to be able to defend himself, or at least put a round into his own head, should it come to it. "How many of them are out there? How many milk-mutants did you see?"

The woman walked casually across the room, sheathing the sword as she went. "Too many," she said. "They're lurking in the shadows; a couple of them are out in the open. I guess even *they* can't stand the heat."

"Maybe they don't want to curdle," Harkness said. "I mean, their insides are practically made of the stuff. If they go all clumpy, it might be like a stroke to them. They might lose the ability to function. Maybe that's why they're sticking to the shadows."

"Maybe," said Red. She reached Lou, who suddenly became very coy, trying to shield his exposed body from the woman, who he now recognised as the girl that had come by earlier asking about Kellerman.

"Where are your friends?" he asked, hunching over the tarp and squeezing his right nipple. The flow increased momentarily before settling again.

Red sighed as the deaths of her Los Pendejos brothers finally sank in. "They…they didn't make it." She had a reputation to uphold, though, and so added, "Bunch of cunts anyway." She didn't mean it. El Oscuro had been, on occasion, a very considerate lover. Sometimes he even gave her the opportunity to finish.

"Sorry to hear that," Lou said.

"Kellerman's dead, too," Smalling said.

"Well, at least that's something," Lou said, though it wasn't the response Smalling had been going for. "Look, I don't know what you want from me, but I'm almost positive I can't give it to you, and I'm finding this whole thing a little embarrassing, if I'm being totally honest."

"Do you have anything to eat?" Red said, optimistically. "Something to drink that isn't *that*?" She pointed at the milk-flooded tarpaulin.

Lou smiled. "That I *can* do. There's food in the basement, but don't go crazy. We don't know how long we're going to be here. Oh, and don't uncover the body down there. It's not a pleasant sight." The thought of the mother-beast down there, head all but decimated, oozing pink slime all over the place, sent a shudder down his spine and brought bile up into his throat.

Red walked across the room and lifted the trapdoor. Her stomach growled in anticipation of the food it was about to receive. Down she went, into the darkness, in search of tinned goods and anything to quench her thirst that *wasn't* milk.

31

"The rooftops?" Roger Fox said, hoisting himself up onto the adjacent gable. "You think we can get all the way to Lou's by using the roofs?"

Zee reached down latched onto her father's wrist. Pulling him up, she said, "Do you have a better idea? There are twenty houses between here and LOU'S LOOT. I'm pretty sure there are no major gaps between, nothing too difficult to traverse. Up here we're safe, away from those fucking...I mean *effing* monsters." She turned to face the others, who all seemed to be examining her as if she had lost her senses. "What?"

"Well, this *is* a little far-fetched," Rita said. "Jumping across the rooftops like cowboys. Sounds like something from one of those terrible novels you read."

"Like I said...does anyone have a better idea?" Zee waited a few seconds, and when no-one was forthcoming, said, "That's what I thought. Now..." She glanced off into the distance, over to where Lou's store would be. "...Okay, follow me. But keep low and away from the edge. If one of those things spots us up here, we're for the chop. Stay close, and whatever you do, don't sneeze, cough, or fart, and absolutely no talking. Does everyone understand?"

They all nodded in unison, apart from Clint, who had fallen asleep in Rita Fox's arms. He was snoring gently, but it was nothing to be concerned about. There were pigeons on the next house making more noise, and the milk-mutants didn't seem to be concerning themselves with them.

Zee walked slowly across the rooftop, keeping low, heeding her own advice.

"It's *your* fault she's like this," Rita told her husband. "If you hadn't found that Action Man™ (other militarized and cockless action figures are available) in that skip all those years ago and given it to her as a Christmas gift, we wouldn't be up here now. We'd be inside, making pastry and talking about boys."

Roger didn't like the sound of that. "Don't blame *me*," he said. "It's all those books she reads. Blame Lee Child."

"Keep your voices down," Mickey said. "I can hear them down there, scrabbling about the place. The last thing we want is to let them know we're up here. Just try not to argue for, like, five minutes. Once we get to the store, you can go ballistic if you must. We just—"

"Hang on a minute," Rita angrily whispered. "Are you giving us advice on our marriage? Is that what's happening here? Because I'm not going to take advice from a man whose cock and balls are constantly on show." She reached down and covered Tom's ears with both hands, even though she had no intention of using further profanities, and Tom had heard the previous ones just fine.

"I think she wants us to follow," Roy said, pointing to where Zee crouched at the end of the rooftop, gesticulating frantically.

"Come on, then," Roger whispered. "Let's go a roof-hoppin'." He wasn't looking forward to it in the slightest.

The first three jumps, if you could call them that, were relatively simple. Two foot gaps between buildings, necessitating only the smallest of leaps, were all that stood between the roof-hopping 'haveners and the next stop on their crazy excursion. By the time they reached the fourth rooftop, all of them – Tom included – were feeling unstoppable. *Bring it on! Fucking milk-mutants, don't make us come down there and show you what a mistake you've made in messing with the people of Oilhaven!*

Then they saw the ten foot jump required to make it onto the next roof – Oilhaven Catholic Church – and six hearts sank simultaneously.

"You can fuck that *right* off," said Roy, examining the empty space between the buildings. "What do I look like? James fucking Bond?"

"Who?" Tom said. His mother covered his ears. Once again, she was a little too late, and Tom had a new word to add to his vocabulary.

"We have to keep going," Zee said. "It's our only hope."

Rita Fox stepped up to the edge of the building. Down there, in the shadow of the old church, something moved. She couldn't quite make it out, but it was big, and had several large appendages, which it was swinging around the place the same way a drunkard took a piss. "I don't think I can do it," she said, backing away from the edge. She looked nervous, and rightfully so. The roof opposite slanted sharply down; even if they made the jump, there was a good chance they would roll off the roof when they landed, falling straight into the tentacles, or mouth, of the thing waiting in the shadows.

Zee shook her head. "You don't have to jump," she said, pulling the coil of clothes-line from her pocket. "It's only a few feet." She searched the rooftop, looking for anything she could tie it to. Everyone watched in silence. Down in the shadow of the church, the milk-mutant plaintively keened.

"Over here," Mickey said. Zee paced across the roof to where the nude man stood pointing at a hook just over the lip of the roof. "That what you're looking for?"

Zee grinned. "That'll do nicely." She tied one end of the clothes-line to the hook, double-knotting it not once but twice, then made her way across the roof, to where the rest of the survivors stood, nervously waiting. "Right, here's what we're going to do. I'm going to jump across and tie the other end of this line to the church. Anyone that can make it across with a jump, please, be my guest. Those that feel like they can't do it are going to have to shuffle over on the clothes-line."

"What about your brothers, Zee?" Rita said. "How are they going to get across?"

Zee was about to answer when a voice said, "I'm already over," and all eyes turned to the church roof, to where Tom Fox was leaning against a gargoyle's ass.

"Tom Fox, you get back here right this minute," Rita said.

"He's over!" Zee said. "He made it. Which means that we can all make it, Mom." Zee tucked the end of the clothes-line into her back-pocket and pried Clint out of her mother's grasp.

"What are you doing?" Rita asked. "You're not going to…" She trailed off as Zee turned and rushed toward the roof's edge, her sick brother clutched tight to her chest. Then she was off the end, floating through the air, an involuntary grunt escaping her as she went. Behind her, hearts leapt into mouths, Rita Fox's mouth opened so wide that she would suffer with it for weeks to come; Mickey applauded, which was always a dangerous game to play when bereft of clothes.

Zee landed on the church roof and managed to keep her feet, despite one of the ancient slates shifting beneath her. She propped Clint up against the stone gargoyle and instructed Tom to look after him.

"Okay," she said, surveying the church roof. Mickey landed on the church roof next, a little heavily – three slates rattled their way toward the edge and disappeared over the side – but safe.

Lining the rooftop were six-inch stone crosses, perfect for tethering to, and so Zee wasted no time in securing the other end of the line. When she was done, she gave it a little pluck. The *boyoyoyoyng!* noise it made told her it was plenty tight enough.

Her father made the jump across, and was steadied by the waiting Mickey.

"Did you just rub your penis on my leg?" Roger said, frowning.

"Accident," Mickey said, taking a step back. "Just trying to help."

"That ought to do it," Zee said, joining Mickey and her father. The line between the two buildings looked good. To her mother, she said, "You'll be fine, Mom. Just don't look down."

Rita gave her the finger and took a deep breath. "Okay," she whispered. "You can do this, Rita. You can do it. Do you want to go first?"

Roy Clamp frantically shook his head. "I'd rather slide down a bannister made of razorblades and land on a bicycle with no seat." In other words, ladies first.

Huffing nervously, Rita lowered herself slowly down, crawling under the clothes-line next to the roof edge. She wasn't good with heights, or falling from them, so it took a moment to compose herself. During said composure, however, she had plenty of time to think about the beast skulking about down there next to the church, and what it would do to her should she fall.

It was the least fruitful attempt at equanimity ever.

She shuffled slowly backwards, clutching at the clothes-line with both arms. Her eyes remained closed for the entire journey, which lasted just under twenty seconds. When hands pulled her to safety on the other side, she exhaled deeply, and said, "Gerghhh."

"I'm so proud of you," Roger Fox said, pulling his wife to her feet. "You did great."

"Don't ever make me do anything like that again," she replied. She had been able to hear the milk-mutant beneath, licking its lips and god knows what else, hoping for a misplaced hand, an accidental slip of a leg.

"I won't," Roger said, though it was a promise he wasn't sure he could keep. Who knew what they would have to do next in order to survive the day.

"Come on, Roy," Mickey said. "Shuffle your fat ass over here."

The landlord regarded the line as if it were a snake, liable to bite and poison him if he made contact with it. "I can't do it," he said. "I thought I could, but I can't."

"What do you mean you can't do it?" Roger said. "There's an eight-year-old boy over here that cleared it, and Zee did it while carrying Clint."

"But I'm *tubby*," Roy said, patting himself in the belly. "I'll break the line; I *know* I will."

"Then jump!" Mickey said. "We'll catch you." He moved up next to the roof edge, as close as was humanly possible. One more step and he would have fallen into the tree- and monster-lined abyss below. "I'm seventy-five percent sure that you'll make it."

"Just seventy-five?" Roy said, fear etched across his face.

"Like you said, you have got a bit of timbre to you." Mickey patted his own belly; his willy did a little dance. "But I'm sure you'll make it. Like, seventy percent…"

"*Seventy* now?" Roy gasped. "What happened to the other five?"

"The longer you put it off, the less likely it is that you'll get across." Mickey held out a hand. "It's now or never, buddy. Let's do this while you're at sixty-five percent."

Fuck, Roy thought, but he knew he had to jump. He couldn't stand the thought of being left behind, left to battle those things alone…and the boy, Tom, *had* made it look relatively easy. Maybe the naked dude was right; he was building it up, making it more difficult than it actually was.

"Okay," Roy said. "But you'll catch me?"

"We'll have a go," Mickey said. "Just make sure you get some good elevation, otherwise we won't reach you."

"Elevation?"

"Yeah, it's what people get when they jump," Roger Fox said. "When was the last time you jumped anything?"

Roy shook his head. Possibly *never*. But he was going to jump now, and failing was not an option. With the others on the adjacent roof, urging him on, giving him strength, he knew he had a good chance of making it.

At least fifty percent…

"Fuck it," he said, and then he was running, running, running toward the roof's edge. He wished he hadn't taken so much of a run-up, for he was officially knackered by the time he leapt off. And, for just a moment, he was flying, confident that he was going to make it. The outstretched arms and wide eyes on the opposite roof told him otherwise.

Down, down, down, he slammed against the side of the church. A hand reached down and grabbed onto his wrist just before he dropped into the void between the buildings. He looked up to find Mickey's face, contorted and terrified, staring down at him.

"Pull me up!" Roy gasped. "I didn't get enough elevation."

"No shit!" Mickey said. "You didn't get *any* elevation." Mickey had seen better leaps from legless crickets. "Don't let go."

"Same to you," Roy said.

"Okay, everyone pull! Pull! Pull!" Mickey said to Roger and Zee, who had a hold of the naked man's ankles, and also a graphic view of what he'd had for breakfast. As he was dragged slowly back, away from the edge of the roof, his member grazed the tiles beneath his body. It hurt like a sonofabitch, and reminded him of the time he'd spent a night with Abigail Sneve, Oilhaven's geriatric whore.

Roy's face appeared at the end of the building, and then his shoulder…elbows…it was working.

"Just a little more," Mickey said, wincing with pain. "We've *got* you, Roy."

For centuries, people had been known to jump the gun, to speak too soon, to generally jinx the fuck out of something, and as Roy's mouth filled with blood and his eyes bulged from their sockets, Mickey knew he had joined the ranks of those premature celebrators.

"Gaaaahhhhh!" Roy screamed, spitting and drooling blood onto the church roof. He dropped a few inches, as if something was pulling him down. Mickey slid forward, desperate not to let go of the poor bastard.

"Hold on, Roy!" Mickey yelled, but Roy was out of it, unconscious, his head slumped listlessly to one side. "Everyone PUUUUUULLLLLL!"

And pull they did. Zee had one ankle; Roger the other, and Mickey had both of Roy's wrists. Surprisingly, Roy came up over the side of the church roof without too much trouble...

At least, the top half of him did. There was nothing below his waist. Intestines and viscera trailed out from his savaged torso.

And down in the shadow of the old church, the milk-mutant ate noisily, clapping its tentacles together with joy at such an easy meal.

Rita Fox screamed.

32

"This is great," Smalling said, chewing on another piece of Spam. "I didn't even know this stuff was edible. I always thought it was for plugging holes in plasterboard."

"It can be used as food *and* sealant," Lou confirmed. "But I wouldn't recommend puttying windows with it."

Red was busy working on her second tin of sardines. "I think you've stopped leaking," she said, gesturing to Lou's sagging, red breasts.

Lou looked down, caressing one nipple and then the other. "I think you're *right*!" he said. "Oh! Thank *god* for that! I thought it was *never* going to stop."

The tarpaulin in the centre of the room was full, as were three large jars that used to hold miscellaneous nails and fixings. The stench in the room would have been enough to knock a crime scene investigator off their feet, but the three sitting around the counter were used to it, had been there as it worsened. And Lou, well, it was his milk. How could he be disgusted by something that was going on inside, and then coming out, of his body?

Lou climbed into a string vest and slumped against the ODDS N SODS rack. He was exhausted, and not looking forward to the next session. He didn't know how women coped, how they voluntarily made their breasts available for tiny humans with the same suction as a Dyson vacuum cleaner. There was nothing hanging off Lou's tits as the milk pumped from him and he was sorer than a hooker on halfpenny night.

"It's getting dark out there," Harkness said. "Must be getting late."

"Do you think they're going to come for us after dark?" Smalling said.

Red forked sardines into her mouth, chewed thoughtfully for a second, and then said, "If *I* was one of those things, that's when I'd attack. They're pretty good at sticking to the shadows during the day. They're obviously wary of us, otherwise we would be dead already."

"Have you always been good at pep-talks?" Lou said, his voice drenched with sarcasm. "I've got goosebumps over here."

"Just saying it like it is," Red said, tucking blonde hair behind her ears. "If those things want to get in here, they will. Ain't no amount of barricade going to keep them out. There's too many of them."

"Seriously," Lou said. "Keep it up, girl. I'm about ready to take them on singlehandedly."

Red pushed herself up from the chair in which she sat and wiped tomato sauce from her lips. "What do you want to hear? That everything's going to be okay? That the effects of your titty-juice is temporary, and that each and every one of those fucking things is going to go back to normal?"

"Now we're getting somewhere," Lou said.

"Well, it ain't going to happen like that." Red brushed the blade of the sword with her hand. "It's going to get messy, and we might not all make it out of here in one piece, but we have to try. We have to fight back. We *have* to."

Mordecai, over in the corner of the room, whinnied, for no other reason than to get a word in edgeways.

"Well, I think we'll be okay here," Smalling said. "At least until morning. I say we wait it out and then make a run for the hills."

"I agree," Harkness said. "I'd rather be out in the middle of the desert, putting some distance between us and Oilhaven, than hiding out here. It's only a matter of time before they come a-looking."

"Well, I ain't going nowhere," Lou said, climbing to his feet. "I was born here, and I'm going to die here." The trouble was, he hadn't expected it to be so soon. "If those fuckers get in, then I'm going to take as many of them with me as I can."

"That's your choice," Red said. "Just don't expect us to do the sa—"

A sudden thump on the roof above caused her to choke on the rest of her sentence. Smalling and Harkness leapt to their feet. Lou lunged for the duel pistols beneath the counter.

Another thump, and another, and several more, and then footsteps, like there was a small army up there, looking for a way in.

"Shit!" Lou said. "Well, I'd like to say it was nice knowing you, but you ate the last of my sardines and parked a horse in the corner of my shop, so I can't."

"Shhhh," said Red, moving around in the semi-gloom. The last of the day's light trickled in from above, through a small skylight, projecting a perfect square on the store's floor. Red couldn't believe that she was only just noticing this. It was a way for those bastards to get in, and they hadn't done a damn thing to seal it up.

Tiny footsteps rushed from one side of the ceiling to the other. Lou followed them with his antique pistols, resisting the urge to shoot, to blow a hole through the roof and subsequently the thing up there trying to find a way in.

"Stay back," Red mouthed, which was not a problem for Smalling or Harkness, who were about as far back as they could be without stepping outside.

A small shadow appeared in the illumined square on the floor, and then another. A gentle rapping of the skylight's plastic suggested that something was about to come through it. Something big, with the intention of killing those within.

Tat-tat-tat...tat-tat-tat...tat-tat-tat-tat-tat, went the rapping, which was enough to make Lou frown.

"Was that The Lone Ranger?" he said.

Red shrugged. What the hell was he talking about?

Lou sighed. Youngsters these days. You couldn't have a conversation with them about *anything* if it didn't involve sand, heat, The Event, or bandits...

Tat-tat-tat...tat-tat-tat...tat-tat-tat-tat-tat...

"It is!" Lou said. "It's the fucking Lone Ranger theme tune. Grab that ladder!"

The ladder to which Lou referred was leaning up against the racking behind Kellerman's henchmen, and after a bout of intense confusion, the men brought it forward, carrying it like a World War One stretcher.

Lou, seemingly unconcerned that the milk-mutants were trying to gain access via the skylight (not only that, but also knew the theme tune to an old show or film neither Red or Kellerman's goons had ever heard of), placed himself directly under the clear, plastic square.

Squinting up into the semi-gloom, he smiled and said, "I don't believe it."

Friendly faces stared down at him, if one could, in fact, be friendly while maintaining the look of abject horror.

"Who is it?" Red said, sword gripped tightly in her hand, still awaiting the moment anything remotely mutated came through.

"'haveners," Lou said, smiling. "We might not be dead just yet, after all.

33

Outside, the milk-mutants gathered. Hundreds of them, all differing in shape and size, all ugly as sin. Their raucous clamour was impossible to ignore – it sounded like there was a conkers tournament going on out there, but instead of conkers, they were using hyenas. Occasionally, something – an appendage, a hulking arm slathered in blood and milk – would slip across the blocked-out front window, screeching like nails down a chalkboard. No-one had had the temerity to take a looksee through the small hole in the door, in case they were spotted. As far as those things knew, the store was empty, *sans* people, *sans* food, and thusly completely useless to them. They could loiter around all night, as far as the survivors were concerned, just as long as they didn't get curious.

Curious would be very bad indeed.

In the darkened store, where they could defend the rest of the building and the neighbouring apartment against attack, the 'haveners sat around in a circle, as far away from the front of the store as possible, just in case that whole 'curious' thing happened.

Clint and Tom Fox had fallen asleep, nestled up against their mother like piglets. The sick one – Clint – had been medicated by Lou, which might have played a small part in his unnaturally quick descent into unconsciousness. Mickey had thrown on a pair of Freda Decker's granny-pants, for no other reason than to make everyone else comfortable, and was sitting closest to the door, one of Lou's historic pistols in his hand, trained on the front of the store. If anything came through, he would blast it to kingdom come, or whatever the milk-mutant alternative was.

"Sounds like they're having a party out there," said Roger Fox, who was eating decades-old raisins from a bowl. "Reminds me of Metallica '92."

"Oh, I remember that one," Rita Fox said, grinning like the Cheshire cat on mushrooms. "Back when they were good, before Lars got really, really ugly."

"I'm just glad they don't know we're in here," Mickey said, sleepily.

"Oh, I doubt Metallica survived The Event," Rita said, but the thought sent a shudder down her spine all the same.

There was a moment of silence – one to add to the many already endured – as the 'haveners tried to figure out, in their own heads, how best to escape this madness.

"They're all dead, aren't they?" Lou finally said. "Dead or…turned?" He was having a hard time coming to terms with what he'd unleashed upon Oilhaven. Sure, he wasn't to know that his milk was bad, but that didn't make it any easier. Now he knew how those big corporations felt, having to recall batches of glass-peppered yoghurt or cars with no brakes.

"Pretty much," Red said. "Not since the monks brought whiskey to the Irish have so many lives been ended prematurely by a simple beverage."

"Thanks for that," Lou said, bitterly. "Another one to add to your forthcoming book, *Words of Great Comfort: A Brief History of Putting One's Foot in One's Mouth*."

Red sniggered. "Hey, you *asked*. I think the sooner you all come to terms with the fact that your dusty-ass, piss-ant town in the middle of nowhere is now a lot less crowded, the better. Now all we have to do is figure out how to kill those fucking milk-mutants."

"*Can* they be killed?" Lou said. "I mean, sure, I killed my m…I mean the mother-beast, and you took a few out on your way over, but so many? How could we possibly take them all out at once?"

"Don't suppose you've got an old nuke knocking about, have you?" Smalling said, glancing across his shoulder. "*That* looks like a missile. What is it?"

"That's the Lady-Pleasure 3000™," Lou said, "and I'm pretty sure that's not going to work on the milk-mutants."

Mickey sat forwards. "Lou's *right*," he said, animatedly. "There has to be a way we can take them down all at once. Something we've missed."

"Short of going out there with swords high and guns blazing," Roger said, "I don't see that there is."

Mickey sighed and relaxed. "I just wish we could blow the fuck out of the lot of them. Paint the town red, so to speak...and a little bit white..."

Since the beginning of time, people had been hit by the eureka effect (otherwise known as a eureka moment, or the aha! moment: see also: *fuck me, how could I have been so bloody stupid?*). Archimedes was the first after discovering how to measure the volume of an irregular object. Subsequently, he ran home from the local swimming baths screaming "Eureka! Eureka!" Since then, millions upon millions of people have had eureka moments, including Barry Chester from Wisconsin, who had managed to figure out how to dunk a cookie in his coffee for more than five minutes without it drooping, breaking, and falling in. And now, it was Red's turn for a eureka moment.

She jumped to her feet, her face filled with wonderment. "There might be a way!" she said.

Everyone shushed her, for she was making far too much noise for their liking. Still, they were intrigued.

"How?" Lou whispered. He hoped she was right; that they could do something, anything, to begin putting this mess right.

Red turned to Smalling and Harkness. "When we were out there earlier," she said, "and the whore was fighting that big sonofabitch. What happened?"

Harkness shrugged. "She had her head batted off as if it was a balloon," he said.

"After that?" said Red, slightly aggravated.

"The milk-mutant blew up," Smalling said. "What's this got to do with anything?"

"What caused the milk-mutant to explode?" Red said, so excited now that she had changed colour. She was making little loops in the air with her hands, urging the goons to catch her drift.

"Well, the only thing I remember was that it was chewing on Abigail's neck-stump," Harkness said. "And then it went all moany and burst all over the place like a TNT-stuffed watermelon."

"Exactly!" Red said, once again checking her volume. "The thing blew up because it drank the whore's blood. She must be infected to high heaven, riddled with enough STDs to turn one of those things into a giant bomb."

"So we should all get STDs and let them eat us?" Rita said. "That doesn't sound like much of a plan."

"The whore's body, or most of it, is still *out* there," Red said. "If we can get it and bring it back here…" She paced across the room to the filled tarpaulin. "We can chop it up. Mix it in with this lot, and feed it to the fuckers. They want more milk? Well, we'll give it to them!"

Everyone was up on their feet now, except for Rita Fox, who was bogged down by two very tired little boys.

"So what you're saying is that if we go out there, past the army of mutant giants, and pick up the headless dead corpse of the geriatric prostitute, then bring it back here, without being gobbled up by the mutant giants, chop it up into little pieces, then drag it outside, without being killed once again, and wait for them to eat it, and then explode, we might have a way out of this?" Lou liked the sound of that.

"In *theory*," Red said. Lou *didn't* like the sound of that. "We're pinning a lot of hope on the fact that your town whore was extremely diseased."

"Oh, she was!" Harkness said. "Even her warts had warts." He wasn't exaggerating.

"Then we might…just *might*…have found a way to take those fuckers down." Her spirit lifted, Red smiled.

"Okay, so how are we…I mean, how are you going to do this?" Smalling said. "Sounds awfully dangerous."

Red exhaled. "Well, the best way would be to take Mordecai," she said, nodding toward the horse in the corner, which huffed and took a few steps back. "Gallop on out there, pick up the whore, gallop on around the back of town, avoiding the main streets. There's more sand out there, so you won't hear the horse's hooves as much. We'll come around back, but we might need a

261

diversion to get those things away from the front of the building so that we can get back in."

"I can take care of the diversion," Lou said. "Hell, I'm thinking I should be the one going out there. All this is my fault—"

"No offense, old man," Red said, "but I wouldn't let you ride a carousel horse."

"None taken," Lou said, secretly relieved that he had been let off the hook.

"You kept saying 'we'," Harkness said. "'We'll come around back'...'we might need a diversion'...Who the hell are you taking with you?"

"I'll go," Mickey said, stepping forward with his hand raised. How they were expected to take him seriously dressed in a pair of Freda Decker's huge panties, they didn't know.

"Yeah, *Mickey* should go," Smalling said, nodding frantically. He sure as hell wasn't going to volunteer for what was starting to sound like a suicide mission.

"You sure?" Red said.

Mickey nodded. "I'm a lot fitter than these guys," he said, gesturing to the rest of the 'haveners. "If all we have to do is grab the decapitated body and bring it back here, I think I can manage that."

"You going out there dressed like that?" Red said, pinging the elastic waistband on the huge panties.

"Overdressed?" Mickey said, grinning. "If those things come after us, we can always use these as a net."

"Okay, then let's go corpse-fishing," Red said. "Mordecai, come out from under that shelf. Honestly. If we don't do this, we'll have no choice but to eat you, and you don't want that, now, do you?"

The horse reluctantly came forward, head down, a look of defeat in its eyes.

When this is over, it thought, *I'm running for the hills, and I'm leaving your crazy ass behind...*

34

"MIIIIIILLLLK!" one giant arachnid milk-mutant growled into the darkness. Once, it had been Petulia Clark, a delightful woman of fifty years whose charity work in Oilhaven was unsurpassed. Pity, then, that she was reduced to this hulking beast of many legs, craving something it neither understood nor truly liked the taste of.

Cries of *MIIIIIILLLLLK!* came from all around; a horrible chorus that made Reverend Schmidt's choir sound like angels.

More mutants arrived in front of the store, each with their own peculiarities. One was a big slobbering mess of teeth and eyes; another was much smaller, but with a wingspan to rival any of the great flying beasts from mythology. One had two heads, another had none – the one with none regarded the double-headed creature with contempt, and would have frowned had it had the tools to do so.

Suddenly, the door to the store flew open, and out galloped a horse with two riders. The milk-mutants turned to see what the kerfuffle was about, but by the time they realised their food was escaping, it was too late. The horse, though clearly nervous, was like shit off a shovel, heading up the street and into the darkness faster than the milk-mutants could muster, despite their many-legged advantage.

The door to the store slammed shut just as a four-armed mutant crashed against it. It was all over in less than ten seconds, and several of the milk-mutants were left shaking their heads, moaning and groaning, wondering if the whole thing had been some sort of clever illusion, a side-effect, perhaps, of the great milk which had birthed them.

*

"Can this thing go any faster!?" Mickey called from the back of Mordecai. He didn't know the workings of a horse, but there must be a second gear somewhere below all that hair.

Red slowed the horse down, which was not what Mickey had had in mind. "It was around here somewhere," she said, surveying the ground for the mangled remains of Abigail Sneve.

"Great," Mickey said. "Whatever happened to 'pick up the body and get back, no fucking around'?" There were bodies everywhere, scattered along the road, lining the street like macabre Christmas decorations, but none of them were missing heads. "Are you sure it was here?" he said. "I mean, the streets around here all look the same."

"It was *here*," Red said, confident that she had the right spot. "Something must have dragged it away." She climbed down from the horse, pulled the sword from its sheath, and began checking through the bodies strewn across the road. What if she was gone? If one of those things had eaten the whole thing? It would have killed just one, then, instead of the hundreds Red had hoped to take out.

"This fucking sucks," Mickey said. He was sweating terribly, through heat and nerves. "We can't stay out here all night. Those things will come for us; it's just a matter of—"

Something thumped into the sand a few feet in front of Mordecai. The horse reared up, tipping Mickey from its back end. Red rushed across, grabbing onto Mordecai's reins, trying to calm the beast down before it worked itself up to the point of running away, very fast, in any direction...

Once she had managed to calm the horse (Mickey was back on his feet, scraping sand from his butt-crack and cursing the practicality of Lou's mother's knickers) Red shuffled toward the thing in the sand, the projectile that had spooked Mordecai so badly.

A headless corpse wearing a short skirt. Its shoulders were now missing, too, along with both arms, but Red recognised the rest of it as belonging to the whore.

Not too far away, there was a deep gurgling sound, and then a meaty pop.

"I guess they didn't like the whore much, either," Red said.

"Is this her?" Mickey said, scrutinizing the body as if he knew what he was looking for. "How can you be sure?" There was no point, he thought, dragging a body halfway across town only to find out it was useless.

"That's the whore's skirt," Red said. "And I recognise that tramp-stamp from earlier." She pointed at a small tattoo on the corpse's right leg: *Hos Before Bros*. "Now, if you would be so kind as to grab the legs. I'll get the...the...*erm*...this bit here."

She was a lot lighter than Mickey had expected, possibly because there was only around sixty percent of her remaining. They managed to sit the body on the horse – once again, Mordecai audibly revolted; once again, to no avail – and climb up, sandwiching it between them.

Something growled in the shadows just as Red urged Mordecai forwards.

"Please," Mickey said, checking across his shoulder for possible tails. "For the love of god, and all that is good and pure, get us back in one piece." And all the way, he tried not to focus on the armless, headless, stinking corpse grinding back against him, begging him for one last fuck before it was too late.

*

"Okay," Lou said, sand whipping him in the face, even up there on the store roof. He saw the horse through the gaps in buildings, skirting around the town just like Red said they would. "Tell them to get ready!"

Smalling, who was standing on the ladder, half-in, half-out of the store, ducked his head back in. "They're coming," he said. "Await further instruction."

"This is *soooo* fucked up," Zee said. She was standing by the door with her father. Both looked nervous. Her father shot her a disapproving look, to which she said, "I mean, this is sooooooo darned tooting messed up," before grinning.

Up on the roof, Lou peered down into the sea of bloated limbs and tentacles. Slime-slathered bodies ebbed and flowed, a sickening tide that threatened to envelop them all. Lou knew he had only one shot at this…one chance to put things right, to save at least a few lives…

"Oi! You ugly bastards!" He waved his hands, frantically vying for their attention.

"MIIIIILLLLLK!" one of them said, which was, he thought, pretty much their entire vocabulary.

"That's right!" Lou bellowed. "Milk is on its way, but I need you to come over here. Come on…this way!

That's right! Follow me to the east side of the building! You too, Cthulhu!"

It was working. The milk-mutants had all spotted the crazed man on the roof, flailing around like a novelty kite. They followed him across the roof, away from the front door.

"Keep it coming!" Lou said. "You know you want some of Lou's milk." He whipped his shirt off and began to tease his nipples. It wasn't long before a torrent began to spew out of him. It hurt like a sonofabitch, but Lou just bit his lip and did his thing. "Here we go!" he said, squirting his titty-juice into the mass of writhing bodies below. "Yeah, you like that? You like that, you dirty fucking milk-mutants?"

The lip-smacking emanating from the sea of bodies told him that, yes, they liked it very much.

"MIIIIILLLLLK!"

"What do you think *this* is?" Lou said. "Ginger fucking beer? Come on, drink up. Plenty more where that came from." He continued to spray the beasts with his milk, avoiding the tentacles and giant arms that lunged for him. One creature tried to climb the exterior wall, but only managed to get halfway before dropping back down into the thirsty throng.

It's working! Lou thought. *It's fucking working! Who would have thought it?*

*

"It's working!" Smalling informed the rest of the survivors. "They're taking the bait!"

Rita Fox exhaled. "Oooh, that is a relief," she said, which was something of an understatement. To her husband, she said, "Do you think this is going to work? Honestly?" She looked terrified.

"Honestly?" he said. "I think we have to *try*. We can't live in a world where those things exist. I'm pretty sure they won't let us." He ran a hand gently down Zee's arm. "But whatever happens, I want you to know that I love you all dearly."

"Love you, too, Daddy," Zee said.

"Love you, Roger," Rita said.

"Love you all," said Harkness, before realising it was a family thing and backing out of the conversation quickly.

The sound of a galloping horse got nearer, and nearer, and...

*

"They're not going to open up!" Mickey said, clinging to the decaying corpse for dear life. "I don't think they've seen us."

Red pointed Mordecai toward the shut door. "YAH!" Off to her right, she saw the mutant horde. They were fixated by the figure up on the roof – Lou – and the milk pumping from his hairy breasts. He'd kept his part of the deal; that was something, at least.

"I'm *telling* you," Mickey said. "They're not going to—"

"They *will!*" Red screeched back over her shoulder. She hoped she was right, for hitting a door at forty miles per hour would not be a pleasant way to end the night.

Mickey closed his eyes. If this was how he was going to die, he didn't want to see any of it. At least he was wearing underwear for once. It would have been terribly embarrassing to go out naked.

Come on, come on, come on, Red thought. "COME ON!" she squealed. "OPEN THE FUCKING DOOR!"

Just then, when Mordecai was twenty feet away and had decided that he, too, would close his eyes, the door opened. Red sighed and tapped Mordecai on the back of the head. "Open your eyes and steer us at that door," she said. "And whatever you do, don't look right."

Mordecai looked right, saw the fleshy tangle of limbs lurching toward them, and said, "Herfff!" by which time they were back inside the store. The horse slammed into the back wall, unsettling several shelves and sending jars of tacks and screws clattering to the floor. Surprisingly, it remained on its feet, unlike Mickey, who had once again toppled off and lay on his back next to the half-chewed hooker.

Roger and Zee secured the door once again, but those things knew, now, that there were people inside. Whatever happened next, it needed to happen fast.

Red climbed down from the dazed horse and dragged the remains of the whore toward the tarpaulin by its broken ankle. On the tarp, the milk was beginning to congeal. It was a lot thicker now than it had been, thanks to the tremendous heat, and now resembled a giant omelette more than anything else. Those bastards would have to eat it, not drink it, not that it mattered.

Smalling climbed down the ladder and was followed shortly after by Lou. The store owner's nipples looked like slices of salami. "Thank god that worked," he said, sighing audibly. "I tried to keep them busy, but they must have seen you coming. Once they spotted you, I couldn't get them back."

"It's okay," Red said. "We made it. That's all that matters."

"I don't think I can watch this," Rita said, gagging at the sight of the mangled hooker. Roger pulled her away to one corner, to where his wife couldn't see or hear what was happening from across the room. The kids – Clint and Tom – had slept through the entire thing, which was amazing, since it usually only took a middle-of-the-night fart to wake them both.

Lou handed Smalling and Harkness rusty saw-blades he'd found in one of the racks. "They're not much," he said, "but they should cut through that." He pointed to the corpse. "I might sit this one out, if you don't mind. Cutting people up has never really been my forte."

"Who am I?" Zee said, gripping her machete in both hands. "Jack the Ripper?" She'd heard a few things about the infamous London slasher, stories here and there that might have been made up, for all she knew.

"Let's do this," said Red, circling the half-dismembered corpse as if it might suddenly get up and start a fight. "And whatever you do, don't get any in your mouth."

*

"It looks like a *blancmange*," Zee said of the pink pile sitting atop the tarpaulin. There were a few bones visible, but as a group they had decided it wouldn't make much of a difference. The mutants wanted one thing, and only one thing.

The milk-cum-omelette. It might be pink, but it still smelt the same. Those fuckers were going to lap it up like yesterday's leftovers.

"It looks disgusting," said Rita. "And you've all got red on you."

"So what *now*?" Smalling said as the door rattled in its frame. The mutants were eager to get in; growing increasingly impatient. "How are we going to get this outside?"

"He's right," Roger said. "It's not like we can just drag it out there. We'll be dead before we get three feet."

They were in quite a predicament, inasmuch as they had the C-4 but were shit out of fuses.

"Shit!" Mickey said, kicking the floor. "Well this is just great. We risked our lives to get that fucking body, and for what? Now it's just going to sit there, rotting in the milk, which is already rotting. What we have there is a rotting pile of milk-corpse."

"Calm down," Red said, moving across the room. She had an idea. Whether it would work, or not, was another matter. "If we can tie the four corners of this thing together, we can make a sack, right?"

"What, like Santa Claus?" Zee said. She was old enough to know that Santa wasn't real, but she was also old enough to know that milk-mutants had no right to exist, either.

"*Exactly*," Red said. "It'll be big, but it should fit through the skylight. We get it up onto the roof and we can just tip it out over the edge."

Lou clapped his hands together enthusiastically. "That's the spirit, girl," he said. "See, I knew you had it in you."

"Well, what are we waiting for?" said Zee, grabbing onto one corner of the tarp, and also something that looked a little like a milky giblet. "Let's send those things back to whatever hell they came from."

"Amen!" said Lou.

"Fuck yeah!" Harkness exclaimed.

"Kill those cunts!" said little Clint Fox, who had woken up and was punching the air with two tiny fists.

*

"It's heavier than it looks," Mickey said, getting underneath the sack and pushing it inch by inch up the ladder. Everyone else was up on the roof, pulling as hard as they could. And still they struggled.

"Just a little bit more," Lou called down, though his voice was muted by the giant sack of curdled milk and guts wedged in the skylight. Only a little was seeping out, and that was up by the opening, not through any unfortunate holes in the tarp.

Something *thunked!* against the front of the store, something big and heavy and not at all human. Mickey wobbled unsteadily on the ladder, fearing, for a moment, that the whole thing was going to give under the weight of both him and the sack of milk-mutant pesticide.

"They're getting a little feisty out there!" Mickey called up. "Can we hurry this up?"

The sack lifted a couple of inches before stopping again. "Shit!" said a voice. Mickey thought it belonged to the father – Roger Fox.

"What?" Mickey said. "What do you mean, 'shit'?"

There were mutterings, almost inaudible over the din of the agitated milk-mutants, and then Lou said, "We think it's stuck!"

Mickey groaned. "*Think?*" he said, "or *know?*" He had a feeling he knew which it would be.

"Don't worry," Lou said. "We'll think of something. Just don't move."

A long, thick tentacle punctured the door. On the end of it, six hands began feeling around the room, grabbing at anything that could be grabbed at.

"Pull this thing out of here!" Mickey screamed. He had never screamed before, and he wasn't sure whether it suited him. It was bad enough that he was wearing a pair of big panties...

"What's happening down there!?" Red said. "Are you okay!?"

"Just get me out of here fast!" Mickey yelled. He was certain a yell fitted him better than a scream. "There's a...a fucking tentacle in here, and it's looking for..."

The many-handed tentacle must have heard Mickey's voice, for it shot across the room at preternatural speed and stopped just short of him. *No, please, no! Please just go the fuck away!*

The tentacle moved this way and that, like a snake about to pounce upon a lame rodent. The fingers on each of the hands wiggled back and forth. One hand was flipping Mickey the bird.

And then it attacked. Hands were under his arms, tickling him, the way a playful grandfather tickled his daughter's firstborn. "Fuck off!" Mickey screamed, for a yell didn't seem to be enough. "Stop tickling...!"

He lowered his arms for just a second, but that was all it took. The sack shifted above him, and then its momentum did the rest.

The last thing Mickey heard as he hit the floor, the sack landing on top of him with a meaty, sickening thud, was the front door buckle and splinter, and then a cacophony of cries, all moaning the same single word.

"MIIIIIIIIILLLLLLLLK!"

35

"Shit!" Lou said, stepping away from the skylight. "I thought you were holding onto it!"

Red looked incredulous. "I thought *you* were!"

Lou shook his head. "I think that's where we went wrong."

"You don't say." Red stomped across the roof and glanced down over the side. "They're fucking *in* there, Lou! They're in the store!"

"But Mickey…" Zee said, trailing off. Rita pulled her daughter in to a tight embrace. Zee hadn't been comforted like that since she was a kid, and in that moment, she wanted to be free of it.

The entire building beneath rattled and creaked as more and more milk-mutants forced their way in. Their guttural moans elicited whimpers and gooseflesh from the 'haveners nervously waiting on the roof.

"We're fucked!" Harkness said. "I mean, that's it. We might as well just jump to our deaths right now. It'll be much nicer than what those things will do to us when they get up here."

"They won't get up here," Lou said. "They don't know we're here, so if we all just settle d…"

Suddenly, a huge hand punched up through the skylight and firmly attached itself to the rooftop. Another followed, and then a third. Lou scrambled to safety. His nipples had started to leak again, proving that when it rained, it poured…

"Holy shit!" said Roger Fox, pulling his family backwards across the rooftop. "This isn't happening! This can't be happening!"

The rest of the creature came through, dragging itself forward, a giant bubble of flesh with three arms, four legs and more eyes than the rooftop survivors combined. It was massive – like three creatures in one – and Lou was perplexed as to how it had got through the tiny square in the roof in the first place. *We struggled with a small sack of gore-milk*, he thought.

"Everyone behind me," Red said, stepping into the centre of the roof. Her sword gleamed as the moonlight bounced from it. The creature looked momentarily confused, as if it had not anticipated much of a battle. "You want me?" Red told it. "Come and fucking get me."

The beast growled, tensed up like a steroid-using bodybuilder, and leapt into the air.

Red swung the sword, knowing that she was dead either way; that the sheer weight of the thing would kill her as it came down on top of her. Well, at least she'd tried…and at least she'd outlived El Oscuro. For a brief time, she had been the leader of Los Pendejos…but that was only because there was no-one left to compete for the crown. Still, it was nice while it lasted.

The creature was still roaring as its bowels gave way, and then the whole thing exploded. Limbs flew off in all direction; eyes darted through the air – a squelchy ball-bearing bomb gone off a tad too soon. Red dove for cover, just missing a hurtling arm as it whipped past her. The stench was unbearable, but in that moment she would have snorted shit direct from a pig's anus if it meant living to fight another day.

Once the dust (meat, innards, milk-blood, detached limbs) settled, Red slipped and slid her way to her feet. The roof was an absolute mess with body-parts and viscera, but she had never been happier to see so much gore.

"What just happened?" Smalling said as he peeled a strip of charred meat from his bald head.

Harkness finished vomiting over at the corner of the rooftop before turning. "Do I have any of it on me? Is it on me? Is it?" He spun around; it was almost balletic.

Lou wiped gore from his forehead. "It must have eaten the mixture," he said. "It must have eaten the fucking whore-milk cocktail! That's why it exploded!" His mouth fell open, but he was clearly smiling.

Just then, something down on the street roared plaintively. Then came the pop, and milky blood shot into view before raining back down.

"Come on!" Red said, rushing toward the roof's edge.

They lined up just in time to see the horde pushing its way from the building below. There must have been a hundred of them, all puking up from whatever constituted a mouth, all limping groggily away, but not too far before...

Pop!
Pop!
Pop!Pop!Pop!

"I don't believe it," Zee said, watching as the milk-mutants exploded on the street below. "It worked! They must have all had some!"

"Couldn't resist Lou's Milk," Lou said, smiling. "Look at that one down there. It's going to..."

Pop!

"Told you."

And so they stood, watching as the things...the creatures that had once been tax-paying citizens of Oilhaven...detonated, decorating the town in frothy white goo and so much baggy flesh. It would take one hell of an operation to get the place cleaned up again, but at least they had the opportunity.

A chance at a fresh start, without taxes and mining, without Kellerman's bully-boy tactics. Lou didn't know what he was going to do about his little problem, but it was only truly a problem if people drank the stuff. Maybe there was another use for it. Lou had noticed some clean spots down in the store where it had made contact. Maybe it was good for cleaning with...maybe, just maybe, there was a business in it after all. All in all, Oilhaven had potential, and with a little TLC...

"Did I miss much?"

Everyone turned to find Mickey standing just in front of the open skylight. Naked again, but covered from head to toe in thick, yellow milk and bloody remains. In his hand, a bone that could have been either a tibia or fibula; it didn't matter which. Zee rushed across and threw her arms around his neck.

"Zee!" Rita yelled. "Be careful! His willy's out!"

Mickey eased the young girl off and smiled. "What was that for?"

"We thought you were dead," Zee said. "How…?"

"I was under the sack when it opened up," he said, clutching at his ribs, which were visibly bruised. "I got trampled, but they didn't even know I was there. I just kept my mouth shut and waited for them to take the bait."

Pop!

"Well, we're all glad you're alive," Lou said from the edge of the roof. "Mayor Mickey."

Mickey almost choked on his own tongue. "Now, wait a minute," he said. "I walk around naked all day. Are you sure that's what you want for Oilhaven?"

Smalling and Harkness shrugged. As far as they were concerned, it was a step in the right direction.

Pop!

"Get over here!" Clint Fox said, his face all lit up like a Christmas tree. "All these cunts are going to blow!"

"Clint Fox!" Rita screeched. "If I hear you use that word again, I'll…"

Pop!
Pop!
Pop!

MILK

Adam Millard

Lightning Source UK Ltd.
Milton Keynes UK
UKOW02f0016060616

275696UK00003B/3/P